First World Problems in an Age of Terrorism and Ennui

or

The Revolutionary

Dominic Peloso

Dark Mountain Books

Publisher's Note:
This is a work of fiction. Names, characters, places, and
incidences are either the product of the author's imagination
or are used fictitiously, and any resemblance to any actual
person living or dead, organizations, terrorist plots, events,
or locales is entirely coincidental.

ISBN: 978-1-931468-31-2
First Printing

ISBN: 978-1-931468-80-0
Electronic Edition

First

World

Problems

in an

Age

of

Terrorism

and

Ennui

Chapter 1:

WELCOME TO THE REVOLUTION!

Greetings to all those who've had enough of the status quo, to all those who have a message the world needs to hear, to all those who are sick and tired of being lost in the background noise of the internet generation!

CHOAS is your one step source for all terrorist-related information. If you're planning an isolated event to get someone's attention, or if you're looking at a full-scale revolution, everything you'll need to know is right here at your fingertips. Bomb recipes, equipment suppliers who don't ask questions, bulletin boards to meet up with those who share your goals. You'll find it all inside. Just click on a topic below to get started on your way to glory and social change.

Make a difference! Support your local revolution! Embrace CHOAS.

Tyler rolled his chair to the back edge of the clear, plastic pad. He looked at the screen from different directions— straight on, then with his head cocked, then from off to the side. He didn't like loading his home page. It messed up his stats. Already, over a third of all the hits he had received in the first month of CHOAS had been from him, from his computer. He felt like a fraud. His computer skills were strong enough to add the small hit counter at the bottom of the page, but not strong enough to figure out how to reset it. Every time he checked on his handiwork, the counter rose by one. He knew that he shouldn't feel bad about that. He should feel good. The higher the hit counter, the more legitimate his website seemed. But he felt like a fraud. He had seen other websites around, dumb-ass home pages of bored high-school kids mostly, whose hit counters read tens of thousands of hits. It was so painfully obvious that the sites hadn't legitimately gotten all that traffic; the kids had manipulated their counters so they looked more impressive. Tyler didn't want that. He didn't mind *being* more impressive, and he wasn't above lying about his impressiveness in order to appear more impressive. But what he feared the most was getting someone like him coming to the CHOAS website, someone like him who noticed the small things. Someone who actually *was* connected with serious terrorist organizations who would *know* that there was no way the site had garnered that many hits and summarily label him a fraud. Someone who was so well respected in the industry that their word would be considered gospel and the CHOAS Terrorist Handbook website would forever languish in obscurity, ignored by everyone.

Tyler was also concerned with what his friends might think, even though they almost certainly didn't care. They probably didn't even notice. He wasn't sure if any of them had even ever bothered to go to the site. He had sent out an email to about fifty people when he first got it online. People he knew well and those he didn't know so well. He had lost touch with a lot of his old friends, the ones from the college days and before. He still had some email addresses but those could well be out of date, dusty and unchecked. Sometimes he would send out a message to someone and not hear back for weeks or even months. Were they too busy to write back? Were they dead? Did the message get lost somewhere in the ether that makes up the Web? There was no way to tell. Not until months later, when he would receive a short reply, filled with murmurings about how the person had been overwhelmed with work or marriage plans or something connected to real-life in some way. Something that Tyler almost certainly had very little direct experience with.

He decided that he was satisfied with his newest upgrade. The words, "WELCOME TO THE REVOLUTION" now blinked on and off. It probably wouldn't make that much of a difference, but Tyler was a perfectionist and a tinkerer. Plus, what else did he have to do? He lifted his logo-less coffee mug from his desk and brought it to his lips. He had let it get cold of course, as usual. He got up out of his chair. Almost as an afterthought he reached back across his desk to the keyboard and opened a work-related spreadsheet to cover over the revolutionary website, just in case someone nosy looked at the screen.

He left his blue, plastic cubicle and walked down the hallway to where the carpet changed color from muted blue to muted green. He placed his cup in the microwave and pushed the buttons. All around him activity swirled. His boss's boss walked by hurriedly in suit and tie. There must be an important meeting today. Another co-worker whose name is unimportant walked past and jokingly told Tyler to get back to work. It was typical big company humor, bland and pointless. Tyler watched the timer on the microwave count down the seconds to hot coffee. It was a waste of time waiting here in the hallway, but Tyler had timed it once and if he were to walk back to his desk, and then walk all the way back to the microwave, he would only have ten seconds at his desk before he had to come back. It wasn't really worth it in terms of productivity. He might as well wait.

Above the microwave was a hand-made sign that said in Helvetica font, "Clean up after yourself — your mother doesn't work here." Tyler fingered the pen in his shirt pocket. Every time he heated his coffee he stared at that sign. He wanted to deface it somehow. Write something like, "My mom works in accounting, can I leave a mess?" or something like that. But he couldn't quite come up with anything that was funny, anything that really said what he wanted to say. There was a joke in there somewhere, but there was no point in expressing it unless he could come up with a way to say it that wouldn't be misinterpreted by everyone. Everything Tyler did was misinterpreted by everyone.

The counter on the microwave counted down to one second. Tyler hit the 'cancel' button and took out his coffee. He never let the counter drop to zero. If that happened, the microwave would beep loudly. He felt sorry for the people in the green plastic cubicles directly across from the microwave. It must be horribly disturbing to hear that incessant beeping all day. Tyler was the only one thoughtful enough to spare them. They probably didn't even notice enough to ever thank him, but that was ok.

He sipped the coffee on his way back to his desk. It was too hot of course, and he burned the tip of his tongue like he always did. It was easier to just push the minute button than it was to type in the forty-two seconds that were required to heat the coffee to its optimal temperature. Every time he burned himself, he would think, "stop the timer at eighteen seconds, not one second dumbass." But he would always forget by the next time his coffee needed heating.

Back in the safety of his cube, Tyler sat in zen-like silence staring off into space. He wished that he had read up on how to meditate. It would be so easy to do in this place. He calculated he could bang out three hours of good meditation per day on average. But he never remembered to do any research when he was at home. He never remembered to look for a book when he was at the bookstore. It was like there was some mental block, something that stopped him from remembering his work life in any detail when he was not at work. So, he sat, in meditative ignorance. It was only two p.m. He had another three hours to go before he could go home. He checked the hit counter on CHOAS again. It was the same. No one had joined his revolution during his trip to the microwave. He checked his email to see if any revolutionaries had sent him a message, or if any search engine had responded to his request to be added to their directory. Nothing. He checked his hit counter again, still nothing. Sometimes Tyler would get caught in this loop for hours. Checking the email, then checking to see it anyone had gone to the page while he was in email, then checking to see if anyone had emailed him while he was at the page, then back to the page to see if anyone had gone there while he was checking his email. . . . He tried to stop himself. Logic dictated that if no one had written him in over a week, the chance that someone sent him an email in the three seconds since he checked last was very slim. But it never really hurt to check.

He got up again. There was no point to sitting there until his coffee cooled to a reasonable temperature. He walked down the muted blue hallway to the corner of the floor. These were the only areas in which there were actual offices. His boss's door was open. Tyler peered in to see if he would be bothering him. The boss was sitting with his back to the door, staring at the computer screen. Tyler never understood why anyone would sit with their back facing the door like that. Someone could throw something at the back of your head and knock you out before you even noticed them. "But then again," Tyler reminded himself, "most people don't think like me. Most people are too self-absorbed and distracted by trivialities to consider something like that."

Tyler didn't want to disturb the guy. What if he was doing something important? What if he was in the middle of a memo and Tyler broke his concentration? Tyler stood in the doorway for a few seconds, staring, waiting. His boss didn't turn around. Tyler tried staring at him harder, as if to psychically alert the man of his presence, but nothing. He lifted his hand to knock, but then decided to give his boss a few minutes to finish compiling the memo. Tyler quietly backed up, sighed inaudibly, and headed for a walk around the floor.

All of the floors in this particular building were made up of a single large room. At each of the four corners were two real offices with real doors and real walls. The elevators and bathrooms were in the center, also made up of real walls. The rest of the space was like a giant dutch-style door. A labyrinth of offices from the floor to the five foot line, and then above, open space. It took exactly eleven and a half minutes to circumnavigate the floor, passing by all eight of the real offices and returning to this spot. "That'll be enough time," thought Tyler, "Then I really have to do this. I'm going nuts here."

The floor was split into four different zones, each with a different color. Tyler was in the muted blue zone, with faded royal blue carpet and turquoise felt covering the cubicle walls. There was also a muted green zone, a tacky orange zone, and a dull gray zone. Out of the four, Tyler decided that he liked the blue zone the best, or more accurately that he was offended the least by the blue zone. He pitied the people stuck in the orange area. But they were a different department and he didn't know any of them, so he never had a chance to joke with any of them about how they could stand all that orange day after day.

Even though he didn't know any of the orange workers, he felt comfortable meandering through their space. They all shared the fifth floor and so were technically part of the same community. He felt the most awkward on those occasions where he had to go to other floors of the building. On those floors there were even more colors: red, yellow, purple. He was used to the blue, green, gray, and orange of floor five. The colors on the other floors seemed unnatural to him, like he was in some kind of weird alternate universe. If he were ever made President (a very unlikely scenario he admitted), he would make all of the cubicles the same color. That way, people would feel comfortable no matter where in the company they were, and the amount of interdepartmental socializing would increase. Think of the upsurge in information swapping that would occur. Think of the new dynamics of synergy that would be created, all from dissolving these artificial, color-based barriers that kept people isolated and inbred!

As he walked, Tyler hummed a song that was stuck in his head. He almost always perverted the lyrics of songs he liked when he hummed them, so he was singing "*I am humid and I need to be loved*" in his head as he meandered around the floor.[1] He sometimes tried to force himself to sing the songs the correct way, but it wasn't nearly as entertaining to him.

Tyler completed his circuit and returned once again to the door to his boss's office. He peered around the corner carefully, in order not to intrude on an important meeting or phone call. His boss was sitting at the large, cherry-stained table, munching on some fries out of a McDonalds bag. "Come on in," said Tyler's boss.

Tyler was embarrassed that he had been seen. He wouldn't want to disturb someone when they were eating. Especially if they weren't eating until almost 2:30. It implied that they were very hungry and they had been too busy earlier to eat. "Sorry to bother you Mr. Moore," Tyler said cautiously. "I can come back after you've finished eating."

---

[1] Ed. Note— The correct line is "I am human and I need to be loved." The Smiths, "How Soon is Now?"

"No, I've got a meeting in ten minutes. If you've got something to say, you'll have to do it now." Tyler's boss had the annoying habit of talking while he was eating. He stuffed another handful of fries into his maw. Tyler would have much rather waited until he was finished.

"I'm wondering if you know anyone who might need some help with something? I've got some time available if anyone is overbooked and needs some help." Tyler put his hands in his pockets in order to wipe the sweat off of them. He hated having to ask for more work. It seemed to him that everyone else was busy around here and somehow he should naturally be busy too. Not having work to do made him feel guilty that somehow he was a fraud who wasn't earning his salary. Asking for a new project felt like a confession.

"I though that you were helping Ken out? What happened with that?"

"I finished that white-paper he wanted a few days ago. I gave it to him for review. But he was out yesterday, so I guess he didn't have time to look at it. But I'm sort of twiddling my thumbs waiting to see if there are any changes he wants done."

Tyler's boss closed his eyes for a second and thought to himself. "I don't want to overbook you with other stuff and then have Ken come to me and ask why you don't have time to help him." Tyler knew that wasn't going to happen. Ken had a PhD and thought that he was God's gift to pretty much everything. Like most PhDs, Ken liked doing all the work himself. He didn't want to farm crucial tasks out to untested people like Tyler. That's why Ken worked eleven hours a day. That's why Ken only gave Tyler minor assignments that amounted to nothing more than busy work. That's why Ken didn't even bother to review Tyler's reports. He had explained all of this to his boss several times. Each time it was decided that Mr. Moore would have a chat with Ken and get Tyler more involved in the process, but nothing was ever done. People were forgetful, people were too busy with other things, people were on vacation for two weeks. Nothing ever happened. That was the reason that every month or so, Tyler would make the same trip to Mr. Moore's office and have the same conversation. It ended this time the same way it always ends, "I'll have a talk with Ken. I've got a meeting all afternoon, but I'll do it first thing in the morning. I'll write a note to myself. In the meantime, talk to Amir and Bob. I've heard that those guys are starting up projects soon."

Tyler left and went back to his office. He was drained from his meeting with his boss. He checked the hit counter again. It had gone up by one since the last time he had looked! "Woo-hoo," he thought to himself. That hit, by some anonymous person somewhere out there, gave him the energy he needed to get back up. He walked over to Amir's office, but there was a note on the door saying that he was out of the office all week. Bob was busy trying to get something completed and looked too harried to talk to Tyler for more than a minute. He said that he did indeed have a project coming, but he wasn't expecting the contract to be signed and the money to show up for about a month. He promised to get back to Tyler once that happened. A dejected but not particularly surprised Tyler went back to his office. He sat in his chair and looked at the clock on the wall. It was made by blind people at a factory in Illinois. At least that's what it said on the face. It showed three o'clock. "Only an hour and a half to go," thought Tyler. No point in doing anything else today. He sighed and reached for his coffee. It was cold. He tried to decide if he had the energy to walk down to the muted green area to heat it up again.

Chapter 2:

City Center Shutdown!

Number of Conspirators:	*5-10*
Danger Level:	*Low*
Arrest Level:	*Medium*
Lethality:	*Low*
Annoyance Level:	*Medium*
Economic Damage:	*Low*
Equipment Required:	*5-10 Hardened Steel Bike Locks (Kryptonite Brand)*
	Some hammers

Want to shut down a major metropolitan area but only have a few operatives? The most vulnerable target is often the subway system. Subways are carrying tens of thousands of people to and fro all day and are often timed so precisely that even a small glitch will result in hours and hours of delays.

Near the beginning of early morning rush hour, position an agent at a hub station. Wait until a train pulls up. Have the agent calmly walk to the front car and inform the conductor that you are stopping the train. Show him the bike lock. Then jump onto the tracks and attach the lock to one of the rails. Remember to stay away from the electrified third rail! Once the lock is attached, use the hammer to crush the key. Either have the agent wait to be arrested or have them run.

The train can't move with the lock on the tracks, and it will take the police a while to break the hardened steel lock. Have agent number two waiting at a second hub station. After a certain amount of time, or on a prearranged signal, have the second agent repeat the procedure. Continue to stop trains at various stations around the area for as long as you have agents.

Make sure that you alert the media as soon as the first lock is in place. They will broadcast the delay to the public who will then not use the trains but instead drive and gridlock all of the highways into town. It will be total CHOAS!

Tyler was driving. The sky was that dark grey color, which was as dark as it ever got in the city. It was late, maybe about eleven pm. He had work the next day but it didn't really matter. People barely noticed if he showed up, so performing more sluggishly than normal wasn't going to make any difference. He was more concerned that he was missing sleep. Tyler liked to sleep. He never got enough sleep. Not on the weekdays, not on the weekends. It was always up too early and to bed too late. As he drove, he wondered if he could live life more fully if he got his eight hours per night. Would he be more productive? Would things taste better? Would he be able to do more? Experience more? Live more? "Probably wouldn't make much difference," he decided.

The light changed from red to green. Tyler crossed the bridge and entered the city. He always laughed to himself as he crossed the Memorial Bridge. It led straight to the Lincoln Memorial. A long time ago, the Italian government created a set of statues and gave them to the city. They were all of shirtless muscular men astride fat horses. The city planners were so delighted by the gift, they ringed them all around the Lincoln Memorial, facing the great, marble Parthenon. As you cross the bridge, you approach the statues from behind, so your first sight as you enter the city is a pair of larger-than-life, corpulent, bronze, horse asses. It was a fitting tribute to the people of the city, the people who ran America. Tyler wondered if maybe it had been intentional, an inside joke of some sort by the conspiracy folks who had designed the entire city to be a magnet for attracting and

15

distributing orgonic energy. Tyler didn't really believe the conspiracy theorists, but it amused him to do the research. He enjoyed pretending that Pierre L'Enfant actually drew out the streets of the city to make a giant pentagram whose apexes included the White House, the Capitol Building, and the Masonic Lodge on 16th Street. He would tell stories about the evil conspiracy to anyone who would listen. Of course, he usually reached the limit of his listener's patience within a few sentences. No one wanted to believe, no one wanted to listen. It was quite rare for him to get someone to sit still long enough to get to the part about the hermetic symbology on the back of the one-dollar bill.

He drove across the bridge. A light rain was falling, which wasn't unusual for this time of year. It was one of those drizzles that is annoyingly light. Without the windshield wipers one couldn't see, but with them on, even at their most infrequent pace, they scratched across the mostly dry windshield making an annoying noise. He sprayed the wiper fluid in hopes of lubricating the blades, but that didn't help much. He turned up the volume to compensate. "...*Freedom for those who can find it! Sex for those who can buy it! Television today... never lies!*" blared the singer.[2] Tyler banged his fist against the steering wheel to get out his aggression. It was so much easier to get out one's aggressions when loud music was playing. He turned the car out of the circle surrounding the Lincoln Memorial and gunned the engine, trying half-heartedly to get the tires to screech a little.

As the song ended, he pulled up to a building. It was the same large, brown office building that was ubiquitous in that part of town, indistinguishable from all the rest of the buildings for ten blocks in all directions. But this one was

---

[2] Atari Teenage Riot, "Atari Teenage Riot"

different. This one had an employee he knew. He sat and waited in his car. He looked at the building next door, trying to count the number of offices it contained. "100, 200, 300 maybe? Three hundred offices, three hundred people who come here every day, come here and work and laugh and live their lives. And I don't know a single one of them. Their lives are totally independent of mine." He tried to grasp the size of the building, the number of people involved. Then he tried to extrapolate that number to include all of the buildings in the city. Tyler had once secretly wanted to know everybody. It bothered him that life was being lived without him. It bothered him that somewhere, someone was having a party, eating dinner, having sex, moving out, watching tv, mourning a dead loved one, all without Tyler's knowledge or consent. He had long ago accepted the fact that he simply couldn't achieve omnipotence, now he was just trying to get an idea of how much he didn't know, trying to understand exactly what percentage of the world he was forced to be satisfied with.

He was interrupted by the appearance of a silhouette of a figure in the doorway of the building. The short, long-haired woman in an ankle length skirt came out, lugging an overpacked bag stuffed to the seams with papers and reports and brown folders. She walked to Tyler's car and pushed the bag into the trunk. As she came around to the passenger's side door, Tyler realized that the music was still blasting. She didn't like loud music. He turned the volume down to inaudible. Then he thought that there was little point in letting the tape run if he couldn't hear it, so he just shut the radio off entirely. The girl tried the door, only to find it was locked. The locks on Tyler's car were wired together, and he usually unintentionally leaned on the driver's lock at some point during his trip, resulting in a sympathetic locking of the passenger door. He hurriedly reached over and fumbled with the handle for a few seconds, managing to get the door open.

"Hey," she said scooting herself into the seat. He leaned over perfunctorily and kissed her cheek.

"Did you have a good day?" he said to her.

"I'm sorry to make you come and pick me up, it's just that it's raining and the Metro's already closed." She apologized every time she made him pick her up, as if it were a special occasion. She knew as well as he did that he would be here again the next night, and the night after that, and the night after that.

"It's ok," he said mechanically, "I love you. I told you, I'll pick you up every night."

"No no, I feel bad making you come and get me all the time. This is it. I'm not going to work late anymore." That wasn't true. Ann always said that this was the last time, that she wasn't going to work late anymore, that she would be around more. Every night she said this, and every night Tyler knew that in 24 hours he'd be picking her up again. Their relationship was well into its third year and all it consisted of was bed. Everything revolved around bed. That was the only time that they were together. They lived a third of their lives next to each other, but always asleep. Everything about Ann reminded Tyler of sleeping. The only outfits he saw her in were pajamas and work clothes. Just seeing her made him yawn. "Tell me about your day," she said to him in a peppy voice. She tried hard to be alert, to enjoy their thirty minutes together before bed claimed them. "Did anything exciting happen?" They pulled away from the law firm and onto 16th Street.

"I came up with a new acronym for CHOAS — Corporate Headquarters of the Organization of Anarchists and Saboteurs. Pretty cool, huh?" He smiled and chanced a quick glance at his girlfriend, trying to keep one eye on the road. The drizzle ended.

"I *meant*, what happened at work? Did you get any new projects, win any awards? Real life stuff." Tyler didn't respond. Ann lowered her head and fiddled with something in her purse. The couple's work situations were polar opposites. For everything that Tyler didn't do, Ann did. Being a lawyer in a large firm meant twelve hours, fourteen hours a day of work, of being 'on.' She didn't have time for fantasy games, and for running websites about made up conspiracies and anarchist nonsense. She actually *worked* at work, was expected to work at work. She didn't understand how Tyler was able to get away with not doing anything, how he was able to just quietly accept not doing anything, how he was able to go to work every damn day to a place that didn't care if he showed up or not, and still have the stones to cash his paycheck every week. Or maybe that was just how Tyler interpreted in his mind how she felt about him. He never asked, and she never volunteered.

After a few blocks of driving with nothing but the squeak of the windshield wipers to break the silence, Tyler finally spoke. "Nothing then," he said flatly, "nothing happened at work. I was sort of working on this one project, but I finished that the other day and I can't find the project leader to get him to review it. So I mostly just sat around. I ate those leftovers for lunch." Tyler was aware of how lame he sounded. Long ago he had wanted to succeed, wanted to live up to the expectations of his teachers that told him he was destined for greatness, wanted to get kudos and promotions and plaques that said, "Corporate Employee of the Month." But it didn't quite work out that way. The people he worked for were all lazy, all incompetent, all unable to keep up with him. In the beginning he found it odd that it often took people more time to review his reports than it did for him to write them. After a while he got tired of being frustrated. Soon after that he realized that no one cared if he did his job or not, no one cared if he showed up or not. The place ran entirely on inertia, fuelled by lucrative government contracts that were signed before Tyler was even born. He also understood that his girlfriend was a corporate lawyer. He didn't *have* to work. If management ever got around to firing him, he could always fall back on her six-figure salary. Once he realized that his effort didn't matter, and failure didn't mean ruin, he stopped caring. He stopped trying. He did less and less and the more he stopped pushing the system, the more the system forgot about him. He was R.I.P; Retired In Place. If he still had any pride left in his job performance, in his standing in society, he would have been ashamed to be washed up before his thirtieth birthday. The only thing that excited him any more was his half-assed attempts to smash the state, and few people cared about that either, it seemed.[3]

"Tell me about your day," he said perfunctorily. It was the same thing night after night. Nothing ever changed for the two of them, nothing ever grew. He had long ago stopped caring about his days, and her days were too wrapped around her job to change much. Life needs light and fun and freedom to move forward and she had none of those things, cooped up in her office from dawn to past dusk. She seemed caught in a recurring nightmare of minutiae. Every day was the same, or at least it all sounded the same to Tyler. "I got this project, and then this emergency happened, and then I was too busy to go to lunch because this conference call came in and blah blah blah. . . ." It usually went on until the couple was well into Virginia on their way to Ann's neglected townhouse. Tyler nodded in agreement now and then, cueing off the way the inflection in

---

[3] Ed. Note— When pressed about why he wanted to smash the state, Tyler often would repeat a quote he wrongly attributed to Jean Paul Sartre.

her voice changed. He wasn't listening to the words. They were driving by the State Department. Tyler looked at the van the police had stationed in front of D Street to block traffic from passing in front of the main entrance to the building. The security weasels were afraid of a car bomb. The van had maintained its station for over two years now, with the driver doing nothing but patiently waiting to back up and let the occasional important diplomat's limousine through. Two years. "Why don't they just build a gate or something?" Tyler thought to himself. He was already toying with ways to defeat the system and get a bomb into the main lobby.

Chapter 3:

Nom de Plume!

I'm sure you already realize that the purpose of your organization is to rally people to your cause. But a lame name can hobble you right out of the gate. In this age of the internet, what doofus decided to name their group the Moro Islamic Liberation Front? MILF? Seriously!?! Obviously they've never used a search engine before. That's why CHOAS is such a great name. It's easily recognizable, imminently googlable, and proves itself. What is more chaotic than refusing to spell 'chaos' correctly? Too bad for you that we've already taken it.

But potentially more important than the name of your organization is your personal nom de plume. One problem the modern terrorist has these days is that all these computer databases make it really easy for law enforcement to track you. But here's a great tip that'll totally confuse the hell out of them... My sources tell me that if law enforcement doesn't know your first name, they will just fill in the blank space in the database with FNU, for 'first name unknown.' So if you are only known as Mr. Smith, you'll be in the database as FNU Smith. Similarly if they only know your first name, they'll call you LNU for 'last name unknown.'

Can you see how to subvert the system? Obviously, just start calling yourself Fnu Lnu in all of your communications. They'll dutifully add all their data about the exploits of Fnu Lnu to their databases, but you'll be completely unsearchable because your name will blend with all the other thousands of FNUs and LNUs that are already in the database. There's no way they can parse out your data. You'll be completely and totally untraceable. No one will be able to tell you even exist. Enjoy your new-found invisibility.

The smell of cigarette smoke hung thick in the air. That was the one thing that Tyler hated about this place. Why in god's name did people feel they had to keep lighting fresh cigarettes? The smoke was so thick already, how could someone think to themselves, "boy, I could really go for *more* smoke!?" Tyler had never smoked though, so maybe he just didn't get it.

Paradoxically though, the fact that you could smoke here encouraged the presence of a certain class of hipster, and that made this place cool. The coolness was the reason that Tyler came here. He sat and stared out the window. The coffee was terrible. It always tasted like the milk was bad. The muffin was halfway decent but not remarkable. He stared out the window and looked at his car parked across the street. He still had about fifteen minutes left on the meter by his reckoning. He never could concentrate when he had a time limit. He looked around the cafe to see if anyone was looking at him. They were all absorbed in their own little worlds. One thirty-something couple chatted quietly. Another man read a newspaper. A group of three people who obviously thought that they were neo-communists sat at the large wooden table and smoked over their iced coffees. Music was playing through hidden speakers, but at a level maddeningly inaudible. Tyler could tell it was a familiar song, but couldn't hear clearly enough to place it. The waitress behind the counter reached up above the register to erase yesterday's 'special of the day' from the chalkboard and replace it with a new blend. One kid just sat there staring into space holding his cigarette like it was a joint. He probably wasn't even old enough to smoke legally. A young couple sat in the corner and ignored each other as they poured over textbooks on psychology and biology respectively. Tyler saw right through them. This wasn't a good place to study; they were just here to make themselves appear cooler than they really were.

That's why Tyler was here, wasn't it? He didn't even like coffee that much, he definitely didn't like the smoke, he could've read his book at home. He could be out doing something more interesting. But he wanted to be seen. He wanted to feel like he existed. He picked up the book he was reading and held it such a way to advertise to the world, "I'm reading Don DeLillo, I'm cool, come talk to me." Tyler wasn't stupid, and he was quite self-reflective. He knew exactly why he was here, even if he would never admit it to anyone. He'd woken up this morning subtly craving the approval of others to validate his existence. He didn't like the fact that he needed approval, but he could only control his brain, not his heart. He was lonely. Ann was working yet another Saturday, and he had nothing better to do and didn't want to be home alone.

It wasn't even that he read DeLillo because it was enjoyable. Tyler found him mildly entertaining, though nothing special enough to be specifically sought out. But he had heard some interesting-looking people enthusiastically talking about him on the Metro the other day and he figured that if he wanted to be taken seriously as a cool person, as an interesting person, he should read something interesting-looking people talked about. Almost all of Tyler's reading was motivated by a desire to have something interesting to say when asked, despite the fact he was almost never asked. And even when someone did ask, it was usually someone so non-literary that they had never heard of whatever author Tyler was reading, and so any coolness points Tyler could have otherwise received were lost. He read a few sentences half-heartedly, but put the book down and decided that he was too bored to read. He began to think of something he needed to add to the CHOAS page. Where was his pen? He wished he'd brought a pen.

A girl opened the door to the little avant-garde cafe. It was hot outside, especially for this time of year. She moved confidently and ordered something appropriately cool, both in temperature and status. She sat at an empty table and rummaged through her canvas bag, pulling out a day planner. But instead of planning her week, she just absent-mindedly doodled in the margins.

Tyler fixated on her from the moment the screen door had opened. He was always looking at people, sizing them up, watching to see if they were looking at him, thinking about him. His imagination played scenarios in his head about how after he left, the people in the coffee shop would discuss how cool and unapproachable he looked, how all of the single girls would tell their friends that they wished they had had the nerve to talk to him. Every week he checked the 'I saw you' section of the City Paper, hoping that one of them was desperate enough to place an ad:

Dear mysterious stranger. I saw you at Donatello's last Saturday afternoon. I read DeLillo too. You left before I gathered up the nerve to talk to you. Please call.

There were always ads like that, but as hard as he scoured, he never found one that seemed to be looking for him. The smoking kid got up and left. As he opened the door the street traffic drowned out the softly-playing music over the speakers. As the door swung closed again the song came back into focus. "What a cold and oh rainy day. Where on earth has the sun hid away?"[4] It didn't really match the summer sun outside.

Tyler often flirted with other women. It wasn't that he wanted to break up with Ann, or be unfaithful to Ann, or make Ann jealous or anything. It wasn't that he even had any hope of success. In fact, it was the fact that he *knew* he'd

---

[4] 10,000 Maniacs, "Like the Weather"

fail that made him try. He wanted emotion; he wanted those butterflies in the stomach feeling you get when you approach a pretty girl for the first time. "It's harmless fun," he thought to himself, there's no way she'd be interested in me, DeLillo or not. One day it had almost backfired on him. He had been at a concert with Ann when a girl sidled up next to him. She was unbelievably attractive. She wore bright red lipstick, Tyler's favorite color (Ann rarely wore any makeup at all). So there, mere inches from his girlfriend, he leaned over to the stranger and said, "Sorry to bother you, but I wanted you to know that your lips are so beautiful, they're distracting me from the show." She demurred and moved away from him of course. Later on, Ann saw a co-worker of hers that just happened to be the beautiful girl's boyfriend! Tyler felt a lump of embarrassment in his throat, but she played it cool and was polite enough not to mention it. No harm, no foul.

Tyler leaned over the table, still holding the book in a position to allow the girl to read the cover clearly and said, "Do you have a pen I could borrow?" He smiled and chanced a quick glance at her breasts. She was wearing a spaghetti-strap, sleeveless purple top. The straps of her bra were suggestively visible underneath. He could see the shimmer of sweat on her chest, but she didn't lean over enough to allow him to see down her blouse. She reached into her bag and pulled out a white Bic pen, with the end chewed off.

Tyler looked for an opening. The bag had Tibetan writing on it. She looked vaguely Asian. "You don't happen to be from Tibet would you?"

"No," she said flatly.

"I'm sorry to have asked. It's just that I saw your bag and I've got a question about that language and I'm looking for someone who speaks it." She didn't turn away or wave him off, so he continued. "I was in an argument with this guy at work. He said that the language is called Tibetan, and I thought that it was called Devenagari. There's no resolution of course, until I find somebody."

"I don't know." She shook her head. "I got it at that Tibetan festival at the Smithsonian last summer. I don't know what it says." She turned back to her date book. Rebuffed, he leaned back in his chair. He took the napkin and wrote up a comment he wanted to add to the Ricin section of the CHOAS page. The napkin was not designed to be written on and tore a few times. But he got enough of the thought down to be able to remember it later. He placed the napkin in his book as a page marker and leaned back in to return the pen, and take a second swing.

"You don't happen to be a Mormon are you?" he said, pretty well knowing that she wasn't a Mormon. She stared at him blankly. "I had an argument with this other guy at work about that statue you always see on Mormon temples. The angel with the trumpet. He said it was Moroni, who's the patron angel of Mormons, while I told him that Gabriel was the only angel with a trumpet. I'd call the church directly of course, but Mormons are pretty pushy and I don't want to have missionaries sent over to my house, you know?" She put the pen back in her bag, and without saying a word, returned her eyes to her doodling.

Tyler was pretty satisfied overall. He had gotten the butterfly feeling, he had made an honest (if somewhat lame) attempt to pick her up. He felt good that he was rebuffed because it made it seem more innocent that way. He couldn't be accused of trying to cheat on Ann if nothing happened right? It also helped strengthen his relationship with Ann in a way. Every time he tried and failed, he became more and more certain that he couldn't find another girl, a better girl. It made him hold Ann all the more tightly because he wasn't deluded into thinking that he could do better. That always happened to guys. Once they get a pretty good thing going they get full of themselves and start to think that they can do better, that since they got this one girl they could get any girl they see, that they can get that really hot girl at the coffee shop and Bang! they're broken up, and then they try to get that hot girl at the coffee shop and Bang! they get rejected, humiliated, and they're back to being alone, moaning and groaning about how they can never get a girl. He looked at his watch, seven minutes to go before the time expired on the meter. He took another sip of the bad coffee. He pretended to read, but he stared over the top of the pages at the girl and her date book. Her hair was short and straight, but all messed up as if she had just gotten out of bed. She had a necklace with a sort of crystal thing on it. She was the complete opposite of Ann in a lot of ways. The grass is always greener right? The song coming over the radio changed.[5] Tyler knew this one by heart. He could sing it from memory. Not that he ever would, mind you. But part of him wished that there was some way he could make everyone else know that he knew the song by heart, that he had listened to the Smiths for a decade, that he was cool long before they were. There was no way to alert the crowd though. They'd go on believing that he was just as much of a poseur as they were.

"What're you reading?" she said unexpectedly.

"DeLillo," Tyler responded. He was going to give his talk about how he liked this book, but not as much as DeLillo's other works, and then he'd go into details about how DeLillo wasn't as good as Pynchon and blah blah blah. In an effort to look well-read he prepared and rehearsed a little speech for each book he was reading. That way he

---

[5] The Smiths, "This Charming Man"

wouldn't come off looking like a dilettante. Of course, he rarely got the opportunity to actually state his comments to someone. No one ever cared enough to ask. Not even Ann. She knew better. "It's ok, but it's not as good as. . ."

"I've never heard of that," she interrupted. "Is it like Anne Rice?"

Tyler was flabbergasted. How could someone who looked so cool make a comment like that? "No, Rice is mass-produced crap. This is actual art," he said.

"I don't read *art*. Too hard. I just want to relax and be entertained."

"That's totally the wrong reason to read." Tyler immediately changed his posture. When she'd first walked in, he had been cowed by someone who was clearly higher than him on the coolness meter. But now the tables had turned. She had slipped. Now he was the hip, interesting one, the one to be emulated and held in esteem. "If you just want to be entertained, watch 90210 or something. You should get something out of reading. It should make you a better person."

"I don't want to be a better person." She took a cigarette out of her purse and lit it. This was supposed to be the non-smoking end of the cafe.

"How can you not want to be a better person? Everyone wants to be a better person. That's what life's all about. Growing and changing and becoming better; physically, intellectually, spiritually. . . ethically. If you're not becoming better than you're wasting everyone else's time. If you don't want to become more than you are, you must be so far down on the evolutionary scale that you don't even know what you're supposed to be doing here."

"You're never going to get to fuck me if you keep talking to me like that." she said matter-of-factly. Tyler was taken aback. He wasn't used to hearing women say things like that in real life, especially not to him. He looked at her blankly, trying to gather his thoughts. By bringing sex into the equation, she had reversed the tables once again. Now she was in the superior position.

"It doesn't matter you know. I'm not going to fuck you anyway." She closed her date book and looked him square in the eye. "I only fuck prisoners."

"Prisoners?" Tyler stammered, trying to regain his composure. "You mean, like people in jail?"

"Yeah. Convicts. Felons. I've got some letters right here." She reached into her sack and pulled out some crumpled pieces of loose-leaf paper with writing on them in blue pen. They weren't actual prisoner letters, they were just some old notes from class, but she didn't keep them in view long enough for Tyler to read them.

With butterflies suddenly as strong as a punch to the stomach, Tyler sputtered, "Why do you do that? Is your boyfriend in prison?"

"They're so desperate. . . ." She dragged on her cigarette. ". . . so lonely. It's not like fucking you or some other self-important loser who tries to impress me with fancy books and a tongue ring. Prisoners can't have their pick of females. They appreciate me. They spend an hour just smelling my skin, their fingertips longingly exploring every inch of my body. They love my flaws— the hair on my thighs, the smell of my feet. They don't consider me just another score, another conquest. Most pretty boys are already looking forward to their next lay before they even come, but

30

prisoners know that I'm their only chance, so they savor the moment." She looked around. "I keep correspondence with some, they pass me around and each time I need to get off, I head over and fuck a different one. I get the pick of the litter each time."

Much later, Tyler would come to the conclusion that she was lying. That she had never even seen a prison, didn't even know where one was. He would guess she told him the story because she wanted to shake him up a little bit. She seemed to be the type of person who was so genuinely hip that she loved deflating pseudo-intellectual assholes who prowled hipster hangouts looking for a quick score. She had Tyler all wrong of course, as most people did, but she almost certainly couldn't tell what Tyler was really like on the inside because he spent so much time decorating his outside to camouflage his true self. She looked him directly in the eye and bit her lip suggestively.

Tyler looked at his watch. The meter had expired one minute ago. As much as he enjoyed the conversation, he had to go. Any minute now someone would come by and give him a ticket. And he didn't feel like paying forty bucks for his cup of horrible coffee. He stood up. "Well, this has been great and all, but I've got to get going." He considered telling her about Ann, telling her that he had had no interest in her, that she was wrong. That would give him the upper hand once again, wouldn't it? He couldn't just walk out of there and let her win, could he? He decided that he could, or more importantly, he decided that he couldn't come up with anything stunning enough to say in a moment's notice. Something that wouldn't sound like a desperate, pathetic attempt to regain the upper hand. "Maybe I'll see you around sometime," he said as he sidled past her. He was already fantasizing about the conversation by the time he got to the door. It was the beginning of the arduous process of working it over and over in his head, trying to figure out where he had scored points and where he had lost them. How he could've done things differently, and how the outcome would've been different if he had. It was all part of his constant attempts to become a better person, or at least what Tyler thought a better person would be like.

When he got to the door she called out to him, "Hey!" Tyler turned around, half-hoping that she'd decided that she wanted to sleep with him after all. His mind flashed, attempting to analyze all the possibilities. To Tyler, a conversation was a chess match, something that needed to be planned out several moves in advance. "Call me if you ever find yourself in prison!" She turned back around and threw a hand up in the air as a half-hearted wave. Tyler smiled. Halfway out to the car he began to wonder if she had been serious about that last comment, if he should've gone back and asked for her number, just in case. It was too late now. There was no way he could go back without looking like a complete doofus. He glanced back just once and saw her looking at him expressionlessly through the window as he got in his car across the street and pulled away.

Chapter 4:

Fuck the Post Office!

Number of Conspirators:	*1*
Danger Level:	*Low*
Arrest Level:	*Low*
Lethality:	*Low*
Annoyance Level:	*High*
Economic Damage:	*High*
Equipment Required:	*Powdered magnetic ink.*
	Stamps

Who doesn't hate the Post Office? They are a monopoly, they suck, and you can't even sue them. But how can you, one solitary man, bring such a large institution to its knees? The answer is way more simple than you might think! Get some magnetic ink. It's the sort of stuff that they use for printing checks. Put some in a bunch of leaky envelopes and then mail them around the country. That's all. When the powdered ink leaks out of the envelopes in the mail handling facility, it will start to stick to the magnetic bar code readers in the processing equipment. This will break the reader. If you send a few dozen letters and hit all of the main mail handling facilities, the post office will have to return to hand-canceling all the mail. They won't be able to deal with the volume and the whole system will shut down for a few weeks at least. People won't get their credit card bills, parents won't get their Mother's Day cards, companies won't be able to force feed their advertising and junk mail into people's homes. Total chaos ensues!

Tyler lay open-eyed in bed, waiting for the sound of the sirens to wake him. A car screeched to a halt on the street outside. Tyler listed closely for the bang, but there was no bang, just a screech. It happened almost nightly; it was a dangerous intersection. But no matter how many times the screech sound permeated the night air, it was never followed by the bang, by the crash, by the emergency. Tyler desperately wished for an emergency. He wanted something to happen— Something to watch, something to talk about the next day at the water cooler, something to use to become a hero. If there had been a major accident on the street, he would've been ready. He had imagined it in his head a thousand times. After the screech and the bang and the screams there would be silence. He would jump from under the covers and rush to the window. "What's happening?" Ann would mumble in a barely audible, half-sleep. "It's an accident, a bad one too from the looks of it," he would reply. "I'd better go out there and see if I can help." By the time he had put on his shoes and got to the scene, there would of course be the requisite number of witnesses, but there wouldn't have been time for the police or other 'officials' to arrive and take over. It would be the duty of the bystanders, the good Samaritans, to remain calm, take charge, and save lives. Of course, the majority of the gawkers would be sheep, would be lemmings, would be too scared, too lazy, too unprepared to do anything but stand there blankly and wait to give a police report. Tyler would swoop in like an angel. A cry of, "Oh no, a baby's trapped in that burning car!" would come from the crowd. And well, blah blah blah, you can figure out how this fantasy goes from here.

More and more Tyler found himself envying victims. He envied the people who were at the wrong place at the wrong time. He wanted a chance to be the hero. But it never came. He never saw a person choking in a restaurant, he never found a young boy floating face down in the shallow end of the community pool. His town was never ground zero in an earthquake, tornado, hurricane, flash flood or an alien invasion. They say that a virtue never tested is not a virtue. Does that apply to bravery, stoicism, and heroism? Can you be a hero without a catastrophe to ennoble you? Until something happened, some reason to step up to the plate and put your nuts on the table, Tyler would never completely feel like a man, never feel like someone worth knowing, worth being.

Ann rolled over, taking most of the blankets with her. "That's fine," Tyler thought to himself, shivering in the dark, "I don't really deserve to be comfortable anyway. What the hell did I do to earn a warm bed today?"

Tyler lay wide-eyed, waiting desperately for the sound of the sirens to wake him. It didn't matter what type. Where the hell were the air raid sirens? Would anyone even know what to do if an air raid siren went off? Did Virginia even provide air raid sirens to its citizens? "Nothing ever happens here," he thought. "How depressing is it for these people to know that the world is going to be just the same tomorrow as it is tonight. That you can go to sleep confident in the knowledge that tomorrow your house, your job, your family, your life, will all be exactly the way it was the day before. People have things happen to them all the time. It's always on the news, every damn night. Wars, fires, airplane crashes. It all happens all the damn time. But not here, not to me. Where's the air raid sirens? Why couldn't I have lived during the Blitz? Boy, that would've been something!"

He spent ten minutes or so lying in the darkness imagining himself to be a dashing young American in London during the Nazi air raids. He imagined that Ann was some British girl he was seeing. He patted her sleeping body as if she were a prop, pretending that he was comforting her and helping her get some sleep, knowing that the air raid would drive them into the underground at any minute.

Sometimes when he was at work, while he waited the forty-two seconds for the microwave to heat his coffee, he'd stare out the window at the parking lot below and scrutinize the people down there to see if any of them was a gun-wielding maniac coming to enact revenge for some perceived slight. He'd daydream about possible scenarios for where he'd hide in order to tackle the shooter when he came around a corner. Some days the shooter would hit him and cause some non-fatal injury, sometimes not. But every time, Tyler would wrestle the guy to the ground and save his coworkers.

Sometimes, when he was stuck in traffic on the bridge going to the office in the morning, he'd watch the planes flying overhead and imagine one of them coming in too low and hitting the bridge just in front of his car. He'd jump out, brave the flames, and save a small child from a burning car seconds before it fell into the waters below. He would be humble of course, and tell the Mayor that he wasn't really a hero, I mean, who wouldn't have taken similar actions if they could save someone?

Almost every night, when he wasn't thinking about the sirens or the Blitz or an airplane crash, he wondered if somewhere out there, some girl he barely knew was lying in her bed, eyes wide open, pining away for Tyler, not realizing that she could never have him.

He had been in an earthquake once, a real one that is, back when he was living in California. When he moved to California his parents and his friends told him, "Don't go there! Aren't you worried about earthquakes?" Tyler smugly claimed that he could handle it. That it wasn't a big deal, that they didn't happen that often and implying that anyone too scared to live there was weak. Then one night, two in the morning maybe, Tyler was fast asleep when a picture fell off the wall, waking him with a start. He lay in bed for a few seconds trying to determine the cause of the noise, and then, the cause of the accident. "Damn," he thought, "I bet that was an earthquake. A small earthquake. And I missed it because I was sleeping. I've been here a year and I missed my first earthquake. That sucks." Then the real earthquake hit. It wasn't like you see in the movies or on TV, it wasn't several minutes of prolonged shaking and rumbling and people having time to run for cover in doorways and duck under tables. It happened all at once, BANG! There was a tremendous sound too, as if a large bomb had exploded nearby. Then a fraction of a second of absolute silence followed by the sound of all the pictures in the entire house crashing to the floor. Then nothing. Tyler waited in the darkness, unsure of what to do. "Is that it?" he thought. With elation at being part of such a momentous event he leapt from the bed to inspect the damage. In the living room he turned on the television to catch the coverage. Was San Francisco in flames? Was the National Guard on the way? An old movie played, seemingly oblivious to what had just occurred. A cowboy in an outlandish costume crouched behind a tree. Tyler walked out the front door. He expected all the lights in the neighborhood to be on, he expected people to be standing in the streets, too scared to go back into their houses, or at least sipping coffee and exchanging 'Where I was when the earthquake occurred' stories. But the avenue was dark. Was the power on? Of course it was, the TV was playing wasn't it? He sat on the couch to try to calm himself down. He wasn't scared, he wasn't panicked; he was giddy. He had something to tell people. A story, something that *happened* that he could say he lived through. At the commercial break, a sleepy-looking newsman came on to report that a small, 3.2 earthquake had occurred, no damage reported. There wasn't a single other earthquake reported in the Bay Area until after Tyler had left for good, a year later.

Tyler told that story many times. It wasn't a great earthquake story, but it was the only one he had. It was really the only disaster story he had at all. The only thing that he could hold up in front of his friends and co-workers and say, "See how calm I remained in the face of overwhelming danger?" He slid out of bed and walked to the kitchen in the darkness. He grabbed the half-flat 2-liter of Coke and drank it straight from the bottle. Ann wouldn't care, she only drank Diet anyway. He walked to the window and watched the street below. Even at 2 a.m. there was still activity. Cars still passed by, stopping at intersections, waiting for red lights. Pedestrians still walked the sidewalks. There was no evidence of that screech heard a few moments ago. The drivers had flipped each other off and continued on their merry way, to whatever destination they were headed to in the middle of the night. Tyler looked at the clock. He still had four hours to go before he had to get up for work.

Chapter 5:

Caltrops!

Number of Conspirators:	2
Danger Level:	*Low*
Arrest Level:	*Medium*
Lethality:	*Low*
Annoyance Level:	*High*
Economic Damage:	*Medium*
Equipment Required:	*Van or Truck*
	Big box of nails

The most vulnerable part of a city's infrastructure is always, ALWAYS, the transportation network. It is large, easily accessible, and easily sabotaged. Want to cause major hassle in your community? Just get a large box of nails from the local hardware store (caltrops work better but are harder to find). Then go to a major commuter highway in your area just before the morning rush hour and pour the nails across the road. You'll cause a reasonable number of blown tires. There will be so many that the cars won't be able to find places on the side of the road to pull off. They'll have to stop in the middle of traffic. And if somebody manages to squeeze by, they'll get their tires popped too. You can tie up a major artery for hours while cleanup crews get all the nails off the road. Aluminum nails work best because they are non-magnetic and so harder to pick up. These techniques also work well as a force multiplier for a larger attack. You can selectively hit certain buildings or areas that provide emergency response capabilities in order to degrade response times. For example, say you were a foreign government planning an invasion and you wanted to slow down the American military response. Simply send a van filled with nails to the one entrance leading to the Pentagon parking lot. If analysts and strategists can't get to their offices, they can't order counterstrikes, or inform decision-makers on how to respond. This easy, non-lethal technique can give you hours of fun and a lot of visibility for your organization with very little money or time invested.

"That girl over there is pretty cute."

"Yeah, I guess she's not bad."

"Are you going to talk to her? You should go over and talk to her."

Tyler and Jason sat on high stools at a small table in a bar more smoky and loud than Tyler was really comfortable with. Tyler would be hard pressed to say exactly why Jason invited him out for drinks regularly. Their personalities were quite different— the things that Tyler was self-conscious about Jason was not, the things that Tyler dreamed about Jason did not. Tyler's impression of Jason, which wasn't nearly as accurate as Tyler believed, was that Jason was a hedonist, he was happy-go-lucky, he didn't worry about who he was, where he was going, why he was here and what he *should* be doing. He just was. Like a Taoist master, Jason was too disinterested in philosophy and too distracted by life to have ever bothered to learn what the word Taoism meant.

Jason sat and smoked and the two sat and watched the night go by. Tyler looked at his watch. It was just after ten. 10 p.m. on a Friday night. Ann was still at work. She had given permission for Tyler to be out, had encouraged him to go and explore and live a life separate from her. Tyler had the impression she felt guilty making him sit home alone, night after night, waiting for her to finish her duties at the law firm. She wanted him to have a life, she wanted him to know people, to interact with people, to experience the things that he needed to experience but couldn't with her. She couldn't be everything to him, couldn't understand all of his needs. And even if she didn't like Jason all that much, she kept saying that she wanted Tyler to hang out with him, to have his *guys' night*, to have his male bonding experience, to talk about the things that he wanted to talk about yet she didn't want to hear about.

The irony of course was that Tyler found it just as difficult to have a conversation about his interests with Jason as he did with Ann, or with pretty much anyone for that matter. Just because the two shared a gender and the same muted blue cubical walls didn't mean that they shared much else.

Tyler sat at the small table, trying not to spill beer on his cell phone. He looked down at the LCD face to see if it had rung. The booming bass of the bar's speakers made hearing difficult and it would be easy to miss a call.[6] No messages as of yet. Jason was coolly staring over at the pool table where two attractive young women still dressed in work attire were playing a game. They were a little on the pudgy side, but the girl taking a shot was quite top-heavy and showed significant amounts of cleavage when she bent over. Jason's eyes followed her bosom as she moved around the table to get a better angle, his eyes straining to see over the pint glass he had on his lips. Tyler repeated himself.

"Go over and talk to them, man. I'm telling you, it's your chance."

Jason put down his beer. "If you're so interested, then you go over and talk to them."

"I completely fail to understand you," Tyler countered, "you are totally single. Those girls are clearly not with guys,

---

[6] Crush, "Jellyhead," but mixed so poorly that the lyrics were inaudible by most of the bar patrons.

they must have come here to meet guys. I don't see what the problem is."

Jason pushed his unkempt, blonde hair out of his eyes. "You know man, you are the most desperate guy I've ever met who had a girlfriend."

"I'm just looking out for your interests, that's all," Tyler said defensively. "I figured that you would *want* to talk to girls. I just hate to see an opportunity being missed. I mean, those two seem totally, and I mean totally, ripe for the picking, and here you sit. Are you gay? I mean, if you are that's ok, I don't mind. We can find you some guys if you like. I'm cool with that."

Jason just stared at Tyler, rolled his eyes, and went back to his beer. Tyler let it drop. He was aware that sometimes his desperation to live life vicariously made him try too hard to push people into doing things that they didn't want to do. He needed to relax.

They sat in silence for a while. Jason finished his drink and pushed the glass away from him. It left a wet streak on the table. "Dude, you don't need to try so hard. Look around, there's plenty of talent in the bar, you don't need to just jump on the easiest target you see. What are you, a cheetah? No wonder you're in a serious relationship, you throw yourself at anything that tosses you a glance. Have you ever said 'no' to a girl ever in your life?"

The waitress came by. The two guys ordered another round of Bass. Bass wasn't Tyler's favorite, but it was the best they had there. Like with everything else Tyler often found himself attracted to what wasn't available. His favorite beer was Newcastle, which, while popular in England, was rare to find on tap in DC. Liking it gave him more ammunition when he complained about how America didn't understand quality and how nothing he liked was popular. Jason firmly believed that Tyler picked things to like on the basis of their unpopularity, just so he could justify his own outsider status in society.

"Ok," Tyler said, "What about that waitress? She's pretty cute?"

"First of all, she is pretty skanky. I mean, she's a waitress in a sports bar. Second, she's a *waitress*. You can't hit on the waitress. I mean, she's working, she ain't here to meet guys. Third. . . "

Tyler interrupted, ". . .I disagree with you on that point. I mean, you always hear, 'waitresses get hit on all the time', but I don't think that it is true. I think that people *think* that and so no one ever does it. I bet that she'd be quite flattered if you asked her out."

"I'm not going to ask out the waitress."

"Do it subtle. Like when she brings the bill write something like, 'Hey, you're cute, here's my number' or something on it."

"Look, if you like the waitress so bad, then you ask her out man. What the hell are you bugging me for?"

Tyler retreated. "Don't get pissed. I mean I'm just saying man, you've got an opportunity that's all. If you're not interested, it doesn't matter to me."

Jason pressed the point. "But clearly you *are* interested man. You keep bringing it up. I told you, I'm not looking to hook up tonight. I got a date set up for tomorrow, I'm cool man, just enjoying a beer for now. Why are you always trying to get me laid? It's like some weird obsession with you."

The two just looked at each other. Tyler tried to put on an air of disgust, as if to say, "I know the real reason you aren't making a move is because you're not brave enough." But Jason didn't get it. He wasn't listening. He was trying to put on an air of, "why are you trying to live through me? If you want something, then do it for yourself." Jason put out his cigarette. "I gotta go see a small man about a big horse, if ya know what I mean," he said to Tyler. Then he got up and walked across the bar to the bathroom. Inside they had hung pages of the sports pages above the urinals to give guys something to look at while they relieved themselves, or maybe just to distract people so they wouldn't write on the walls.

Tyler sat playing with Jason's empty cigarette pack. Tyler didn't understand Jason. Hell, Tyler didn't understand anybody, nevermind Jason. He just hated to see an opportunity go to waste. Of course, for himself there was always Ann, but Jason would be going home alone that night. Why would he *want* to go home alone? Why would he want to just sit there and not talk to girls and not meet people and get phone numbers and learn about new things and possibly kiss new lips and all that? It didn't make any sense in Tyler's mind.

"Why do I have to do everything myself? If I don't push push push, put in 100% of the effort, it doesn't get done. I'm trying to help these people for god-sakes! But they refuse to put in even an ounce of effort on their own behalf. I just don't get it. Do they want to be lonely? Do they want to be failures? Do they want to look back on their lives as a series of 'coulda beens'? Why do I have so much energy but so little opportunity? Why can't I ever meet one person who eggs me on, pushes me harder, challenges me to do more, live more, be more, challenges me to do the things I don't want to do? Strike that. . . things I don't have the guts to do. Everyone is so fucking complacent and I hate it. I hate seeing others allow opportunities to simply pass them by the dozen when I have so few opportunities, so few choices in my life."

Determined to make something happen, anything happen, Tyler stood up and walked straight over to the two girls playing pool. If for nothing more than to prove to himself that he had no problem just walking up and talking to a girl. "Excuse me," he said to the busty one. "My friend over there is really shy, but he's been talking all night about how cute you are, and try as I might, I can't convince him to come over here and talk to you." The girls both looked in the direction of the now empty table with confusion. "He's in the bathroom now, so I figured I'd take this opportunity to talk to you on his behalf," he said, bringing them back to the conversation. "Do you think that it would be possible for you guys to come over and introduce yourselves to him when he gets back? It'd really make his night." Tyler smiled in anticipation.

"No, that's ok," said the girl. "We're really not that interested." She then went back to her pool game. Tyler scurried back to his seat quickly, so that Jason wouldn't suspect anything when he returned from the bathroom.

Chapter 6:

Sign Guestbook   *View Guestbook*

Rating: 1 out of 5 stars
From: Jason Koldberg, San Francisco

This site totally sucks! What the hell are you thinking? I mean, I suppose that I could forgive the amateurish nature of this pile of filth if you actually had something reasonable to say. But you don't.

What the hell do you think you're trying to accomplish? I mean, do you think that any real terrorist is going to go on one of your dumb ass schemes? They are totally unworkable in the real world. And no real revolutionary is going to come here because the IP Address is probably being tracked by the Feds anyway.

And even if this thing does work like you planned, what the hell are you thinking? Do you really want someone to cause this sort of chaos? Why are you supporting terrorists? Are you crazy? Why would you want to cause another Cole bombing? Maybe you should seek some professional help asshole. Or at least find something more productive to do with your time. Get a job or a girlfriend or something.

"But I've got a job," thought Tyler as he read the entry in his electronic guestbook. The guy didn't get it, he clearly didn't get it. Nobody fucking got it. Not one single god-damned person got it. Tyler felt his lip quiver a little bit. He wanted to cry, he wanted to have that emotional release, he wanted to bang his head on the monitor until it shattered and covered his face with blood. He wanted to hunt down this jerk and kick his ass. He adjusted his tie and started to squeeze a pencil until it broke, but gave up once he heard a slight crack.

"Who the fuck is he to be so critical? He doesn't even have his own website. At least I'm trying to accomplish something," Tyler thought, "This guy's got nothing better to do than criticize." He stared at the green screen for a while. "Probably lives in his Mom's basement." He scrolled down to the only other entry in his guestbook. It was much more positive. Of course, it was written by Tyler himself (from Ann's computer so it couldn't be traced back to him). As the owner of the site he had the power to erase the comment. He could delete it so that other people who might come this way wouldn't be swayed by the arguments of a cretin who almost certainly still lived with his mother. But then again, Tyler thought, "I need to be able to accept criticism. I can't silence voices because they don't agree with me."

Tyler took a half-assed swing at the screen, making a 'thump' noise that was audible in the other cubicles, but not loud enough to be disruptive. He did it more to hurt himself, punish himself, than to hurt the anonymous comment writer. "What the fuck am I doing?" he thought. "Am I so fucking insane that I won't erase this comment because of some higher goal? Because I'm *better than that?*" Tyler flashed back to grade school. He was always small as a child, small and spindly and uncoordinated and fucking useless when it came to sports. In gym class the teacher would pick two students at random to be 'captains' who would then pick their teams and set the batting order for the daily tee-ball game. One day, the teacher, obviously trying to be more PC than usual, picked Tyler and the second biggest geek in class to be captains. It was really Tyler's chance to shine. Of course he put himself first in the batting order. The other geek, whose name might have been Craig or Chris or something unremarkable like that, instead accepted his lot in life and put himself last in the batting rotation, which was his usual place in the playground pecking order.

Of course Tyler popped out three times and his team lost. Afterwards the teacher pulled him aside and praised the opposing captain, saying that he was a better sport, that he was a team player, that he put the team ahead of himself and that's the way it should be and implied Tyler was a jerk for putting himself before the team and that's why they lost and he should try to be more like the other captain in the future.

"Fuck that," Tyler thought. "If I could get my hands on that Mr. Moore now I'd kick his ass too, I'd wring his neck." Tyler never, NEVER had a chance to shine, had a chance to show people what he could do, had a chance to be the game winner, to hit the homerun, to be the envy of all the little people like Tyler who sat on the sidelines and watched the bigger, stronger kids win glory and praise and cheerleaders and all that crap. He would never be given a chance by the athletic elite, he would have to take it himself. That was the only game in which he had a chance to make a difference. Sure he didn't even get to first base, but it was the *opportunity* that was important. He had to take what he could get and he should never be apologetic for it. Mr. Moore's words had rung in his ears for too long now. He hit the screen again, harder this time, trying to make a noise that people *would* hear. He wanted to create a reaction. No one ever reacted to him.

He moved the mouse over to the delete key, ready to defiantly remove this jerk's hateful and unproductive comment in a big 'Fuck You' to his grade school gym teacher. But he hesitated. "What about those people who've already read the comment? If they come back to the guestbook they'll see that it has been deleted and they'll think that I can't accept criticism and that I'm silencing people who don't agree with me and I'll lose all of my street

48

credibility and I'm fucked. His hand backed off the mouse. "If I leave the comment there it's saying, 'bite me, I don't care what you think.'"

But Tyler immediately second-guessed himself, admitting that no one ever came to his site. He only had three hits today, and one of them was this jerk. The chance that either of the other two people read the guestbook was slim. The chance that either of them was important enough to matter, or even notice was even smaller. He clicked the delete button. Immediately he regretted not writing down the guy's email address so he could send him a nasty email later. Although he would probably never have gotten around to actually sending it, he wanted to maintain the capability in case he just happened to get pissed enough to do it.

"Lunch?" came a voice. Tyler looked up. Jason was peering over the wall of his cubicle. It came up to just below his nose. A Kilroy with a shock of blonde hair stared at him from over the blue, fabric wall.

"Hey, you want to go to a riot?" Tyler responded.

"Sure." Jason said automatically. "What kind of riot? You starting a riot? Let me know first so I can keep clear of the tear gas."

"I'm not starting a riot. Don't you read the news?" Outside of sports, Jason didn't read news very often, and even if he did, he wouldn't have heard about the protest. It wasn't highly publicized, except in certain circles. "The IMF is coming to DC next week.[7] There's going to be this huge protest. They're going to have half the city shut down."

---

[7] Ed. Note— The International Monetary Fund's annual meeting, April 2000.

"You mean like that thing in Seattle last fall?"[8]

"Yeah, yeah, but bigger! Seattle was just a wake up call. The protesters are better organized now, word is they're going to cause more trouble. This is going to be huge!" Tyler dreamed of being in a riot, of being part of something really big and notable. He couldn't be at Woodstock, or in Dealey Plaza when Kennedy was shot, or storm the beaches at Normandy, but he could be present for this. Part of him wanted to see half the city in flames. Jason gave Tyler a quizzical look that lasted several seconds.

"Sure, I'll go." And then as an afterthought, "What's wrong with the IMF?" Tyler didn't want to explain. He hated people like Jason for their complacency. He hated them because there were things going on around them and they didn't know about them, didn't care about them. They just believe what they're told and they felt that if it isn't on the news then there is nothing to worry about. Jason was the type of guy who figured that the people in the IMF were probably good guys, or at least normal, regular people who could care less about politics. That they just came in every morning at nine and did their jobs like everyone else. It was the theory of social inertia. In a previous discussion, Jason had presented this theory he came up with that there could never be a large, conspiratorial, 'evil' organization because no one cared enough, no one was organized enough, to pull off a significantly evil act. Every individual inside every organization had their own agenda and they did their own thing. For most people, Jason included, their own thing revolved around doing the least amount of work without getting fired. No one was motivated enough to beat through all of the bureaucratic treacle to plan something that actually had an effect on someone else, nevermind hurt someone else.

---

[8] Ed. Note— The World Trade Organization Ministerial Conference, held in November 1999.

50

If anything not right was going on, Jason was sure that it would be on the news somewhere. Some investigative reporter would do some sort of special on it and the truth would come out. It would be in the reporter's best interest to do so. They want to get promoted to anchorman and all, so even if they didn't personally care, they wanted to find the dirt. And then, once the problem was exposed, the politicians would all run for cover and deny everything and pontificate about how they were against it all along and the bureaucrats would get fired or transferred or whatever and the problem would go away. That's the way the world worked. The fact that Jason hadn't heard anything about evil-doing at the IMF was enough to convince him that there really wasn't anything going on worth protesting about.

Tyler was typing away. "There, I just emailed you the URL of the website that talks about how the IMF is screwing over Third World countries. Read it and then we'll talk." Jason just gave him a blank look. He wasn't going to be bothered to read anything.

"So, are we going to lunch or what?" he repeated in a bored tone.

Chapter 7:

Contact exchange!

Are you in need of operatives but just don't know where to find any? I totally feel for you brother. No matter how dedicated a person is to their cause, it can be lonely trying to find other people equally committed. But that's where CHOAS can help! Just sign up for one of those free email addresses (like hotmail or yahoo), and send us an email detailing your personal beliefs, what you are willing to do, and what you need done. Then we'll match you up with others who have similarly-aligned philosophies and goals. These might end up being people far away from you, people that can't be traced back to you at all. Maybe you can join forces to become a revolutionary front, or at a minimum just come to some mutually beneficial deal where you perform some service for their cause and they perform some service for yours. Think "Throw Mama From the Train" but replace the mama with the plutocracy.

Remember, CHOAS is here for all your terrorist and insurgent related needs. Just send an email for more details!

Another weekday evening. Another night of Ann working. Tyler was bored again. He wandered through the house alone for a while, as the daylight slowly died and the rooms became dark. The place was still a mess. He stood in the bedroom looking at all of his ties. They lay across his dresser in a heap. He was supposed to hang them up, but he hadn't done so for what, 7. . . 8. . . 9. . . days, he counted. He considered hanging them up now, but he was still too unmotivated. Most people in Tyler's office, Jason included, had stopped wearing ties every day, but Tyler was always impeccably dressed. In a previous job, Tyler was amazed by a guy who did nothing, nothing at all, but always wore a three-piece suit. Everyone, all the bosses said the guy was a great worker. It was the suit. They guy once confided to Tyler that the suit was the trick. "If you dress like you are a professional, people treat you like one. What you actually *do* doesn't matter." Tyler desperately wanted to be treated like a professional. He wanted people to think he was a great worker. He wanted to actually be a great worker, but he couldn't do that, obviously, until people respected him enough to give him important projects and lots of responsibility. Since that hadn't happened yet, he dutifully wore his ties to remind people how competent and professional he was. He ignored the subtle suggestions from coworkers that he was too uptight and needed to relax. They didn't understand, they all had plenty of actual work products to show off their professionalism.

He thought about paying some of the bills that lay on his desk, but they weren't due for another week or two, and again he remained unmotivated. The dishwasher probably could have been emptied, but he wasn't going to eat anything anyway so who cared? He was still reading that DeLillo book, even though he didn't think it was all that good. The prose was too flowery. DeLillo was desperately trying to write the Great American Novel, and Tyler felt he was trying way too hard. Tyler wanted to tell that to someone, but none of the people he talked to on a regular basis would have any idea who Don DeLillo was. Tyler was probably wrong anyway. He picked up his book and headed to the coffee shop. It wasn't so much that he wanted to read, or wanted to drink coffee, but he wanted to be out there, somewhere, anywhere, doing something. Even if it was nothing, being out of the house made him feel more alive than just sitting there alone waiting for Ann to come home, silently emptying the dishwasher and putting away neckties.

It was pretty warm out, despite the fact the sun was on the verge of setting. It was the deceptive type of heat, the kind that makes you walk out your front door and say, "oh, it's really not as bad out as I was expecting." But then after a few blocks of walking you start to sweat and burn and feel the oppressiveness of it. Of course it didn't help that Tyler was wearing jeans. It was really shorts weather. But every time he tried on a pair of shorts he always felt self-conscious, as if he was wearing lederhosen or kid's clothes. Maybe it was just that he felt is knees were too knobby. But whatever the reason he never ever wore shorts, not even on the hottest days.

He walked down the road only a few blocks before he arrived at the first coffee shop. He called this one the Christian coffee shop because it was next to a church and the first time he went there he could overhear a group of kids talking about God. That first impression was the only connection this place had anything to do with anything religious, but Tyler always had to name things, code everything into his own language, he couldn't call the place by its actual name. He had to make it his. The Christian coffee shop, the Smoky coffee shop, the restaurant where Ann screamed when she saw a roach on the table, etc. Every business he ever went to got a nickname.

Since it was warm out, he ordered an iced tea instead of his usual latté and sat down at one of the tables. It was pretty busy and there was only one table open all the way off in the corner, which was fine by Tyler. Sitting on the outskirts gave him the appearance of being detached and aloof from the rest of the rabble who frequented the place. Tyler was very perceptive; he saw everything and always remembered the important details. He opened his book but didn't start reading right away. He used it as a shield to hide his eyes as he scanned the crowd. Everyone seemed to be in groups of two and threes and fours. There wasn't anyone else here by themselves. They all had people to be here with. Tyler sighed. There were a few tables of cute young girls and he tried in vain to make eye contact with one of them. It wasn't so much that he wanted them, but he wanted in some way to get them to notice him, to smile back, to come over, to hit on him. Tyler had never been hit on by a female, and was always amazed when he heard stories of it actually happening to other people.

Sitting at a table almost directly across from him was this girl he recognized. She was Asian. Tyler thought that she was Thai, but maybe from southern China. She was at one time dating one of Ann's coworkers. Tyler had met her once or twice at different happy hours. He couldn't remember her name. He quickly averted his eyes from her table and went back to reading his book. She was sitting with this guy, chatting. Tyler was desperately hoping that he would be recognized, that she would come over and say hi, just say hi. Obviously he could have gone over to her table, but he didn't want to be the one who made the first move. What if it wasn't the same girl? What if she didn't recognize him? He'd look pathetic. No, he didn't want to take the risk, he wanted for her to come to him. That's the only way he would win. He would say, "Oh yeah, you're so-and-so's friend. I remember you from that happy hour." And they would chat for a moment or two and she would go back to her own table and her own conversation and Tyler would feel more *real*. Having someone recognize him would make him more solid, more important. It would mean that he wasn't invisible.

Of course, as long as she was sitting there, he couldn't concentrate. He spent the next twenty minutes constantly glancing over the top of the book to see if she was staring at him, see if she was trying to remember where she had seen him before. But that never happened. She either didn't recognize him or didn't want to talk to him. Maybe she was cheating on Ann's coworker and didn't want to get recognized. Maybe it wasn't the same girl that Tyler thought it was. Maybe she was dealing with the same set of insecurities that he was suffering from. After a while the pair left and Tyler was once again alone.

That really pissed him off. "How dare she not notice me," he thought. He reconciled himself with the fact that he was much more observant than other people, and she probably just hadn't seen him. That's the problem with most people, they just don't ever *look*. It was like they had blinders on or something. People only saw what was right in front of them. So many times Tyler and Ann would be walking down the street and they'd pass somebody with some outlandish piece of clothing on and Tyler would say, "Did you see those pants that guy was wearing?" and Ann would just be completely oblivious. It was like a clown could pass them by and she wouldn't realize it. It was too noisy to read in here anyway.

He left and walked farther down the road to the other non-Starbucks coffee place in the area. Tyler refused to enter a Starbucks, on account of their predatory business practices. That was part of the reason that he almost never went for coffee with Ann. She couldn't understand why he would walk four blocks out of his way when there was a perfectly good Starbucks right next door. She didn't want to walk that far and he wouldn't give in to the corporate juggernaut.

Tyler called this other coffee shop the Gay coffee shop on account of how he once overheard the owner talking to someone and they both sounded gay.[9] While it was smaller

---

[9] Ed. Note— Tyler once mentioned the name of this place to Ann and she accused him of being insensitive. Tyler felt that his name wasn't derogatory, just descriptive, but refrained from calling it the Gay coffee shop anywhere else but in his head from then on.

and shoddier than the Christian coffee place, Tyler liked this one better because it had a hipper crowd. It was mostly college-age slackers. Tyler really wanted to be a college-age slacker again, hanging out at coffee shops until all hours of the night talking philosophy and politics and literature and music. Not that he ever did that in college, although he wanted to.

As with the first place, Tyler sat in the corner, out of view. He didn't want to sit right in the middle and advertise to people that he was alone. He wanted to be that aloof guy off to the side that obviously is too cool and too busy to be bothered socializing. There weren't really that many people in this place. It had been steadily losing business since that second Starbucks had opened nearby. Both Tyler and Ann agreed that this store wasn't long for this world.

Despite the hipster nature of the place, the radio was playing some crappy '80s dance mix, and not even in an ironic way.[10] Tyler wished it was colder so he could have worn a jacket without looking strange. That would have given him the extra pocket-space he needed to carry his cd player and headphones. He liked wearing headphones, partially because his music was always much better than whatever was on the radio, but also because having them on gave him an excuse for not talking to anyone. A person sitting alone just staring off into space was weird and lonely and desperate and hoping to meet someone. But a person with their nose buried in a book and wearing headphones was clearly self-absorbed with their own thing and not looking to be bothered. It made him feel better about the fact no one ever tried to bother him.

---

[10] Madonna, "Papa Don't Preach"

He probably came to this place once or twice a week, and he always ordered the same thing, a chocolate muffin and a medium latté. He ordered that in the winter and he ordered that in the summer. He recognized the wait staff on sight, but they never seemed to recognize him. Not once had they said, "You want the regular?" No, they never seemed to remember. He ordered his latté and muffin again this time, but the cashier charged him a dollar less than what he usually paid. For a moment Tyler thought that they were giving him a discount because he was a regular and all, but when they gave him his drink, it was just plain coffee. They must have misheard him. Tyler just sighed and sat down in the corner.

Without the distraction of so many people to attract attention from, he fell into his book, and made some good progress. He didn't even bother trying to hold the book up high so that people at other tables could see the cover and know how literate he was. After about fifteen minutes the coffee was mostly drunk and what wasn't was cold. The muffin had been reduced to just a wrapping. The door opened with the tinkle of a bell and in walked that girl Tyler had talked to at the smoky coffeehouse. The girl whom he spoke about Tibet with. She entered with a gaggle of friends.

"...my mom wore this kinda crap all the time," she was saying. Her hands reached down and smoothed her dress. She was wearing what could only have been a bridesmaid's dress from the early '70s. It was teal in color, satin, and reached down to just below her knee. In the back it was tight, but it draped lazily and awkwardly in the front, emphasizing her small bosom and slight frame. It had a sequined starburst pattern that radiated out from her left thigh all the way up to her chest. At first, Tyler thought that maybe she was going to the prom. He didn't know how old she was, and although she looked to be in her mid 20s, it was entirely possible that she was still going to a school dance.

But the fact that she wore it underneath a zippered hooded jacket made it seem unlikely that she had anywhere special to go. Besides, he figured she had more fashion sense than to wear that hideous monstrosity.

"What do you think of this thing?" she said to the cashier, who she almost undoubtedly knew from somewhere, that mythical place where the beautiful people congregated away from the eyes of schleps like Tyler. "I got a new dress at the Salvation Army. Do you like it?" It was hard to judge her reasoning. Was she wearing the dress as a joke? As a punk? As a "fuck you" to fashion trends? But her question was so honest, it seemed as if she were seeking approval, not as a joke, but as a symbol of self-worth. The look on her face made it appear that she would've been crushed if the cashier had disliked it.

She reached for the coffee with her thin left hand. She was wearing one of those beaded metal cords that banks use to stop people from stealing their 4¢ pens. She must have had five of the cords wrapped around her wrist, over and over again. Her red-brown hair was pulled up into the same short ponytail she'd been wearing the last time he saw her. Her ears were aglow with a dozen piercings each, which clashed thematically with the more formal and staid gown. Her feet were completely bare. Tyler looked around, trying to see if she had just discarded her footwear somewhere nearby, but she hadn't. Her feet were very large, and thin, in a way more reminiscent of flippers than feet. Ann's feet were tiny, so maybe they just appeared large in Tyler's mind. Her soles were absolutely filthy.

Several more patrons entered the café, including this old guy with a dog and a plaid shirt. "Hi Molly," he said as his dog went over for its sniff of recognition. She rubbed the fur under his neck and smiled.

It bothered Tyler that he had been coming to this coffee shop for months and no one knew his name. "Why the fuck does everybody know everybody but me?" Tyler thought to himself. He tried to get back into his book and his self-pity, but he couldn't concentrate anymore.

Chapter 8:

From the FAQ:

Q: Why do you do it?

A: This is probably the most frequently asked question here at CHOAS HQ: Why is it we do what we do? The answer dear reader is why not? Why shouldn't we do what we do? More importantly, what else CAN we do? This society is so boring and cookie-cutter that there really isn't anything else to do! Not for people like you and I dear reader. Would you rather sit on your comfortable couch watching reruns of Seinfeld, eating chips and listening to your heartbeat ticking away what's left of your life?

Jean Paul Sartre once said, "In a society that has abolished all adventure, the only adventure left is to abolish that society!"

I hope that answers your question. Godspeed culture warrior!

Tyler sat watching Headline News cycle around for the third time in a row. He was waiting for Ann to call for her nightly pick up. There was nothing else on tv Tuesday nights. He thought about reading a book, but decided against it. It was so hard for him to concentrate on something when he knew he might be disturbed at any moment, and Ann could call at any moment. He looked over at the phone sitting on the coffee table. He bounced a red kick-ball against the wall for a while, but that didn't help. He wanted to play a game, but there was no one to play with. It wasn't raining yet outside. It might rain soon. He hoped that Ann would call him before the rain started. It wasn't so much that he didn't want to get wet, but that the traffic tended to back up once the first drop fell.

He felt that he should be doing something. He should be improving himself. He felt that he should be accomplishing *something*. But there really wasn't anything to accomplish. He had just updated the website, the apartment was pretty clean, so what was left to do? Everyone he knew seemed so exhausted by the simple requirements of daily life that they just collapsed in front of the tv at night. A number of people at work had said that they'd love to have hobbies but they just didn't have the time. Once, a coworker named Lydia told him that she never had time to do creative things on the weekend because she was too busy mowing the lawn. Tyler couldn't imagine how mowing the lawn would take up an entire weekend, nevermind every entire weekend. Didn't these people ever get restless like he did? "That's what I desire most in life," he thought to himself, "I need to surround myself with people that are restless." Of course, that's not something you can really advertise for. And all the truly restless people in this world were probably outside right now doing something, not sitting alone in an apartment bouncing a red kick-ball against a wall.

The television glowed with stock footage of the riots in Seattle, and talked about the police plans for what streets would be cordoned off in DC that weekend. Tyler watched the masked protestors hurling rocks. "Who are these people?" he wondered to himself. "Where do they come from? A lot of them seem to be wearing similar black clothes, a uniform of sorts. It's not a coincidence, they must know each other, but how?" None of the people Tyler worked with would ever consider doing something like this, nevermind decide on uniforms ahead of time. But they must come from somewhere. Maybe it was a college thing, they were all in some club someplace? It wasn't on the internet, that's for damned sure. Tyler had spent hours searching for some website that would offer to connect him to these people, but there wasn't any, except the one Tyler made himself, of course, and that hadn't yet connected him to a single restless soul. He toyed with the idea of dressing in a black uniform for the protest in DC, but decided against it. He figured that they would make him for a poseur pretty quick. They'd call him out and reveal that he wasn't a real radical, but just some jerk who was out to get his jollies. They wouldn't accept him. He wasn't part of their world. He wanted to be, but he wasn't. He didn't even know where their world was.

A commercial came on, advertising a special showing of Schindler's List that was going to be broadcast commercial-free that weekend. He hated that movie. "How do you know you aren't an asshole?" he'd said to Jason one night after having enough beer to override his normal sense of self-censorship.

"That's easy, don't be an asshole," Jason replied.

"No, I mean how do you *know* that you aren't an asshole?"

"That's easy. . . don't be an asshole," Jason repeated.

"Well duh, but is it really that easy?" Tyler looked down into his glass of beer as he spoke. "The problem with that sort of stuff is that you can't ever be objective about yourself. No one thinks they're an asshole, everyone thinks they're a saint. I mean, go back to Nazi Germany and ask those people. I'm sure they all would say they were nice upstanding perfectly reasonable human beings, but objectively they were freaking Nazis, you know? I mean, unless someone is out there, someone objective that doesn't really know you, who says, 'Yes, what you are doing is valid and impressive and helpful,' then you never really *know* do you? You're always just sitting in darkness hoping that maybe you aren't an asshole and what you are doing is helpful and well received by humanity, but you never really know. . ." Tyler trailed off when he looked up and it was obvious that Jason wasn't even listening to him.

He'd never be as lucky as Oskar Schindler, never really have the peaceful sleep that comes with certainty. He'd never really know if he was a saint or a Nazi or worst of all, an asshole. He switched off the tv.

Tyler picked up his blue journal off his desk. It had an 'Amnesty International' sticker on it that they had sent him in anticipation of his donation (which he never got around to sending). It also had the word 'CHOAS' scrawled on the cover in white-out (the only thing that would show up against the blue). It was his 'Choas Journal,' and in it he jotted down all of the ideas he had for his website. He stared at a blank page for a while, trying to come up with something interesting to say, some new form of mayhem to create, but his mind wasn't on specifics. It was on bigger questions.

He was angry that his life wasn't harder, that he didn't have a ready target to fight against. He was just sitting there, doing nothing and yet there was no consequence to his inaction. There was nothing that anyone needed him to do. He hated himself for even complaining about it, knowing that he'd get no sympathy from anybody for complaining that his life was too cushy.

He put down the pencil (he never wrote in pen), and threw the journal against the wall in frustration. It lay next to the couch with its pages splayed out on the floor. Tyler glared at it, hoping it would move, hoping it would limp about like a wounded animal. That would give him an excuse to kick it and put it out of its misery. But it was inert. The blow against the wall had killed it.

The phone rang. It was Ann. She was finally finished. Tyler looked out the window at the blackness outside. A thunderbolt flashed across the sky, and you could hear the first drops of rain splash against the windowpane.

Chapter 9:

Countermeasures!

The biggest weapon the pigs have to break up your protest is tear gas. I know what you're thinking - that you can handle it. You think that if you and your compatriots are strong enough, brave enough, incensed enough, a little stinky gas isn't going to hold you back. Well, I'm here to tell you brother, it will. Take it from me, CHOAS has been in a lot of riots and protests over the years, and every single time we hear from amateur revolutionaries that tear gas isn't going to stop them, and yet, at the first hiss from the first canister, they turn tail and go running home to mama.

But fear not revolutionaries, there are ways to make yourself practically immune from the gas. Obviously a full up gas mask is the best protection, but those are hard to come by and even harder to actually wear properly. However there's a simpler, cheaper solution. Tear gas is a chemical called o-chlorobenzylidene malononitril. And what is it about that particular chemical that the powers that be don't want you to know? It's easily neutralized by acids! So all you have to do to keep yourself safe is just take a scarf, or a bandana or something, soak it in vinegar (a cheap and easily available acid), and wrap it around your face. Sure, it's not the most pleasant smell, but it'll make you pretty much immune to the effects of tear gas. You should even be able to get close enough to a tear gas canister to pick it up and throw it back at the police. See how they like a taste of their own medicine! Ha!

What do you wear to a riot? What to wear, what to wear, what to wear? Is there some sort of etiquette? Tyler sat on the floor in front of his open closet. "Everyone always seems to blend in, there must be some sort of guidelines that people are following," he thought. "I mean, there's got to be a place to look it up. You can't just *know*, can you? Why do I always have a hard time with the stupid stuff?"

He began pawing through his clothing. His shirts were generally organized into piles based on how warm they were: sweaters on the left, long sleeve shirts in the middle, t-shirts on the right. He had already made the decision to wear a flannel shirt on top, sort of like a jacket, so that probably meant a t-shirt underneath. He went to the front door and stuck his hand outside. It was April, but it wasn't too cold out, a t-shirt would be all right. He returned to the closet.

The past few years, Tyler had been mostly wearing more "grown-up" clothing, on the insistence of Ann who disliked it when Tyler dressed like a college student. She wanted him to be "more classy" so that she could take him to fancier restaurants on the fly without having to modify her plans because he was underdressed. There was a time in Tyler's life when he only wore band t-shirts. He wore them like a badge of honor, a not-so-secret symbol to attract people who would recognize the obscure bands he was displaying knowledge of and introduce themselves, and also as a way to scare off and intimidate those who weren't cool enough to know who Nietzer Ebb and Echo and the Bunnymen were.

He decided to start at the bottom of the pile, since those represented the shirts that he hadn't worn for the longest time. There was a U2 shirt that he got way back in high school when they were playing on the Joshua Tree tour. He didn't actually go to the concert, he'd been too intimidated to try to hang with the cool people who actually went, but he was able to get a friend to get him a shirt (which he slyly didn't wear the day after the concert like everyone else did). But U2 simply wasn't cool anymore, having sold out and all, so that shirt was now worthless. He folded it back up. Next on the pile was an old Cure shirt that his eight year-old neighbor had stolen from an amusement park for him years ago. The Cure was pretty cool, in an old school retro way. He could wear it with that pair of black Converse high-tops that he had saved when they stopped making them, and really go for the retro look.[11] But the shirt was flimsy and ratty looking, and it probably wouldn't make that good an impression.

He had a really cool Earth First! T-shirt he'd mail-ordered a while back. However, the design wasn't very interesting, and you could barely make out the words, "Earth First!" written in small type at the bottom. So what was the point really? Nobody would notice. The point was to get someone to notice. The point of *everything* Tyler did was to get someone to notice.

Eventually, Tyler settled on a black shirt that he'd had for a while. It had a giant red star in the middle and was rather generic, but at least it didn't say anything uncool. The red star had a whole Communist vibe to it that should go over well with the other protestors. He decided against jeans. The only ones he had were Calvin Klein and those were simply too corporate to wear. He put on a pair of khaki pants that he had bought without trying on. It turned out that they were too casual to wear to work, so he had never worn them. But just last weekend he had noticed a bunch of skaters on the street wearing casual khakis, so he thought that maybe they'd work. When combined with the pair of canvas "summer-style" combat boots he bought from the Army-Navy store, he looked pretty good— militant yet stylish.

To finish the ensemble, he dug to the bottom of a cardboard box that contained mostly socks with holes in them and found a bandana. He'd read that the well-prepared protestors in Seattle brought bandanas and a bottle of

---

[11] From the Cure's "Just Like Heaven" video.

vinegar to negate the effects of the tear gas. Tyler didn't think that he'd be central enough to the action to get gassed, but he wanted to be prepared, or at least to look prepared. He wanted to look like an old pro, the type of person who'd been to many events like these, the type of person that you could come to for advice and comradeship.

He stood in front of Ann's mirror and tied the bandana around his face, Jesse-James style. He was satisfied. The whole ensemble really worked. The bandana hid a grin. He thought about a hat for a minute, but all he had was a baseball cap with the logo of a fancy university on it. The hat made him look more like a yuppie frat-brother than an iconoclastic rebel. He stared at his reflection for a while, trying to get into the mood. He spent a good thirty seconds standing still, with his balled fist high in the air in a symbol of defiance, just to see how it would look. Eventually it became too difficult to breathe through the mask and he took it off. He didn't think that he would actually wear the thing anyway. He was too self-conscious for that. It's strange, for some people putting on a mask would make them less self-conscious, more anonymous, more free. But that wasn't the way Tyler's mind worked. He thought that it would make him stand out, that the "real" protestors and rebels would look at him and think he was a poseur or an imitator, not a real protestor, just a wannabe. Tyler stuffed the bandana in his pocket, making sure to leave just a little end dangling. That would show people that he *had* a bandana ready, but he wasn't being too obvious about it.

He paced around the living room for a while. It was still early, he had some time to kill before heading out. He wanted to listen to some music, something to get him in the mood. He wished that he had some Rage Against the Machine to listen to. It would be the most obvious choice of course. He hadn't bought the cd because it was simply too trendy, and Tyler would rather die than be trendy. Someday,

69

years from now when it was forgotten, he would seek it out in a used record store and then claim to be old school, but for now, it was forbidden. He settled on Ministry, being industrial, and therefore somewhat in line with the emotional tone of the day.[12] He sat down on the couch, checked his watch, and waited.

---

[12] Ministry, "You Know What You Are" The Land of Rape and Honey.

Chapter 10:

Quick-Set Cement

Number of Conspirators:	*1–3*
Danger Level:	*Low*
Arrest Level:	*Medium*
Lethality:	*Low*
Annoyance Level:	*Medium*
Economic Damage:	*Low*
Equipment Required:	*Couple of Bags of Cement*

Whenever there is a riot or demonstration, the police like to set up barriers around town and close off the streets. This provides the people who are being protested against a buffer zone between themselves and the protestors. What's the point of protesting if you can't even harass the people who you are protesting against? But you can use the barricade concept to your advantage. During the protest, simply hang a block or two back and mix up a batch of cement. Quick set is obviously the best. Then run up to the barricade and dump the cement on it. The cops probably won't stop you because they have their hands full preventing people from climbing over the barricade. The next day, when they try to open the street again, they'll find that the barrier has been permanently affixed to the asphalt! It'll take cleanup crews a few days to fix the problem, especially if you use a lot of cement in a lot of places. Traffic around the protest area will be shut down for days, causing way more damage to the city's economy than they expected. They won't want another controversial meeting in their town for a long time.

"I love the smell of tear gas in the morning," he thought to himself. He couldn't say it out loud of course. It was way too derivative of that line from Apocalypse Now to be acceptable for public consumption. So he just kept his mouth shut. Tyler and Jason were coming up the Metro escalator at Foggy Bottom. They could already hear music playing from the street above. "...I'll jail and bury those committed and smother the rest in greed!"[13] "C'mon c'mon. I don't want to be late!" Tyler started bounding up the steps two at a time. The protest website said that the activities were starting at 9 a.m., and it was already almost 10. If things really went to hell quickly, the whole riot might be over before Tyler even got there. He sniffed the air to see if any tear gas had been released yet. He didn't know exactly what tear gas smelled like, but he figured he'd know it when he smelled it. He looked back down the steps. Jason was calmly riding up, standing on the right to let people pass on the left.

"I'm coming, geez, keep your panties on." Tyler decided that Jason was right. You didn't want to look too eager. This was supposed to be a serious affair. Tyler wanted people to think that he did these kinds of things all the time. He wanted people to think that he was deeply involved in the movement, even maybe a leader in the movement. He didn't want to appear to be just a riot tourist. He wanted desperately to be taken seriously. He wanted to fit in.

Jason on the other hand had no problem admitting he was a riot tourist, and was dressed suspiciously like one of those frat boys that go to goth clubs to gawk at the weirdos. Besides his general pretty-boy surfer hair, he was wearing his Penn State baseball cap, and a t-shirt that had a "Mr. Zog's Sex Wax" logo. He was chewing gum. It never even crossed his mind to bring a vinegar-soaked bandana, but then again he hadn't spent the time that Tyler had spent reading up on the subject. If you asked him, Jason would've probably told

---

[13] Rage Against the Machine, "Sleep Now in the Fire"

you he was only there to meet some hippy girls, or maybe to score a little free pot.

Tyler's hands were full of flyers. He had this great idea for publicizing his website. "After all," he thought, "who would be more interested in my revolutionary tips than these people?" He had found this ACLU brochure online that gave a bunch of advice for what to do when you get arrested. It talked about what your exact rights were and how to be uncooperative without getting beaten. Tyler had copied the entire thing down. At first he was just going to give it to Jason, since he figured that Jason wouldn't be as up on civil disobedience procedures as he was. But then he thought some more and decided that if he just put a tag line at the bottom that said, "This information brought to you by CHOAS - http://www.choas.com" then people would think CHOAS was pretty cool and knew the score and they'd go to his website and they would start conversations on the message boards, and he'd gain some notoriety and a platform to say the things that he knew people needed to hear.

He had printed the flyer out at work, and then used the copier to make a hundred copies. The news media had said that there was supposed to be a hundred-thousand people at the riot, so one hundred flyers didn't seem like all that much. But he didn't want to print out too many at work. Not that anyone would've noticed really, but he felt guilty about using up all of the supplies, even though it was sort of their own fault for leaving him with so much time on his hands. If they didn't seem to mind that they were paying him for not working, why should they mind that he was stealing a ream or two of paper? But after nervously standing by the copier for what seemed an eternity as 100 copies slowly printed, Tyler gave up and scurried back to his desk. He didn't want to be on the photocopier for too long in case someone else wanted to use it and inquired too closely about what he was printing. "That should be enough to plant the seed," he thought. Maybe it was enough to reach a critical mass. Every person who sees it would tell two friends who would tell two friends and so on. Maybe a news reporter would even pick it up and mention it on the news? Tyler considered that a longshot, but you never know.

"...The field overseer, the Agent of Orange, the Priest of Hiroshima...."[14] The sun was shining pretty brightly that day. Spring had some of the best weather of the year in DC. Tyler was starting to wish that he had brought sunglasses, but he hadn't. He didn't know exactly where the IMF was, but he knew that it was somewhere near the George Washington campus and the metro station. He'd heard on the news that GW closed down for the weekend and made all the students leave. They claimed that it was because they didn't want any students to get hurt, but Tyler knew better. He knew that the school had been pressured by the police to get rid of their students to lower the number of possible protestors. That really sucked. If Tyler had been a GW student he would've locked himself in his dorm room and refused to leave. Or so he would've said if you'd asked him.

"No you wouldn't have," Jason said, "You would've pussied out like everybody else and gotten out of there." Tyler was hurt by that accusation. He knew that he would have stayed. He just never got the chance to do anything like that, so nobody realized that he had it in him. They just knew the meek, boring Tyler, and there was no way that they could tell he wasn't inherently meek and boring. They didn't realize that it was his life, his job, his girlfriend, his responsibilities, that made him *appear* boring. If things had turned out different he would have certainly become a firebrand. He just never had the opportunity.

---

[14] Id.

74

"What the hell do you know? I would too have stayed. Hell, the students paid for the rooms, they don't have anyplace else to go. They're backs would have been up against the wall. It would be easy to stay."

"Whatever dude. You're fucking Che Guevara." The street was pretty empty. There were a few people milling about, wandering to and fro, but not many. It was also strangely quiet. The pair could hear music playing a few blocks away, but that was the only sound. Tyler looked around and realized that there were no cars on the streets. The police had blocked off a quarter of the city in anticipation of the protests. They weren't letting any cars in, even if the people lived there. That wasn't right. Two blocks from the IMF they weren't even letting people in their apartments. That was even more not right. Tyler licked his chops at the thought of the lawsuits that were going to result from this debacle.

"Come on, the barricades are up this way." They moved through the streets. Even the parked cars were missing. It felt not right, it felt like something was happening. It wasn't the same as usual, it wasn't the way it had always been. Tyler could feel it deep inside his stomach. Finally, something was going on, something that he could be a part of. He hoped that eventually he'd be able to tell his grandkids about today. "You know, they say that this is going to be wilder than Seattle."

Jason kicked a rock down the street. "You're kidding yourself, there's no way that this is going to turn into a riot."

"No, it has to. You see, the people in Seattle didn't know what they were getting into, they just showed up. The people at this place, they're ready to just go nuts. They know that to make an impact, this has to be even more destructive. And the cops, they'll be all on edge because they know this could get way out of control, so they'll be more likely to start banging heads early."

Jason shook his head. "You're talking out your ass man. Why don't you just admit that you don't know shit? This ain't going to get out of hand precisely because of Seattle. The cops there got taken by surprise. These guys are ready. They've had time to train, they're not going to lose their shit so easily." He spit on the floor, "plus, the whole place is going to be full of poseurs like us. There's going to be too many gawkers in the way for the real troublemakers to get a critical mass."

"Nah, you just wait, this' going to kick ass." Tyler looked around for someone to hand some flyers to. The people milling about on the street looked young and bedraggled, but maybe they weren't here for the riot. They could just be locals. Tyler figured that he'd better hold on to his flyers until he was sure he had good candidates. It was a practical consideration since he only had a limited number of flyers.

They walked up H Street and saw a barricade. It was pretty lame looking actually, just a waist-high steel fence and a couple of fat looking cops standing around joking. On the protestor side there were a number of people, but no one seemed to be doing anything other than standing around. Tyler and Jason stood around for a while. "So what do you want to do man?" said Jason. He looked bored.

"I don't know, I thought that there'd be more going on than this. Maybe it's early. Lets walk around a bit." They moved down H Street and the density of people started to grow. It was mostly a younger crowd, pretty hip looking, and a bit scrungy. Everyone seemed confused and unfocused, like they didn't know what they were supposed to be doing. Occasionally the pair would pass someone with a sign of some type, handmade out of an old bedsheet and some tempera paint.

"Hey Man!" a college-age stranger said to Tyler, "Rage Against the Machine Man!"

Tyler was confused. "What?"

"Your shirt man, that red star. It's a Rage shirt right?"

"No, at least I don't think so. It's just a red star."

"That's the symbol of the Chiapas people man," said the kid, "It's like Zack's personal cause. He's always wearing black shirts with red stars. Fight the power man!" He slapped Tyler on the back and disappeared into the crowd. Tyler was concerned. He didn't want to appear to be supporting corporate rock consumption. If people thought that he was wearing a Chiapas shirt that would be cool, but he didn't want to appear to be wearing some band shirt he bought at a concert. Dammit. He looked around at what other people were wearing to get an idea if he was dressed correctly. It was hard to get a good read. People were wearing all sorts of things. Some had on traditional hippy attire, but there were others who wore polo shirts or sweats or other things Tyler didn't think were all that cool. Jason was saying something, but he wasn't listening. He quietly decided that he looked ok and resolved not to think about it or act all self-conscious. A guy ran past wearing nothing but a grass skirt.

They meandered down various side streets for about an hour, chuckling at some of the funnier protest signs. Around noon they got to K Street, which was where they'd been told the serious rioters were hanging around. The street was filled with people sitting down. Some were eating, some were talking, most were just loitering aimlessly. There are a lot of storefronts on K Street, corporate stores like Gap and Starbucks. There is a lot of glass to smash and things to loot. None of the storeowners had taken any sort of precautions to keep their merchandise safe. But to Tyler's surprise, there was no smashed glass. A few slogans were written in chalk and marker on the buildings, "Smash the Corporate State," "IMF GTFO," and that sort of thing, but there had been no looting, not even a little bit. Maybe it was just too early. The real looting and anarchist cathartic destruction of corporate symbols probably wouldn't occur until later, once the crowd was whipped into a frenzy by student leaders and police brutality.

Sitting in a large group were a bunch of kids dressed completely in black. They were wearing ski masks or black bandanas. They were well-equipped and carried backpacks probably filled with all sorts of chaos-causing goodies. They seemed grim-faced and purposeful with cold steely eyes. They were waiting for the signal. "See those guys over there?" Tyler whispered to Jason.

"Yeah, you mean the brigade of punk ninjas?"

"Those guys are the hardcore rioters. It's like some secret group. They're like totally into the deal. They've been trained."

"Trained to riot?"

"Yeah, there's this group out in California that trains people in protesting techniques. I've read their website."

"You gotta be fucking kidding. Those guys need to get a freaking life." Jason started walking across the street. "There's some girls over there though, let's check them out. I hear that hippy chicks are usually pretty easy."

"I wonder how you join one of those groups?" Tyler mused as he walked across the road with Jason. "I mean, they've got to be coming from somewhere right? I mean, somewhere there's got to be this guy who isn't part of their group, and they see him and invite him to join. How do you think that happens?"

"Why don't you go ask them?"

"Nah, I'm sure that they're busy. Plus they'd probably think I was a narc or something. I mean I'm hanging with Mr. Zog and all."

"Hey, don't knock Mr. Zog. Mr. Zog is the man." They approached a small splinter group of rioters in black. They had their masks off and were smoking. A female reporter in a business suit approached them, cameraman in tow. She had probably been told to get some interviews and had no idea who she was talking to. As she closed on the smokers they began covering their faces and told her to get the hell out of there. "We don't want to be filmed. We aren't giving you permission to film us!" they shouted. The reporter didn't quite get it. The rioters in black were wearing masks because they knew that the police were going to film the day's events and they were going to cause trouble later. They didn't want their faces on tape because they could be identified and prosecuted. All of this went over the head of the naïve reporter who just kept trying to get them to answer her questions.

Jason jumped in front of the cameraman, using his body as a shield to protect the rioters' identities. "Hey, get the hell out of here!" he shouted. "Are you deaf? They said they don't want to give you an interview." Tyler saw what was happening and attempted to intercede his body as well, but it was too late. The rioters had replaced their masks and blended back into the crowd without so much as a thank you. The reporter turned and left, she'd get her story elsewhere. "Some people are freaking rude," Jason said.

At the end of the block, the serious police presence started. This street was much closer to the IMF than where the fat, laughing cops were, and officers here looked much more professional. These were the real riot police. They stood stoically behind the steel fence, at attention, in a row. Their arms were crossed behind their backs so they wouldn't appear to be taking a threatening or dangerous posture. They were dressed almost like sci-fi space trooper football players. They had shin guards, helmets, shoulder pads and clear shields— a row of futuristic Roman soldiers, ready to do battle against the anarchic, barbarian hordes. Their entire outfit was black, Darth Vader black, except for the bright white POLICE emblazoned upon their chests. Tyler looked upon them with a mixture of fright and wonderment. They were scary. They had bats. They had bats and there was every possibility that they would soon be using those bats to smash Tyler on the head. He examined their belts for guns or tear gas canisters, but he didn't see any. "They probably have them in the fallback area," he thought to himself.

"Those black dudes look pretty hard-core," Jason said. Tyler wasn't sure if he was referring to the police or the protestors. Both groups seemed to be very professional and intent on delivering their message. "I bet that if anything happens, this is probably the place." Tyler looked at him in acknowledgement. They both steeled themselves for the coming conflagration. "Hey," Jason said to relieve the tension, "Why don't you try giving *them* some of your flyers." Tyler looked down and the papers he held. They seemed amateurish when compared to the seriousness of the kids in black and the shiny new uniforms of the riot police. A woman walked past wearing a large white sign that said 'legal observer.' It was her job to record any acts of police brutality that might occur. She had a clipboard and a sheaf of papers.

80

Her information was probably way more official than Tyler's was. He looked over at the grim-faced protestors. They undoubtedly had been well trained in police tactics. They didn't need his advice, he thought to himself. "It's better not to waste the flyers I have on them. I could get a lot more benefit by giving them to less professional protestors." He rolled the papers up into a smaller bundle and hid them under his arm.

Jason and Tyler stood around chatting about work for about a half an hour. They kept an ear out for the sound of a drum. Tyler had read that the way the groups in Seattle coordinated their attack was through the use of drumbeats. The idea of the Roman army came to mind. In those days, they didn't have loudspeakers and radios and GPS and flareguns. They conveyed their attack orders via coded drumbeat. Tyler wondered if the protestors knew the drumbeat codes that were used in antiquity. You could probably find them on the internet somewhere. Maybe he should have printed that out on the back of his flyers, he thought to himself. Although on second thought that'd only be useful if everybody was in on the code, and it was likely that nobody protesting today paid attention to that kind of stuff anymore. Nobody ever paid attention to that kind of stuff anymore.

After a while it became apparent that no drumbeat was forthcoming. There was no attack. Several times people with cell phones and clipboards wandered past. Several times, people got up en masse and milled about in a more deliberate manner, but there was no rushing of the barricades, no forcing of the issue, no taunting and goading of the oppressive police. Just milling about. Eventually, the pair got bored and decided to see if there was anything else going on. They walked up towards the White House, which was some blocks from the IMF, but there was a large field there, and the sound of music wafted from that direction, so perhaps there was more to the spectacle than just watching the kids in black aimlessly wander to and fro.

The lawn in front of the White House was indeed a spectacle, but it was more reminiscent of a rock festival than a riot. There were groups of people camped out in clumps on the stony ground. The grass there had long been worn away from constant celebrations, gatherings, and protest marches. Kids sat on their ratty blankets eating sandwiches and drinking bottled water. They all seemed dirty and grubby somehow, as if they were wildmen just coming out of their caves. They wore what looked like tattered rags. Many of the women had those backless wrap-around tops that you only saw at Grateful Dead concerts. The men all had long, dreadlocked hair. As they walked through the crowd, Tyler had this overwhelming feeling that they all knew each other. Everybody knew everybody but him. It was as if they had all come from the same place, the same strange alternate dimension. These were not the type of people that you saw on the streets everyday, especially not in preppy, status-conscious DC. They were probably all kids from liberal arts colleges up and down the East Coast. Kids whose parents had enough cash to send them to private colleges like Bennington and Swarthmore. Schools cool enough to fill their students with anarchist and communist manifestos. It would all wear off after they graduated though. That's what happened to the baby boomer generation in the 1960s, and it would soon happen with these kids. They'd graduate and have to cut their hair to get a job and, like Sampson, all of their rhetoric would fall away. Tyler's uncle once told him that everyone becomes a Republican as they get older.

There were also large floats and paper maché effigies all over. It was like the staging area for a freaky Macy's Day parade. Some were artfully done too, lending credence to the theory that the majority of the protestors had been bussed in from liberal arts schools. There was one giant pig lying on the ground. It must have been 10 feet tall. On its side were the words, "I.M.F.=P.I.G." Tyler looked around for its owner, but none was evident. "Jason," he said, tugging at the Mr. Zog shirt. "Jason, here, take a picture." He handed Jason a camera. Then, looking around surreptitiously, he stepped in front of the pig and quickly tied the bandana around his head. He lifted a clenched fist in a mock demonstration of anger and fidelity, like the black Olympians in the '60s. Jason, who wasn't as self-conscious as Tyler, laughed heartily and took a picture. Tyler quickly removed the bandana and hid the camera back in his pocket before any of the wildmen took notice.

The pair moved closer to the stage that had been set up. It was angled in such a way that anyone in the White House would be able to look out and see what was going on. Of course, no one in the White House cared. They didn't care about the protests and they didn't care about the message. They did care about getting elected though, and that meant maintaining a posture that would allow the protestors to feel that the government empathized with their grievances, but also allowed the conservative constituency to feel that no one in government was willing to give a bunch of dirty hippies the time of day. Plus, no one was even home in the White House that day anyway. The President and his staff were in Europe at the time. That was probably not just a coincidence.

The stage was currently empty. They were between speakers. Music was blaring from the sound system, hypothetically to keep the crowd warmed up and frenzied.[15] Most people weren't listening though. Across from the stage, there were a number of tables set up. "Let's go over there and get some literature." Tyler said. Of course, it wasn't what

---

[15] The song playing at the time, Indigo Girls, "Galileo" was failing to keep anything frenzied.

they were expecting. Both Tyler and Jason had thought that the tables were set up to get people to join various causes, and to sign various petitions, and to get on various mailing lists. But it was just a bunch of people selling stuff. Even the Green Party table was just a guy selling bumper stickers and pins. There was no literature to pick up and no petitions to sign. Maybe the protest was the petition. What would a list of signatures accomplish that a hundred thousand screaming anarchists couldn't accomplish in person? Tyler bought a large pin that had the letters 'IMF' in a big 'no' symbol. He wanted a souvenir, something to remember the riot by, something to bring into work and leave lying around so that the squares in his office with would know his political leanings. No one ever bothered to ask him directly, so he had to resort to what he considered more subtle tactics to get his message across.

Jason bought a pin too. His said, 'Stop Sucking Corporate Dick!' "There was one of those pictures that goes around the internet, you know. One of those stupid email chain jokes right? And it was of this old Japanese woman, and she was wearing a shirt that had this exact same phrase on it. It was hella funny. She had no fucking idea what it said. Maybe I'll give this to my grandma." Jason was speaking mostly to himself, Tyler was thinking about other things. He was looking for more stuff to buy, more things to say to the world, "I'm cool, I was there." Like the Earth First! t-shirt that he had bought online.

There still wasn't anyone on stage by the time they had finished walking through the maze of tables. "I don't think that there's going to be any tear gas today." Tyler said dejectedly.

"Well, it certainly isn't going to happen here, this just looks like a staging area. If there's any action, it'll be back on the front lines." Jason pointed north. The two wordlessly began moving in that direction. Tyler took one last look around at the spectacle. It was starting to get late in the afternoon, and some of the tables and floats and signs had been abandoned and lay silently in the grass. Tyler consider picking up a sign, but he worried that if the owner saw him holding it, they'd make a comment and he'd feel like a loser for stealing a sign. He slyly dropped his sheaf of flyers on one of the abandoned tables. No one was going to get arrested anyway, so it was pointless to keep carrying them around. Besides, he knew in his heart that he wasn't going to actually hand any out, so he might as well leave them in a place where maybe somebody might pick one up. He wished that he'd had a rock or something to hold them down though. As soon as he started to walk away they began blowing in the wind.

They moved northward up towards where the front line was. On a tree-lined street with ridiculously unaffordable brownstones, they came upon the best the resistance had to offer. The street was blocked off with a three-foot high, steel, crowd control barrier. Behind it stood a number of cops in full riot regalia. On the other side sat a hundred or so protestors, right in the middle of the street. The guy in the grass skirt was there. He was holding a sign that said, "THE GAP RUNS THIRD WORLD SWEATSHOPS." A number of hot girls were there. They had dirty dreads and wore wrap around halter-tops without bras. They all seemed really young and skinny. There were slacker boys there, long dirty hair and scraggly beards masking their age. Birkenstocks all around. Most of the kids who weren't wearing rags they sewed together themselves were clad in the latest styles from Old Navy or The Gap. They sat passively but cheerily. One by one they got up and walked over to the barricade. A police officer solemnly parted the steel barrier slightly and the protestor stepped through. Then the police officer took their hands and tied them with a plastic strap and calmly led them into a waiting blue bus that had steel mesh on the windows. Sometimes the protestor and the police hesitated a second to allow a friend to take a picture. They all had big smiles on their faces as they were led into the bus, like cows being led obliviously to the abattoir. The officers, not having any vested interest in either the corporations they were defending nor any grassroots political movements, took it all in stride, grinning with relief under their helmets that they wouldn't have to do anything drastic enough to get reprimanded for when the fallout came in a few weeks.

All of this was being carefully observed by an older woman with a clipboard and a hat that said "legal observer." Tyler sidled up to her. "What's going on here?" he asked the woman.

"We made a deal with the pigs. We break through the barrier one at a time and they'll arrest us for trespassing."

"What's the point of that?" Tyler said incredulously.

"That way we can get our message across without any violence. It'll save a lot of trouble on both sides."

Tyler walked away shaking his head. He grabbed Jason who was trying to chat up an almost skeletal crunchy-looking girl who was waiting her turn to get arrested. "Let's go," he said.

They walked away from the scene. "I don't get it. Don't these people understand? This is stupid."

"I thought you were all for this non-violent protest thing?"

"Non-violence only works when the other side is violent. Gandhi used non-violence to get sympathy. He got those

86

journalists to write all those articles about how the British were beating unarmed guys with sticks and shooting women and crap. That's when non-violence works. It worked in the '60s when the Man was shooting Kent Staters in the streets. That's why they got wise on the other side. I mean look at those cops on the line. They're standing there with their arms behind their backs. They've been taught not to be provocative, not to cause trouble. They don't use any force. They don't give the protestors any reason to sue them later. It's fucked. I mean, no point is made. They stand there, and we stand there and the damn IMF meeting goes off without a hitch and all of this crap doesn't mean nothing. Not a damn thing. By allowing protests like this, they think that they can co-opt the revolution. They let it all happen, but it doesn't change nothing. Not a damn thing. Even Clinton was saying shit like how he 'respects' the protestors' views. But he doesn't, he doesn't care about nothing but his donors. And since this whole protest thing didn't have any effect, he's got no reason to care about what people think. He knows they can't hurt him. Sound and Fury signifying nothing man. Signifying nothing."

The man in the grass skirt was standing on the street corner, taunting the cops on the other side, daring them to hit him on the head with a club. But they didn't. They weren't responding. They just stood, eyes forward, hands behind their backs, occasionally cracking a smile. On the side of the street, some cops and protestors stood together, quietly chatting about the day, leaning on the barricade like it was a bar railing.

In the middle of the street the line of people willing to get arrested for the cause continued to get longer. It was now a 20-minute queue.

Chapter 11:

Confuse the FBI!

Number of Conspirators:	*1*
Danger Level:	*Low*
Arrest Level:	*Low*
Lethality:	*Low*
Annoyance Level:	*Medium*
Economic Damage:	*Low*
Equipment Required:	*Thermos*
	Liquid Nitrogen

The problem with explosives these days is that the FBI requires chemical companies to put microscopic tracers in their products, so if you use them to make explosives the FBI can track you. But here's a way to confuse the fuck out of them:

Get high quality thermos that seals really well. Fill it to the brim with liquid nitrogen. Seal tightly, using glue or duct tape or whatever. Then drop the thermos into a public wastebasket on a street corner. After a short time the nitrogen will begin to boil creating tremendous pressure within the thermos. Eventually the thermos will rupture causing a huge pressure wave that will make lots of noise and possibly blow the wastebasket apart. Of course those doofuses from the FBI will quickly be on-hand to find out what happened. But their chemical samplers won't detect any explosives residue because there won't be any. You'll have 'em scratching their heads for weeks!

"Hey, uh, I think this whole thing's about done, don't you?" said Jason. "I'm gonna head home. I gotta do laundry tonight. You coming?" He pointed at an escalator to the Metro. It hummed downward into the darkness.

"Nah, I'm going go sulk about the state of the world for a while," replied Tyler.

"Lighten up dude. Ann must not be blowing you often enough. I'll see you at work." Jason was a bit tired with Tyler's constant grumpiness and depression. But he had fun anyway, even though he wasn't really too sure who the IMF even was. It was his opinion that Tyler didn't really have a grasp of what the protest was supposed to be about either, although he'd never tell him that to his face. He pinned his "Stop Sucking Corporate Dick" button to his Mr. Zog shirt and disappeared down the escalator.

Tyler started walking towards Dupont Circle. He didn't really have a reason to go there, but he didn't want to go home, and Dupont was the cool part of town. It made Tyler feel cooler just being there. Maybe he'd buy a book or something. He wished that there was a damn decent record store in town, but there wasn't, not even in the suburbs. It was all crappy chains that sold nothing but hip-hop and teenpop. He wished there was a place somewhere that had all of the cool music that he liked. A place where he could be reaching for a rare Belle & Sebastian e.p. at the same time as someone interesting and they'd bump hands and they'd laugh and they'd start talking about their similar interests and they'd get all chummy. But there wasn't. You could order cds on Amazon, but that wasn't the same thing. Everybody Tyler knew listened to crap.

Well, there was that ultra-cool electronica store in Georgetown that catered to all the rave kids. That place was pretty cool, but it was too insular. You really needed to know what you were talking about if you went in there. They had turntables for customers to sample their DJing skills. Tyler didn't know enough about the electronica scene to really feel comfortable there, although he did have a few Goa Trance

89

cds.[16] In any case Georgetown was further than he really felt like walking.

By M Street, the protestors had faded and the crowd was mostly just people on their normal business. Tyler walked over to one of the benches that formed a ring around the statue in the middle of the Circle. He sat quietly and watched the people that passed by. Mostly it was yuppie Gen-Xers on their way to an early dinner or maybe a late lunch. There were a few gay couples. If you came here on a weekday, the entire lawn surrounding the statue would be filled with scruffy bike messengers and the air would be filled with the smell of marijuana smoke. But they weren't here today. The main thing Tyler noticed was that every person who was in the park was with someone else. There were twos and threes and fours, but there didn't seem to be anyone there by themselves. There didn't seem to be anyone there who didn't have someone to sit with, to talk to, to be with. Everyone except Tyler, Tyler was alone.

There were the bums of course, the park had a few resident bums. Not as many as other areas of the city, but a few. They were all dressed in the same monochromatic brown, dirt-stained clothes that seemed to work as effective urban camouflage, as if the city was purposely trying to hide them from view. They sat on benches, or lay on them, sleeping in the middle of the day, in the middle of all that foot traffic. Tyler had always had trouble sleeping, and if there was one thing he admired about bums, it was their ability to sleep pretty much anywhere, anytime.

But, sleeping bums aside, the park was filled with people who were enjoying some form of human interaction, unlike Tyler. He felt alone and lonely all the time, even when he

---

[16] E.g. Banco de Gaia, "Big Men Cry" and Juno Reactor, "Pistolero"

was with other people. Maybe everyone felt like that inside. Maybe everyone felt that no one understood them and that their friends and associates had no sense of who they were, who they truly were on the inside. Maybe all of the people all over the world were alone really, just pretending to be happy for image sake. Wasn't Tyler just talking to a friend of his? Wasn't he just walking and talking like all of these people here, seemingly connected to the world, a node on the giant social web that connects any two points with six degrees? Were we all alone in a crowd? Tyler just felt unlucky, isolated, and miserable.

He checked his outfit again, just to see what he was dressed for. He felt cool enough to enter the coolest stores in the circle. Most of the time he came this way he was with Ann. Typically, Ann wanted to go to the fancy restaurants, and that meant dressing up in a nice shirt and slacks and all, and that was so freaking dorky looking that he'd be way too embarrassed to be seen in some of the places around here. He wished that he was cool enough to pull off what he called the 'gay guy look,' which was somehow both hip and stylish and fancy all at once, and probably had something to do with Banana Republic. But every time he went into one of those stores, he came out empty-handed. He just didn't seem to have the courage to pick something out. Clothes are a real personal choice. You can't ever wear something that you can't imagine yourself in. Ann wouldn't wear short skirts and hooker boots, even if that was what Tyler wanted, because she simply couldn't create a mental image of herself in those clothes without laughing. Tyler couldn't form a mental image of himself in a skin-tight, collared, V-neck black polo shirt, so he could never bring himself to buy one.

He sighed a little and thought about what he could do. He considered getting some coffee, but he didn't have anything to read. It felt pathetic to just sit there and stare. He could go to the bookstore and stand around the philosophy section, hoping someone would notice him thumbing through Thomas Hobbes and be impressed enough to talk to him. But he was dressed a little too radically to convincingly pass for a student of philosophy. In the end he just decided to go home. Ann was probably waiting for him anyway.

He walked towards the Metro station humming, but not loud enough for anyone to hear. ". . . at the final moment I cried. I always cry at endings . . . ."[17]

---

[17] Belle & Sebastian, "Get Me Away from Here, I'm Dying"

Chapter 12:

"Hey, it's the Tibetan dude."

Tyler turned around. It was the girl from the coffee shop, the girl with the old prom dress, the Tibetan girl.

Tyler glanced down to check what he was wearing, but then he remembered that he had just been to a riot. Well, not quite a riot, more of an almost riot. Regardless, he was definitely dressed for a riot, and any counter-culture person should be able to see that at first glance. So he was ok, despite being thrown into this conversation without any warning. Tyler was perceptive enough to usually recognize people before they saw him, and he liked to quickly script out the first few sentences of the conversation, much like a football coach scripts out the first few plays of a game. But this time he would have to play it off the cuff.

He opened with, "Were you at the protests?" He wanted her to know that he was at the protests. She would respect him for going to the protests.

"What protests?" she responded.

"The IMF protests?" he said incredulously. She looked at him without comprehension. "The big protest they had in DC today? The one they shut down half the city for?"

"I don't really watch the news. I had no idea." There were different levels and classes of hipsters. Some were very political on one issue or another, some were into the music, some were into the art and literature, some were just poseur hipsters like Tyler who were more into the scene than into any particular aspect of the scene. Tyler always worried because it was difficult to tell the difference and accidentally direct the conversation in the wrong direction. The non-political hipsters viewed politics and caring about current events as anathema, and a sign of a deep-rooted seriousness that would kill their buzz. Tyler switched the subject before the girl got the idea that he was too serious.

"Where are you headed then?"

"I'm going to work."

Tyler was puzzled. "On a Saturday?" He immediately realized his mistake. Just because he worked in a 9-5 corporate office, it didn't mean everyone did. He saw this conversation beginning to crash and burn. He really would have been more comfortable if he had had the chance to go over things before he started, but frankly, he never really expected to ever have the chance to talk to this person again. "I mean, where do you work?"

"CVS," she said, pointing at the pharmacy on the corner. Her nails were painted an olive drab color, and a cheap plastic toy bracelet dangled from her wrist.

"huh. I would've thought you would have worked somewhere cooler."

"What's that supposed to mean?"

"You know. You've got the cool hair, the cool dress, the cool shoes, I wouldn't pick you for someone who worked in a drug store. I guess I would expect someone like you to have a job in an indie record store, or maybe a used bookstore or something like that. Something that fits your personality."

"We all gotta pay bills man. You take the jobs where you get them. Do you think I'm working as some sort of art project?"

Tyler looked down at his feet. "No, I guess not." The girl glanced down at her watch. She wore it loose with the buckle buckled at the first hole, like a bracelet. She twisted her arm around to see the time. Tyler thought about asking, "Are you late for work?" It was a calculated risk. It would make him look like he was empathetic and caring, but on the other hand it would give her the perfect excuse to end the conversation. Tyler had no one else to talk to, so he took the safe route and didn't ask.

She looked back up at him and said, "So, what do you do?"

Now Tyler was on familiar ground. He had already played this conversation out in his head a million times. "I run a website for anarchists," he said. That's what he told people who were cool, or at least what he would have said had he really talked to very many cool people. He didn't want to mention the college degrees and boring office job. It made him seem like a tool of the establishment, which was essentially true, but wasn't how Tyler felt on the inside, and it's insides that count.

"What's an anarchist?"

" . . . . "

"Oh," she said, "Like a punk rocker?"

"Well, there's a lot more to anarchism than just punk music," be began, "It's mostly about freedom from laws and getting rid of big institutions. It's about people doing what they want to do without being oppressed by the man." Tyler sometimes reverted to old slang, or hippie slang, or even purposely dumbing his sentences down with words like "ain't" and "y'all." He thought the sarcasm came through and people could tell that he was just kidding. He likened it to adding special effects to his speech. But as Ann told him, most people just thought that he was stupid or anachronistic. The girl just stared at him, waiting for him to say something interesting. He skipped to the summation. "I guess anarchy is just about living and not bothering other people and not worrying about shadowy businessmen in smoky rooms stealing all the money out of the stock market."

"What does that have to do with Tibet?" she said.

"Well, nothing. I mean, I was just interested in Tibet because of all the oppression they've got going on over there." She didn't seem to really grasp him. "The Chinese, they invaded Tibet. There's a lot of folks who are fighting for independence, but it's tough because the Chinese are our trading partners so we don't want to annoy them too much. But I don't have anything about Tibet on my website. It's more of like a how-to guide for people performing civil disobedience."

"So you're like a computer guy then? I really don't know all that much about computers. I can barely even figure out email."

The last thing Tyler wanted to be known as was a 'computer guy.' In his head computers meant geek, and anyone related at all to computers wore pants that were too short and buttoned the top button on their dress shirts. "No, I'm not really into computers that much. I can do a little html and make a web page, but that's about it. To be honest, I really don't like programming and all that. It's too. . . precise for me. I'm more of a free-flowing person. A 'big ideas' guy." She glanced at her watch again.

This time Tyler decided to take the chance, "Are you late for work? I don't want to keep you."

"Nah, it doesn't really matter when I show up. People can wait in line another minute for their Chunky bars and generic shampoo." They both chuckled a bit. Then a moment of awkward silence. "But I guess I really should go. Maybe I'll see you around again."

"So, can I get your email address?" He blurted out. It was so weird how fast this whole email thing came upon people. Only three years before, he and a bunch of other people had laughed at a geeky guy in college who blew it with a girl by asking for her email address. It used to be just for dorky science types. Only a few years later, it was almost universal. "Or like maybe your phone number would be better, if you know, you don't really do email."

"Well, I usually don't give my digits out to strange guys," she said. But, in spite of her comment, she reached into her pocket, pulled out a ball-point pen, and took Tyler's left hand. She opened up his palm and wrote, "bethamphetamine@hotmail.com"

"Ok, gotta scram," she said. Tyler thought about asking if she wanted his email address, or the name of his website. He even thought about giving her one of his business cards momentarily, but only momentarily. In the end he just stood mutely and watched as she wandered down the street.

Tyler headed off in the other direction purposefully. Partly because he wanted to make sure that if she turned around he wouldn't be standing there, he would look like he had someplace important to go to. But also partially because he wanted to get to a restaurant or something where he could get a napkin and copy the email address down. For some reason he really couldn't stand when there was writing on his skin. It made him feel like poisons were leeching into his body.

It was only later that night, as he ate dinner silently at home with Ann did he remember that the girl's name was Molly. He was pretty sure she never asked his name at all, but that was ok.

Chapter 13:

Bacillius awesomeus!

Number of Conspirators:	*1*
Danger Level:	*Low*
Arrest Level:	*Low*
Lethality:	*Low*
Annoyance Level:	*High*
Economic Damage:	*Medium*
Equipment Required:	*Mosquito Pesticide*
	Envelopes

Is there an organization out there you'd love to see destroyed with a biological weapon, but you don't have the PhD science background to make one? Here's a great alternative: "Anthrax" is a bacteria called bacillius anthracis, and it's bad news and a great bio-weapon. But it's got a cousin called bacillius thurnegentius or "BT" that you can get easy. It's not harmful to people, but it kills mosquitoes dead and you can get it at any hardware or gardening store.

Sure it won't actually hurt anybody, but most of the tests the FBI runs to see if that suspicious powder is really anthrax will also test positive for BT. So get a box of it, put it in envelopes, and start sending threatening letters to your targets! As soon as the cops do a routine preliminary test, people will FREAK OUT! The more sophisticated tests could take weeks to get back from the lab, and during that time the place you sent your little calling card to will be in complete lockdown. And it only costs you like $10. Talk about cost-effective!

"Hey, you'll like this, you're into all that freaky weirdo crap."

Jason had a way of just coming into your office talking, as if he didn't want to waste time with the beginning and proceeded directly to the meat of the conversation. Tyler reacted instinctively, closing his browser. Although he didn't have any work to do until Jeff got back to him with the data, he felt guilty playing around on the internet. Not that anyone would really have noticed anyway. He swiveled his chair around.

"Start from the beginning. . . what?"

Jason poked his head around, trying to get a better view of the screen. "Looking at porn there, huh?"

"No. Plus fuck off." Tyler looked down at the paper Jason held.

"Oh yeah, I printed this news story for you." He handed the page to Tyler. "Its about this guy who went nuts."

"What did he do?"

"It seems that he always wanted to be a bus driver right, like it was his goal in life and all. But he failed the test over and over again. He was like obsessed right? So then he finally snaps. He steals a bus right, and then he just drives around all day, picking up passengers and everything. When they tried to stop him he pulled a gun and the cops shot him dead. Take a look at that line I highlighted. I think it's hilarious."

Tyler looked down. "'The weird part was that he must have been the most courteous driver I've ever had,' said one shocked rider. . . ."

"Why would this interest me?" he said dejectedly.

"I don't know man, I mean, aren't you into all that 'people freaking out' stuff? Maybe you could post it on your website?"

"Have you ever been to my website?"

"No."

Tyler shook his head. "This is just sad. I mean what the hell is this world coming to?"

Jason made a feint for the hall. "Oh man, I don't want another one of your gun control tirades."

"That's not what I mean. I mean, how fucking pathetic is this world? I mean, when I was a kid people were supposed to grow up dreaming about being President, or an astronaut or something. I mean, how small do you have to be to dream about being a bus driver? Is that the best he could come up with? If you're going to waste your life chasing a dream, you might as well dream big."

"Dude, the guy was nuts."

"Even so, the guy should have been able to come up with a better fantasy than that you know? Is that what we're teaching people these days? That the best dream you can obsess on is being a bus driver? Couldn't this guy come up with a better cause worth dying for?"

"I don't know what to tell you man."

Tyler immediately changed the subject. "The guy I really like is that dude who killed Versace." Tyler's mind saw connections to things that other people didn't see. It meant that occasionally he seemed to flit around, but in his head there was a smooth-flowing connection.

"huh?"

"The guy who shot Versace . . . ?" Tyler waited for Jason to recognize the reference.

"Wasn't he insane too?"

"Yeah, but in the right way. I mean, you know, he went around settling scores." Jason didn't seem to get it.

"I mean, there's a list of people you, Jason, wants to kill right? I mean, there's got to be somebody, some guy who stole your girlfriend, or that bully from grade school, I mean somebody you'd like to see dead, right?"

"Uh, I suppose."

"But you'd never *do* anything, right, you'd never actually kill any of those people. I mean, maybe you'd get one in a fit of rage, but you'd never go and get them all, systematically. Right?" The question was rhetorical. "But this guy, I mean, he did it. He didn't just talk shit like you and I would. He didn't just sit on his ass dreaming about what he was going to do and bitching about life in his journal. He said, 'fuck the consequences, there are people who I need to settle scores with and I'm going to do it.' I mean, how incredible and liberating would it be to just fuck it all and get all those fuckers that need getting. God, I wish was as free as that guy was."

"You know, I think I know why you like all these freaky people. It's 'cause you're out to fucking lunch yourself. Sometimes you scare me man." Jason said.

"Ahh, you just don't get it. You're too brainwashed by the establishment. You don't have that freedom. Neither do

I. They keep me docile by paying me a huge pile of money just to sit here. They've given me too much to lose." Tyler switched gears yet again. "Hey, let's walk over to Starbucks. We need a break from all this drudgery."

"Starbucks? I ain't paying for coffee, they've got free coffee here."

"I know, but I want to get out, I want to see new people, I want to feel like I'm out somewhere, not just sitting here in this cube wasting my life. At least take a walk with me, you can just sit there, or I'll buy you a coffee or something."

"No can do man, I just got this new project from Jeff. I'm swamped. I just figured I'd come by here for one of your amusing rants." And with that, Jason left. Tyler just sat there for a bit and sighed. He thought about getting up and going over to Jeff's office and asking him about that data he had promised. Jeff had said that he was going to be working full time on getting that data set up so Tyler could finish his stupid project. But apparently he had found something better to do. The least he could have done was to involve Tyler in this new mystery project. Tyler fantasized about walking over to Jeff's office and giving him a piece of his mind. He walked through the conversation a dozen times, rewording the conversation over and over again, anticipating every lame excuse Jeff could have and ripping it to shreds.

But in the end, he didn't bother. There wasn't much point anyway. Yelling at people rarely made them move any faster. Tyler just swiveled his chair around and went back to composing his letter. He had been working on his email to "bethamphetamine" for almost an hour now. He wanted to get exactly the right tone and style. He wanted to use impressive sounding words but not ones that would be so big that Molly wouldn't understand them. He wanted to be accessible and friendly, but not too friendly. If she felt that he was hitting on her she would bolt. If she felt that he was desperate, she would bolt.

Most of the time he had been writing the letter, he had a "what's the point" mentality. He was positive she wouldn't write back, no matter how expertly he composed the missive. It just wasn't like people to write him back. He was always the one who had to pursue friendships and relationships. It was hard and disappointing. And that was just with the dorky people that Tyler knew, it would be even worse with cool fun interesting people that Tyler never had a chance in hell of even interacting with in high school, nevermind being friends with. But he dutifully wrote the letter and revised it and changed it, and read it aloud (in a whispery voice so as not to disturb anyone), and revised it again. He really wished that he could have told someone about it. He'd love to show it to someone like Jason, who seemed to be a real expert with women, but he couldn't. First of all, guys just didn't collaborate on stuff like that, and even if they did, Jason knew Ann, somehow Ann would end up hearing all about it, and Tyler didn't want Ann to know.

It wasn't like he was thinking about having an affair, or leaving Ann for this new girl. It wasn't like he even wanted this girl as a friend. It was just sort of something hard-wired in him. He needed to chase women, make them like him. He didn't know why, and he really didn't expect success. Maybe it was just his id trying to justify his own miserableness. If he hit on women and failed (as he invariably would), it would just reinforce the fact that he was a loser and his life sucked and the whole world was allied against him. That would make him feel better about sulking and being moody and pretentious and hiding in the corners of the room and never bothering to actually put his true heart on the line because it was a forgone conclusion that it would be damaged if he gave anyone the slightest chance to hurt him.

104

Chapter 14:

Cancer Scare!

Number of Conspirators:	*1*
Danger Level:	*Low*
Arrest Level:	*Low*
Lethality:	*Low*
Annoyance Level:	*High*
Economic Damage:	*High*
Equipment Required:	*Ladder*
	Pair of insulated gloves

Buildings are big. Buildings are expensive. Buildings are owned by corporations. Taking out a building can cost a company many millions of dollars and completely disrupt their business. And it's way easier than you might think to do it.

Head out to the rural south and find an area where there are abandoned telephone poles lining the old backwoods roads. Climb up to the top and unscrew some of those glass transformer covers (wear gloves). They are filled with oil, and that oil is filled with carcinogenic PCBs. Collect a gallon or two of it.

Head over to your target building. Out front, or in back, or somewhere nearby should be an intake grate that sucks in air for the HVAC system. Dump the oil in. If you want to get fancy, use some kind of sprayer for better results. Then call the EPA. Tell them the building is contaminated with PCBs.

PCBs cause cancer if you get long-term exposure, so while you probably won't hurt anybody, no one will be able to work in the building until they get it cleaned up. And PCBs are a giant pain to clean up. Chances are good they'll have to condemn the whole

building. That'll cost them millions, plus they'll have to apologize
to all their workers for exposing them to dangerous chemicals.

Every day, every single day, on the drive home, Tyler
fantasized about how he would quit his job. Some days he
would fantasize about doing it quietly with a minimum of
hub-bub— just a short note and a quick goodbye. Other
days he would imagine a huge argument with desks being
turned over and security called to drag him from the building
foaming at the mouth. Sometimes he would think about
simply leaving— no note, no explanation, no anything. He'd
change his phone number and just disappear. It would
almost be worth it to see how long it would take anyone to
notice his absence. It might be weeks. But although the
fantasy changed from day to day, the fact that Tyler
fantasized about quitting his job was a constant.

He would go over every argument and counter-
argument. He would anticipate the questions of the HR staff
and the managerial staff and the co-workers. He imagined
how they would say that he has been doing good work for
them and that they want him to stay. He imagined that they
would plead with him to accept their apologies and ask
forgiveness for not using him properly and for not giving
him opportunities and for generally making his job suck. He
imagined all the ways that they would try to blame him for
his troubles— that he wasn't aggressive enough to ask for
work, that his work wasn't up to par, that his skill set wasn't
as useful as they had thought it would be. He ran through all
of their possible responses and countered them individually.
Over and over again he would go through every word of
every argument. He would imagine what he would say to
prospective employers when he went on job interviews. He
would lay the blame carefully, not accepting any
responsibility himself, but also not trashing his former
employer and thereby looking ungrateful. He would talk

106

about just wanting new opportunities and a chance to prove himself, he would talk about looking towards the future and how he wanted to reach the next rung of the ladder.

On the rare day that he wasn't focused on work, he daydreamed about his life's worst experiences— the beatings, the rejections, the bad dates, the horrible times he'd lived through over the years. Tyler once told a friend that the difference between a strong, confident optimist and a weak, passive, pessimist was the formulation of their remembrances. The confident people he knew, like Jason, always relived the best parts of their life; when they won the race, when they got the girl. The passive, morose people like Tyler always relived the worst parts of their lives, again and again, a repeating hellish movie concatenating one failure after another.

Today on the drive home his fantasies were mild. Just a simple rehash of all the reasons he was leaving to an anonymous manager who listened but presented no challenging questions for Tyler to maneuver his logic around. His mind was mostly on something else today. He was thinking about the girl he met last weekend and the email he had sent her today. She wouldn't write back. He was sure she wouldn't write back. "Spellbound Spellbound Spellbound Spellbound. . . ."[18] The radio was generating background noise for Tyler's thoughts. It was playing the same mix tape it had been playing all week. Over and over again. Tyler usually only drove his car to and from work, and he was too lazy to change out the tape more than once a month or so.

She probably wouldn't write back. They never did. No one ever wrote Tyler back. He was rarely the focus of

---

[18] Siouxie and the Banchees, "Spellbound"

anyone's attention, he was never the one people wanted to be with. He had always had to work hard to get people to notice him. He liked it when people noticed him, but it was always he who had to do the work. He never had the luxury of just sitting there and doing nothing and have people notice him, he had to make all the moves, take all the risks, shout and jump around and fret over all the emails and the phone conversations and the being at the right places at the right times. No one ever seemed to go out of their way to get Tyler to notice them.

He hadn't actually sent the email to that girl yet. He was going to, but he wanted to go over the draft a few more times first. Tyler was meticulous, and bored, and realized that information can be valuable. It's best to know as much as you can going in, it's best to have it all planned out, know every little detail, who knows what would be important? Who knows what gem you would find? As soon as he had gotten home from the IMF protest he did a Google search on her email address, but nothing turned up. Then just to see, he did a search on his email address. His home page on GeoCities came up first, filled with information about every detail of his life, subtly designed like a fishing lure to pull in people from around the world who might share a common interest or two. No one ever contacted him. Then came a torrent of web pages and chat rooms and message boards and the like where he had posted messages with his email attached. He knew that it was a cry for attention, a call to say, "hey, I'm cool come talk to me." But no one ever did. But there was his info, in case it ever came up.

He did a search on Jason. Again nothing. It was like he didn't even exist online. Tyler couldn't understand why people wouldn't make themselves more accessible online. At a minimum a person should be searchable by name. I mean, who knows what childhood friend might be looking for them right now, unable to get in touch? Tyler longed to hear

108

from a childhood friend. Not that he had many of course, but even an old acquaintance would be ok. Just to know that he didn't dream his childhood, just to know that he was alive and his existence had indeed been acknowledged by someone.

After a while he was bored and lonely enough to stop revising and to push the send button. The email was on its way to 'bethamphetamine.' Irretrievable.

Tyler's birthday was coming up in a few weeks. He knew that no one at work would notice. He knew that none of his friends would remember. He was pretty sure that Ann would remember. She was good at remembering things like birthdays, it was her way of proving that she cared. She would certainly get him something nice. Money was rarely an object for her. Tyler wondered what he would get this year. Ann's presents were a small window into Ann's mind. She never got him what he wanted, but he appreciated the gifts because what he did get gave him a glimpse into what Ann *thought* he wanted, which in turn was a glimpse into how Ann perceived him. And insight into how he was being perceived by others was in itself a great gift to him.

Chapter 15:

Commitment

We here at CHOAS HQ just wanted to take a short time-out from our usual fare to say a word about commitment. We've provided plenty of great ideas here for you, from tiny pranks all the way up to full-scale revolutions. But before you pull the trigger on any of these ploys, you have to ask yourself, "what is my level of commitment?" It's pointless and dangerous to go half-way on some of this stuff, if you aren't going to go through with it, you shouldn't even bother starting. And even if you do go through with it, are you prepared for the consequences? You might get arrested, you might get killed, heck you might even succeed and find yourself running a revolutionary government after you've overthrown the old regime. Are you prepared for these consequences? Take the quiz below and we'll help you determine the level of commitment you've got for your cause. Then we'll suggest things you can do to accomplish your goals, factoring in that level of commitment

Question 1: How much do you have left to lose?

"I want to be like William Wallace," he said out of the blue one Saturday afternoon.

"Who?" Ann wasn't really listening, she was more interested in her magazine. Tyler was supposed to be reading his book.

"William Wallace, the Scottish rebel leader?" He stared into Ann's eyes for evidence of comprehension. She blankly stared back at him. It was a game that he liked to play, make some obscure reference and see if anybody was familiar with it. If they weren't it would give him ammunition later, when

110

he ranted about how nobody understood him. "Braveheart?" he said after a pause.

"Oh sure," she replied, "who wouldn't want to be like Mel Gibson." She turned her eyes down to the magazine, hoping that the conversation was over.

Tyler sighed audibly, "Not Mel Gibson, Wallace himself, the actual guy, not the movie star." He waited to see if she would commit to the conversation.

"Didn't he live in a mud shack? Why would you want to live in a mud shack? I saw that movie, everybody was dressed in wool and was wet all the time, who'd want to live like that?" Her eyes didn't leave the magazine. She was reading an article on the "top ten foods that will reduce the size of your thighs." Ann often complained that her thighs were too large. Tyler kept trying to tell her that everyone in the world was too self-absorbed to ever notice the size of her body parts, and in any event he thought she looked just fine. But every morning she looked at herself naked under the harsh, unforgiving glare of the bathroom lights and felt her self-confidence drain away.

"Ah just forget about it," said Tyler. He tried to audibly show his disgust for the fact she wasn't interested in what he had to say. It came out more whiny than he intended it to. His eyes returned to the novel he had been reading.

Ann put down the magazine and looked him straight in the eye. "Ok," she said in an even tone, "why exactly do you want to be like William Wallace?" She knew that she would hear about it later if she didn't at least pretend to make an effort now.

Tyler held up a finger. "Because they pulled out his intestines," he said flatly. It was more of his game. Make an outrageous statement and try to pull the listener into the conversation. Tyler liked it when people paid attention to him and he felt that he had to resort to sub-audible tricks and outrageous statements to do it. Ann wasn't buying it. She had known him too long. He had hoped that she would say something like, "Why do you want that?" or something, but she just stared at him. She knew that there was more to Tyler's statement than what he had said, and he knew that she knew. After a few seconds he continued. "I just saw that movie on cable the other night. It was a scary time to be alive. They did nasty things to people. There weren't cops and laws and safe places like we have now. We're so damn soft. If I told you, 'rebel against the king and we'll pull out your intestines,' you'd stay in line right?" He stopped to sip his latté. "But Wallace, he didn't cave in. He knew what would happen to him and he still did it. He had stones. Not like people today, not like me. You can change my behavior by withholding sex. I moan if my coffee isn't hot enough. There's no way I could've survived back then. Everything is so damn easy for us. We sleep in warm beds. We never go hungry. People don't hunt us down and pull out our intestines or nail us to crosses for thinking differently."

Ann had heard this before from Tyler. "Isn't that a good thing? Why do you want bad things to happen to you?"

"It's not that I *want* bad things to happen to me. I want to be challenged. I want to know that if I fail, bad things will happen. My life is too damn easy. I have no challenges. I get paid at work even if I fuck around on the internet all day. I never have to worry about where my next meal is coming from. I don't have anything to strive for. How can I make the world a better place? What can I do to improve things? There's nothing. Everything has been handed to me on a damn silver platter."

112

Ann had returned to her magazine. "So go live in the woods and kill bears with your bare hands. No one's stopping you."

"That's exactly it. That's it exactly. No one is stopping me. There's no consequence to my actions. Nothing I do even matters. What's the point of being alive if nothing I do makes any difference? I need to stand tall in the face of adversity. That's what I need. And I have no adversity. I've been cheated out of adversity by this damn perfect society. It's made me too complacent to do anything great."

Ann toyed with the white plastic cover to her paper cup. She bent it back with her teeth until it cracked slightly. A jet of steam shot out. It was still too hot to drink. "If you've got to fantasize about something why don't you fantasize about being a rock star? Do something normal for a change."

"Rock star . . . there's no way in hell I'd ever be a rock star." Again, he waited until she put down the magazine and paid attention to him before continuing. "Every rock star is the same. They always get big and popular for a few years, and life is great. I bet it totally kicks ass to be a rock star when you're at the top of your game. But tastes change way too much. Every rock star, every damn one, eventually winds up in the $1 rack at Tower. Eventually people's kids will find your cds in their parents' collection, see your outlandish clothing and say, 'Mom, you really used to listen to this guy?' Of course, Mom will counter with, 'Well, we were young and stupid in our day. I used to think he was cute back then, I can't for the life of me figure out why now.' And then, you're a joke." He paused for a second and an almost imperceptible sigh came from his lips. "I don't want to be a joke. I want to do something important."

"Important? Like what you're doing now?" She chuckled.

"Exactly! This is just what I've been saying. I want to do something important, I want to see a wrong and right it, I want to laugh in the face of danger and fly in the face of adversity. I want to be stoic the night before my execution and scream 'Freedom' to a crowd as they chop off my head. But I can't. Everything is too damn easy. They've made everything too damn easy and they've cheated me out of my chance for glory."

"You're an idiot," she said. "You got it nice— nice car, cushy job, a forgiving and patient girlfriend, and you're moaning because no one wants to chop off your head and you don't live in a ditch . . ."

"I wouldn't mind being a writer," he said, interrupting her.

"Isn't that the same as being a rock star? Won't people make fun of you as a writer?"

"No, it's not the same thing. As a writer you can fade from view, your books can be considered 'not relevant,' but no one will make fun of you for being uncool. Maybe it's because you don't really see how writers dress. Rock stars are too flamboyant. I don't want to be flamboyant."

"You want to start a rebellion, for no particular reason, but you don't want to appear too flamboyant?" Ann said incredulously.

"Yes."

Ann stared at Tyler. He stared back. She shook her head and went back to her magazine. Tyler looked around, but none of the other people in cafe had been listening to their conversation.

Chapter 16:

Infrastructure Takedown!

Number of Conspirators:	*1*
Danger Level:	*Low*
Arrest Level:	*Low*
Lethality:	*Low*
Annoyance Level:	*High*
Economic Damage:	*High*
Equipment Required:	*Aluminum powder*
	Iron
	Magnesium fuses
	A car

America runs on electricity. Even short, localized outages can wreck tremendous damage. Think how much disruption you could cause if you knocked out the power over a large area of the country, every single day!

Impossible? Think again. Using the recipe for thermite I showed you previously, make up a bunch of thermite packs. They are easy to make and perfectly safe to handle. Head out on a cross-country road trip. Once per day stop your car on the side of a lonely road next to one of those giant power towers that criss-cross the country. They are found in pretty remote areas so you should be able to operate unseen. Place some thermite packs on the legs of the tower, light, and leave. The thermite will melt the legs, the tower will fall, and the resulting cascade will take out a significant portion of the power grid.

Can you keep taking out towers faster then they can rebuild them? Damn right you can! Congratulations, you've singlehandledly taken out the power grid for the cost of a couple of tanks of gas.

It was exactly one hundred and seventeen hours before she wrote back.

That was eighty-one hours after Tyler had given up hope. He had a thirty-six hour rule for emails. Over the years he had sent a lot of messages to a lot of people, and in his experience, if someone didn't write back in a day and a half, they probably weren't going to write back at all. Sometimes the person was on vacation or having computer troubles or something, but the rule was true 99% of the time, so he was quite shocked when he saw the message in his inbox.

The first day after sending Molly the meticulously written email, he had checked his inbox dozens of times, even checking the trash folder just in case Hotmail had decided for some reason that her letter was spam. He even checked his work email in case she had written him there, which didn't even make sense since she didn't even have that address. He hadn't been all that surprised that she hadn't responded, but it was still disappointing. After a few days, he had pretty much forgotten about the entire incident, chalking it up to another one of his typical experiences with members of the opposite sex. He was already fretting over some new unimportant social faux pas he had made, and had mostly forgotten he'd ever met Molly. When her email did arrive, he almost deleted it by mistake, lumping it in with all the offers for online porn, penis extensions, lower mortgage rates, discount prescription drugs, and other ads that cluttered his mailbox.

Molly wasn't like Tyler. Molly didn't fret about little details. Molly didn't even usually fret about big details. Molly spent almost no time online. For her, it was just a way to connect up and make a plan or two, and even then it was pretty crappy. Molly's internet connection was spotty and her modem was slow. It wasn't really worth her time. She meant to write more, especially to people from back home, people she never saw anymore and was losing touch with. But she rarely did. There was always more interesting things to do. She had pretty much forgotten about that strange, melancholy boy she talked to on the street the other day. His email was buried down beneath a pile of ads for penis enlargement, lower mortgage rates, and all those alerts from all the various online groups she had joined; filled with information about subjects she no longer cared about and would never read anyway. If she could figure out how, she'd have her name taken off their mailing lists.

Molly hadn't responded right away. It wasn't that she didn't care. Well, she didn't care all that much, but she thought that she would write back eventually. But first she had to eat dinner, and then watch some tv, and when she tried to get on later that day she couldn't connect, and the next day she had work, and that night some dude she occasionally hooked up with had invited her to a ska concert at the Black Cat. Then she forgot about the whole thing until she checked her email again a few days later. Even though it was only a few lines long, Tyler had spent a long time composing it so it'd be just right. He knew he only had one chance, and he had to seem friendly but not desperate, interesting but not unreachable. He used words that were long enough to show he respected her intelligence, yet short enough that he wouldn't seem too brainy. He left it open-ended. Like everything Tyler did, it was a trap to make you come to him, to make himself feel wanted by putting the onus on the other person to continue the contact. Tyler had convinced himself that he did this to allow the other person an out in case they didn't want to talk to him, he lived in mortal fear that the people he talked to desperately wanted to get away, but he kept them cornered and didn't even notice. Ann had tried to tell Tyler multiple times that he was wrong about how other people perceived him, but Tyler couldn't bring himself to believe her.

117

It took Molly about five seconds to skim through the three paragraph letter, she wasn't really a big reader, preferring to get the gist of something rather than study it. This contrasted with Tyler, who would have gone over every single sentence, word for word, trying to divine any secret meanings implied and unsaid.

She would have given him a call, but Tyler didn't leave his phone number. He didn't want to seem too forward and creepy, but more importantly, he didn't know Molly and had no idea what her schedule was like. What if she called late at night when Ann was home? It was all innocent of course, Tyler just wanted a friend, but he didn't want even the appearance of something underhanded going on. He could lie to Ann of course, tell her it was just Jason. But the less lies that one had to tell, the less chance of tripping up later. And what if Jason just happened to call on the same night? That would look weird.

Molly started to reply to the email, but lost interest after a few minutes. The next day she logged on again, determined to respond. But she lost interest again after a minute. She didn't like having to come up with something clever to say. She didn't like monologues. She didn't like interacting with people on a scale of days. She was more of a second-by-second person. She was better on the fly, spontaneous-like. She needed to play off of another person. She needed to see their expressions and know what buttons she was pushing. She needed intonations and eyes and body language. And she was a crappy typist and not a great speller. This was why she never did well on writing assignments in school. There was too much time to get wrapped around her own thoughts and lose track of the subject. She was bored by her own thoughts. She didn't think that she was a very stimulating person, and secretly she wondered why anyone was interested in talking to her. She never came up with anything interesting to say by herself. Maybe that's why she dressed flamboyantly, to make herself more interesting, and to distract people from her internal blankness.

In the end she gave up on trying to respond to Tyler's letter. She didn't even understand all the things he said anyway. She lobbed the ball back into his court. That was easier than thinking too hard about it. Plus, to be honest, she didn't really care all that much. She wrote simply:

Dude, Good to hear from you. Hope your not dead. Call my cell if you want to hang. 703-403-0247.
                                         -zubzubzub
                                          Moll.

Chapter 17:

Self Reliance!

The best revolutionary is the self-reliant revolutionary. If you do your research you will see that most people that get caught get caught because someone in their group betrayed them. Informers, undercover agents, suspicious friends and neighbors, all are potential problems for the revolutionary. The less people in your cell, the less chance that a betrayer is in your midst and the greater your chances of success. It's tempting to think large-scale, with massive plots and gigantic schemes, but remember, a smaller successful attack is always better than a larger failed one. This website has provided you with the tools you need to launch plots that don't require much, yet have a fairly large effect. Many are things you can do on your own or with a very small cell of co-conspirators. Don't be a fool, remain suspicious. Remain vigilant, remain self-reliant!

I know I know, humans have a natural instinct to share, to seek out similar minds, to bounce ideas off each other. And of course you'll have to do some of this if you want your message to resonate. But being a revolutionary is a lonely lifestyle, be prepared to keep your plots to yourself, or to spend a lot of time in a prison camp.

From the perspective of someone lying on the floor, the wooden slats seemed to stretch on forever. It wasn't that far really, maybe only twenty feet, but something about how the sun shown through the window and reflected against its smooth surface made them seem like they went on forever. Maybe it was a ratio thing; the vertical variation of the surface was so many orders of magnitude smaller than the horizontal distance that the floor seemed vast. Tyler lay on his belly for a while, appreciating the vastness, then got bored and stood up. After sliding across the living room in his white socks, he settled down at the table in the dining room to pay some bills.

Ann had left before he had woken up, or at least, before he had woken up properly. It was a Saturday, not quite noon. She had to go to work. She had forgotten to bring some documents home, or had to fix a mistake someone else had made, or handle a new issue that just came up Friday afternoon, or clean her desk, or something like that. She said why she was going in that morning, but Tyler was still wrapped up in blankets and didn't really grasp her not being there until well after she had left. By then it was far too late to say goodbye.

Tyler on the other hand didn't need to go to work. He rarely had to even show up on weekdays, so the thought of having to go in on a weekend was utterly foreign to him. He laid around in the big bed with the moon-and-star pattern sheets for a while. He put the tv on for background and watched, or half-listened to two and a quarter rotations of CNN Headline News. When he got up it was more because he was sick of hearing the same stories repeated for a third time than anything else.

He had walked downstairs wearing his moon-and-stars pajamas, the ones that had the same exact pattern as the sheets. Ann thought it would be cute for the two of them to match the bedding, but her matching pjs were soon replaced by an even cuter set of sleepwear that had a Chinese-food pattern.

There was nothing happening downstairs. Nothing that needed his attention. He cruised from the living room to the dining room and back, then upstairs to the bedroom again to see if anything had been missed. But it hadn't. There were

121

things he could do of course. He had some reading to catch up on. He probably should do laundry soon. But there was nothing that *needed* to be done.

He went downstairs again for a drink of water. Then back upstairs to use the bathroom. He thought about getting dressed, but he couldn't come up with a reason why he should. He knew that nothing in his wardrobe was going to be more comfortable than the moon-and-star pattern pajamas, and he didn't want to bother wasting his cooler outfits when no one was going to be around to see them. Each shirt would only last so many washings. He couldn't risk them for something so trivial as sitting around the house.

He went downstairs again and looked around the kitchen for something to eat, or alternatively something that needed to be put away. He unloaded the dishwasher from last night. One of his cds was still in the cd player, and simply pressing the play button was easier than going through his collection to pick something different to listen to. Music started.[19] In a way this too was a waste like the clothes because there was no one around to hear the music but himself. Nobody would know what he was listening to. At least cds didn't wear out. He went back upstairs to maybe gather clothes for the laundry, but was distracted by the pile of bills that he had left lying around.

They weren't big bills, just a phone bill and a Visa bill that consisted mostly of local restaurants and gas for his car. But they were due soon. At least it was something to do. He grabbed the stack and went halfway down the stairs. Then he went back upstairs and rooted through his desk for his stamps and checkbook. Once he got downstairs he felt like

---

[19] Matt Pond, "Fairlee" The Nature of Maps

lying on the floor for a while, and so he did. Sometimes he liked to pretend that his legs didn't work anymore and he had to drag himself around with his hands. The floor was slippery enough to make that challenging but still possible. But this time he just lay there and allowed himself to get bored enough that paying bills seemed like an attractive alternative.

He sat in the dining room, at the big wooden table that Ann's mother didn't like but that Tyler thought was pretty cool. He laid out his bills and took a pen from the kitchen counter to write things out. But he froze before he could get to the first check.

It was silent. Too silent. The music was playing of course, so it wasn't silent like a monastery. In fact, there was quite a lot of sound coming from the stereo. But it was like the sound was disembodied. Like it was a soundtrack that had been overlaid onto a silent scene. Similar to how in a horror movie the protagonist is sneaking around what must be quite a silent haunted house, yet the silence is enhanced by an eerie orchestral score being played through the THX Surround system.

In Buddhism, the highest state of being one can have occurs when one loses the sense that one exists. In a way, Tyler had reached bottisattva. He looked around the room, and out the window, and at the floor, and at the walls, and at the table that Ann's mother didn't like, and Ann's pen lying on it, and felt the utter and complete stillness of it all. Nothing was moving, nothing was happening. Everything just sat there, calmly and silently.

"This must be what it's like when no one is at home," thought Tyler. Every weekday Tyler and Ann went off to work, and the house was still here. It's easy to lose track of everything that isn't within eyesight, but the house didn't stop existing just because no one was in it. It just sat here, exactly like it was sitting here now, every day. Tyler was only used to experiencing the house during the evenings, and usually with Ann bouncing around somewhere in it.

And Tyler looked out the window and saw that there was wind and light and motion and life outside and he felt like he was in a mausoleum. He felt that this must be what it is like to be dead. You just lie there, quiet, silent. There is no motion or energy or anything. And Tyler felt alone— desperately, bitterly, disturbingly alone.

It wasn't an aloneness like he had felt before, like he felt most days. This was different. It was like a drowning. He had to get out. He had to get near something alive. He considered screaming but he couldn't break his silence. He felt like crying but that required more life than he had to give. He ran upstairs to get away from the music, to get away from the silence, to get away from the window. It was such a nice day. The weather was perfect for being outside. For taking a walk in the park, for lounging around playing frisbee, or having a picnic, or flying a kite. Tyler desperately wished that Ann was around. He wanted to just grab her by the hand and toss the moon-and-stars sheet into the car and head out to the park and spend the day *living*. He picked up his phone and dialed most of Ann's digits. He was going to call her and tell her that he was coming to get her and that they were not going to waste such a beautiful day. That they were going to go to the park and that they were going to call all of their friends and they were going to all get together and play volleyball and run around in circles giggling and have a bar-b-que and light a fire in a big pit and sit around it talking until the wee hours of the morning, with his arms around Ann's shoulders to shield her from the chilly night air. And they were going to be smiling and they were going to be laughing and they were going to be bonding and it was all going to be great and beautiful and something that was

124

going to last them their entire lives. The memories that could be made that afternoon, that very afternoon could be the ones that lasted them until the end of their lives!

He put the phone down without finishing Ann's number. She wouldn't want to go sit in the park, there'd be bugs. And she would be complaining or pouting the whole time because she knew Tyler knew that she had to get work done and wasn't allowing her to do it. And she would be pissed off because people at work were counting on her and she had to earn her pay and shouldn't have to handhold Tyler through every one of his little crises. Besides, it wasn't like Tyler knew a lot of people to make a day of it in the park. And the few people he might be able to call would probably not be interested in going, or they'd be busy shopping or painting their den or watching college football or something and nothing Tyler ever wanted to do, really wanted to do, turned out anyway. People were too busy living their lives or something.

Back when he had just graduated college, during that summer that he couldn't find a job, Tyler used to wake up every Sunday morning in an apartment he was subletting from the Icelandic grad student and head out to the Spanish-style coffeehouse a few blocks away. He would stop at the bodega on the way there and get a Sunday paper, and order a mocha latte (which they served in a pint glass), and he would enjoy his drink and read every page, every damn page of the Sunday paper, culminating with a thorough scouring of the Help Wanted section. Then on the way back he would stop at the bakery and buy a fresh baguette, the kind with lots of seeds, and he'd go back to the empty apartment and sit and make little sandwiches out of the baguette and some cheese and a few peppers that he started eating just to spite himself because he didn't like peppers and because you need a hot pepper sandwich to kill the ogre in Zork, and he'd be content.

Sitting in front of his bills laid out on the big dining room table, Tyler thought back to that time. He thought back to all of the things he didn't have anymore. To all the places that he wasn't, and he just didn't want to be *here*. He wanted something. He wanted a memory. He needed to see people. He needed to be with people. He couldn't stay here in this dead house. He could feel his limbs stiffening. If he didn't leave quickly he would soon be dead.

Not having anything else to do, and not being in a mindset to come up with new ideas, he just put on some clothes, grabbed his book and ran to the coffee shop. Literally ran. He needed to be with people. He knew that the people at the coffee shop wouldn't talk to him. They were strangers. They didn't know him or care about him or even notice if he was there or not. But they were people and they were alive. They were familiar in a way. They were his friends in a way. Not real friends, they didn't know his name, he didn't know anything about them, but he knew that their faces would be familiar. He knew that he wouldn't feel so alone if he could at least overhear someone's conversation.

It was a strange feeling being there, being together yet still being alone. Was it just an illusionary form of togetherness, like on television? The characters on all your favorite sitcoms never watched television. They got together in the cafe and they dropped by each other houses and they actually interacted with other people. They actually *lived*. But it is so easy to transpose their lives onto your own. Television was getting too good at manipulating your brain chemistry, it made you feel like the people on television were actually your friends. You never felt lonely for that half-hour when your friends came to visit and talked about their wacky adventures and told jokes and were just exciting to be around. Tyler, who generally felt that the people on television were inane and vapid, got sort of a similar comfort

126

from being in familiar places. He had seen the waiter or bartender or barista or whatever they hell they called it before many times, and although nothing was exchanged between the two besides an order, no playful banter, nothing more then a 'Hey,' Tyler felt that recognition that came from eye contact, and for a second, he felt a little less alone.

He sat there pretending to read his book, hoping some of his 'friends' would be there. But it was still early Spring and the weather had turned out to be colder and cloudier than it looked from Tyler's window. There weren't any of the regulars sitting outside— the people who knew each other and talked to each other, and although they never actually spoke to Tyler, the ones who gave Tyler's brain permission to secrete those chemicals that made him feel loved, or at least acknowledged.

Tyler considered talking to the bearded guy who made the coffee. He thought that maybe this was a good chance to get to know him, since there weren't all these other people in the way to soak up his attention. But Tyler thought the better of it. He figured that maybe he'd be taken the wrong way. It was impossible in Tyler's mind to talk to a male stranger and not be mistaken for attempting some awkward sort of gay pickup. Plus, this was the place Tyler felt most comfortable. If the conversation went poorly he'd be embarrassed to come back, and then he'd be forced to switch to the coffeehouse down the street that was secretly run by the church next-door and wasn't anywhere near as hip clientele-wise. Or god-forbid the Starbucks.

So, he just sat there for almost an hour, nursing his latte. Tyler hated cold coffee, so most of what wasn't consumed in the first five minutes was going to wind up undrunk anyway. He really wanted to call Ann, but she was at work and he didn't want to bother her. He had called her and begged her to come home before and it was never a good conversation.

She would accuse him of being insensitive to her, since it was obvious that she wouldn't be at work if she had any choice in the matter, and it would end with her telling him that the best he could do was let her go back to work so she could finish faster. Ann had lots of friends at work, and rarely felt lonely. She didn't understand what it was like being Tyler. She never had extra time on her hands. The idea of sitting around the house with absolutely nothing to do all day was heaven to Ann. It was hell to Tyler.

The worst part of being bored and lonely is that you lose the ability to figure out ways to make you less bored and less lonely. He called Jason.

"Yo, talk."

"Hey, this is Tyler . . . come on over, I'm bored."

"Nah. I'm watching the Michigan game." Tyler could hear chewing noises over the phone.

"Seriously, come on over. I've got Madden 2000, we can *play* football."

"Fuck that." Jason said, "you know I don't play video games. I'm gonna watch football." Tyler waited a few seconds, hoping to get an invite over to watch the game. None was forthcoming. If he had asked, maybe Jason would've said yes, but Tyler never asked for things. He wanted to be invited, otherwise he'd feel like he was being a pest. Tyler worried constantly that people thought he was a pest.

"Allright. fine." He gave up and hung up the phone. It still amazed him that Jason, a red-blooded, 20-something American male hated video games. To Tyler videogames were an absolute necessity.

128

Tyler sat at the table with his arms crossed and a scowl on his face. He surreptitiously stared at some of the other people, trying to will them into talking to him. But his psychic powers were pretty limited and no one seemed to notice. He wanted to scream. He wanted to stand on the table and shout, "look at me! I'm here! I'm alive! I am human and I need to be loved!"[20] He didn't move though, other than to try to scowl a bit more than humanly possible. After a few seconds he dialed it down a bit, to put forth a more believable and less comical visage. He didn't want to scare anyone off.

"If only that Molly girl came by. I bet she'd talk to me." He craned his neck and looked past the cafe's garden, trying to see if she happened to be coming down the path, but no one was there. He had her phone number of course. He programmed it into his cell the minute he received that email from her the other day. He wasn't going to call though. First, he was sure that she was just being nice and didn't really want him to call, or maybe she was being mean and it was a fake number. Second, he didn't really want Ann to find out. Not that anything was going to happen, or he was going to do any betraying or anything, but he'd have to explain himself, and explain how he met this girl, and it was just too much trouble. Ann probably wouldn't care of course, but it would end up with Tyler trying to describe how lonely and alone and lame he was that he had to take such a drastic step, and he really didn't want to admit his frailties to people, even those people who already knew his frailties by heart.

He did call, of course. There wasn't much else he could do really. He liked to believe that he was in control of his

---

[20] As noted in Chapter 1, Tyler stole this last line from The Smiths, "How Soon is Now"

emotions, that everything for him was an academic exercise. Pros and cons were carefully weighed. All possibilities were meticulously considered and reconsidered. He knew in his mind that calling this girl was a bad idea. The most likely end result was that she wouldn't be home. Second most likely would be that she wouldn't be interested in meeting him for some reason. Third most likely was that she would come, but that they wouldn't get along, or she'd be disappointing in some way and he'd regret having ever called her in the first place. Fourth most likely would be that he would get along with her, and she'd become a pest, calling him all the time and getting underfoot. Tyler wanted people to want to be with him, but he really did relish his privacy and preferred to deal with people only when he was in the mood to deal with them. Historically, when he did find people who liked him they tended to call him at annoying times, such as when he was watching his favorite show or something, and he'd feel obligated to do stuff with them that he didn't like doing, like seeing a crappy movie or going to a loud, crowded bar and demanding that he awkwardly dance. What Tyler really wanted in life was a few clones of himself that wouldn't cause so much trouble, but who would be around when he needed someone to play Quake with.

But all the scowling and willing in the world hadn't brought him any attention, and he could feel the knot in the pit of his stomach. It was that feeling that something was really wrong in his life, the feeling you get when your girlfriend dumps you, or when the opposing team has just scored the go-ahead touchdown against the 49ers and you know they are going to lose and there isn't a damn thing you can do about it. Fuck.

He dialed the first six numbers on his phone. It was in speed dial, but he wanted more control. He wanted a few more seconds before he had to commit. Maybe something would happen, or he'd get another call, or that feeling would go away, or something. He hesitated for exactly eight seconds. He knew that if he waited longer, the phone would figure he had given up and reset. But finally, he pushed the last digit.

Tyler knew that most answering machines picked up after the fourth ring, so he usually hung up after three, especially if it was someone he didn't really know. He always came off as a doofus on voice mail, and he preferred to talk to live people. But just after the second ring, someone answered the phone.

The first sound Tyler heard was a crash, which was Molly dropping the phone on the floor. Then a disembodied, distant cry of, "shit," then the sound of fabric being drawn across the phone's microphone. Then finally a proper hello, or at least a, "yo."

"Hey Molly, this is Tyler." He usually rehearsed the first few sentences of his conversations, but he hadn't done that this time. Since he didn't know her very well, didn't know her at all really, and she didn't give him much to go on in her email, he didn't really know what to say or how to approach the situation, and he was feeling far too needy right now to have rationally thought this phone call out very thoroughly.

"Who?" she replied sleepily. Tyler thought that maybe she sounded a bit stoned. It was hard to tell.

"Tyler." There was silence at the other end of the phone. Molly was rummaging though her head trying to come up with some connection. "The guy from the email . . . from the other day."

Something almost audible clicked for Molly. "Duuuude." she said, stretching the word out a bit.

Tyler didn't want to seem too eager, and he wanted to wait just the right amount of time before continuing, but wound up hurrying and stepping over her words. There were several different entreaties he could use to get her to come to him, but after the 'dude' response, he decided to go with short, simple, and disaffected. "I'm down at the Consecrated Grounds. Come hang out."

Molly stood up, perhaps a bit too fast, and her head swam a bit til she sat back on the bed. "Crap. I just woke up." Tyler braced himself for the inevitable rejection. Well, it was better to have loved and lost than to never have, ". . . gimme like an hour. I mean if that's cool with you. I don't know if you've got better stuff to do."

"No no," Tyler said, half-surprised. "I've got a book, take your time. I'll be here all day." He hung up the phone. He looked around for a leftover newspaper or something to read. He didn't want to sit around for an hour by himself. But at least the knot in his stomach had gone away.

Almost immediately his phone rang. He figured that it was Molly canceling, but it was Ann. "I think I'm going to come home soon," she said enticingly.

"Oh." Tyler's reply was the result of surprise, but it came off sounding as if he were a bit dejected.

"Don't you want me to come home? I thought you were bored. I can stay at work if you don't want me there." She really couldn't figure Tyler out sometimes. He had said on several occasions though that his inflection was bad, and sometimes he sounded unenthusiastic about things he was really happy about, so Ann just assumed it was another one of those days.

"No, of course I want you to come home. I'm bored off my ass. It's just that I just ordered this latte at the coffee shop and all. But maybe I'll get it to go. . ." he knew what her response would be.

"No, don't rush on my account. I've got to do some clothes shopping anyway." Ann was always shopping for clothes, mostly because it took twelve trips to the mall to buy one outfit that didn't make her feel fat. "I'll come home soon."

Tyler hung up the phone. He was going to get antsy. He checked his watch, and tapped the face, hoping to somehow make it go faster. Ann wouldn't be home for like two hours, so he had to hope that Molly would come, he could have a short but intellectually stimulating conversation, and could get home before he had to explain himself to Ann. He felt his mug. The coffee was already cold.

Chapter 18:

Hard Currency Shortage!

Number of Conspirators:	*1-10*
Danger Level:	*Low*
Arrest Level:	*Low*
Lethality:	*Low*
Annoyance Level:	*High*
Economic Damage:	*Low–Medium*
Equipment Required:	*A few tubes of glue*
	A mask

Even though our corporate masters would probably rather have us use easily trackable credit cards, cash is still an incredibly important part of our society. We need it. We crave it. We feel incomplete somehow if we don't have a big wad of it in our pocket. If you remove the cash from a society, you will bring it to an entire halt. Luckily for the enterprising anarchist, this is remarkably easy to do.

Simply wander around town and mark the locations of all of the ATM machines in your target area. Most banks will be happy to provide you a list of their ATMs. On a Friday night, after the banks are closed, wander around to all of them, and squirt a small amount of crazy glue or epoxy into the slot where the card goes. You have now disabled this ATM for at least several days. It should not be too hard to cover a large area in one evening of hard work. A dedicated team of anarchists should be able to disable all of the ATMs in a small city overnight. Of course, the banks don't open again until Monday. Cash will become in short supply. Hording, chaos, looting, and theft may result as the denizens of the city realize that they can't pay for all the shiny baubles they need to feel a sense of fulfillment.

It was another one of those good behavior nights. Sometimes, if Ann was able to leave at a reasonable hour on a Friday night, a night where she wasn't accosted by a partner on the way to the elevator exhorting her to stay until midnight on what was almost certainly a one-time, rush, emergency project, if Ann was able to leave at a reasonable hour, she would get invited by a coworker or two or three to go to dinner. And Ann loved dinner. Of course, since the firm was downtown, and since they were all classy high-priced lawyers, and since they were used to the best, it meant dinner at a fancy restaurant. Ann and Tyler had different definitions of 'fancy.' For Tyler the term was used for any restaurant with cloth napkins. For Ann, it was any restaurant where the waiter came by after the main course with a crumb sweeper and put your scraps into that small pocket in his apron. Tyler, who couldn't see much of a difference between a $10 meal and $100 one was unimpressed, and he hated to have to play by the rules. He hated having to dress up in what Ann called, *medium* clothing. Before he met Ann, Tyler had two levels of clothing; business suits that he wore to work and t-shirts that he wore everywhere else. But Ann liked to eat at places where neither of those levels of dress was appropriate. She was drawn to those restaurants where you had to wear something akin to 'business casual.' She had harangued Tyler into taking numerous trips to Banana Republic in search of at least a few outfits that he could reasonably wear. He was a failure at it. Whenever he went in there he noticed the gay employees and customers, and they always looked quite stylish, but Tyler could never pull off the look. He always felt like a complete tool. It was as if he was trying pass himself off as something he was not. Nothing ever quite fit right, and the separates never quite worked together, even though Tyler would usually resort to finding a mannequin in the store and just buying everything it was wearing as a package. Ann often made the situation worse by suggesting after dinner that they go to one of the coolest, hippest spots in town, the places that Tyler would normally love to go. Dressed uncomfortably in his preppy clown clothes, he would just feign tiredness and demand to go straight home after fulfilling his duties as a dinner companion. After all these years Ann still couldn't figure out why he didn't take advantage of her offers to do the things he wanted to do in return for his putting up with her culinary demands.

This night they were walking down Eye Street. It's really called 'I' Street on the maps, but because the letter I looks like a 1, or maybe because it looks like a J, all the storefronts on the street listed their address as Eye. There were six of them in the party tonight— four of Ann's coworkers, plus the couple. The coworkers were all male, all single, all pretty attractive in an ivy-league educated, preppy law firm associate way. Tyler had experienced many evenings like this before, and he knew Ann's coworkers even better than he knew his own. They were quite friendly, but their main interest was always finding some women to hook up with. If this night turned out the way nights like this inevitably did, it would end with a cab ride to Adams-Morgan and some of the clubs with beautiful people and crappy music and cover charges and Tyler just sort of standing around uncomfortably with nothing to do while Ann talked shop and the guys tried to meet girls or drink themselves stupid.[21] Tyler rarely spoke. He just didn't have anything relevant to say. He didn't know or care much about law, and, like any gathering of coworkers, the company's business was always the main topic of conversation.

---

[21] God, the thing Tyler hated most was those bars that played retro-80s alternative music and all the pretty 20-somethings would dance around and pretend like they listened to bands like Depeche Mode and Echo and the Bunnymen when they were in high school which they totally did not. In fact, these were the same people who probably mocked people like Tyler for listening to music outside the Top 40, TRL-Live norm. Hypocrites.

They were walking down Eye Street on the way to Galileo's, which they had decided to 'look at,' holding off on their final decision about where to eat until they saw the menu. They were walking down the street in a row, with Tyler on one end holding hands with Ann. She was wearing a pantsuit. Tyler hated her in pants. She looked much better in skirts and Tyler often told her that he liked her in skirts and that she should wear skirts more often. They didn't have to be the micro-mini skirts that Ally McBeal wore; heck, even ankle length was fine, but he liked girls that dressed like 'girls.' Every time he mentioned it though she shot back with a diatribe about how skirts make her look fat and he was being sexist and how he didn't understand her and if he did he wouldn't ask her to wear things she didn't want to wear. Tyler often wondered how she failed to remember that he didn't like wearing his dorky medium clothes, but did it just to please her. But he wasn't a girl so maybe he just didn't understand. Ann claimed it was totally different, and Tyler never had the strength to continue the argument.

It was dark out, but winter was over and the nights were starting to become warm again. The streets in that part of town are well lit. From the outside, to the casual observer or tourist, it looked very fancy and swank with its marble buildings containing white-shoe law firms and high-end restaurants. But like all cities, decay and disorder were there, half-hidden but visible if you put your mind towards noticing them. Sometimes the trashcans were piled high, McDonalds bags and discarded newspapers cluttering the floor around them. In the shadows cockroaches the size of your thumb could sometimes be seen scuttling out of view. Now and then a rat would brazenly and defiantly walk down the sidewalk next to you, as if it had as much right to be there as you did. And then there were the bums.

Tyler had first seen some bums in DC when he was in seventh grade and he went on a school field trip. It was bitterly cold that day and the class trudged across the great lawn between the Capitol and the Washington Monument. Right in the middle of one of the dirt paths that criss-cross the field, a homeless person had constructed a makeshift tent over a Metro vent. Steamy, hot air, dusty and stale, swelled up from below. Tyler had wondered back then how the President (who he assumed walked to work this way every day) would allow something like this to happen. It just seemed not right somehow. He could understand bums living in the shadows of far-off frontier cities, but it seemed wrong to have them living a few yards away from where people who were supposed to be looking out for them were working. It just seemed that someone should care. Now Tyler was less naïve.

They were walking and talking about something or other related to some client or law thing or whatever, the conversation wasn't all that interesting. Tyler tuned it out. In a few minutes he would tune back in and try to make a witty comment at least tangentially related to the topic of conversation, just to show that he had been paying attention. Lying in the entrance to an alleyway was a bum. He was a young man, couldn't have been more than twenty-five. He was dirty and unkempt, but he wasn't completely in tatters. The clothes he wore looked reasonably new. He lay on his side with his back arched at an uncomfortable angle. He craned his neck in pain. He was almost in tears. As they passed by, he said to no one in particular, "Please, I'm sooo hungry." There was an obvious tone of desperation in the man's voice, as if he was pleading for his very life. The strange thing Tyler noticed was that the comment wasn't directed to himself and his companions. It was directed to the demons in the man's head. He was begging his own psychosis to leave him alone so he could get something to eat. But the hallucinations had no pity on the wretch. He just kind of writhed around a little and whimpered.

138

Tyler hesitated a moment, but only a moment. It seemed as if the other people in his group hadn't seen the man lying on the floor. It was as if he didn't exist, or that he was as inanimate as the other bags of trash that littered the street. They didn't turn their heads or slow their stride or skip a beat in their conversation. Tyler couldn't understand how they could be so blind. He had to attribute it to blindness, to inattentiveness, to too much focus on the inane conversation at hand as opposed to the world around them. People were like that. It had to be blindness, a sort of selective blindness, because no one in their right mind, no one with any sense of consciousness or decency could have walked by after hearing the psychotic man bleating for help. Tyler wanted to help, he wanted to lean over and say, "I'll help you man, I'll make it better." He wanted to get the guy some food, but more than that, he wanted to make some kind of lasting difference. He wanted to do something positive. It would be so easy to get this guy some Zoloft or Prozac or some anti-psychotic something or other and he'd probably be fine. He'd probably rejoin the rest of society and become a productive member of the community. Tyler right then and there decided to become an advocate for the homeless, to campaign for free medication, to lobby Congress (which after all was right down the street) for better health care for the mentally ill. But the feeling of guilt he had in the pit of his stomach didn't subside. "No," he thought, "I need to do more. I need to care more, as a functioning moral actor I need to do more to help." Tyler decided to go back to school and get a PhD in psychiatry or psychology or something like that (a little research would point him in the right direction). He didn't really like his job anyway, his career was pretty much going nowhere. Sitting at a desk all day playing on the internet and collecting an unearned paycheck wasn't satisfying, so why shouldn't he just drop out and go back to school and really make a difference? A difference on an intimate personal level. Not on some sort of societal level, building bridges or formulating policy or whatever, but on a personal level, a one-on-one level. He wanted to be the sort of person who would get down on his knees in the filth and the grime and pick up the limp hand, blackened with dirt and muck. He wanted to make a positive, direct, measurable difference in the life of this person, in the lives of many people, one-on-one. What a glorious change that would be for him, to make a difference! Not to be stuck in a cube everyday staring at a computer, producing nothing but meaningless reports that wouldn't be read anyway. A mountain of paper that amounted to nothing more than a field of wasted trees and a check mark on some suit's monthly progress report. Tyler didn't see how anyone else could not feel this way. How could all these otherwise intelligent people he was walking with not feel this way?

He walked on towards the restaurant with the rest of the crowd, but internally resolved to talk to Ann about it in the morning. She wouldn't understand, but that didn't really bother him. He would do it anyway. He eyed each of his companions in turn, followed the lines of their mouths as they smiled and talked about the best place to get a $4 cup of coffee, the best place to meet some high-class yet easy women, the best place to shop for their crapulent toys and doo-dads that they used as a crutch to delude themselves into thinking that they were happy and satisfied. Tyler was smarter then they were, he was more aware than they were, he was more awake than they were. If there had been an admissions form in front of him he'd fill it out this very second. He'd show them all the meaning of compassion!

Of course, by the time the dessert came, he had pretty much completely forgotten about the plan. Or maybe he had convinced himself that he could do more good in other ways. Maybe campaigning for the environment was a better way to spend one's life than campaigning for human rights. Maybe he didn't really have the money to spend another five years in school. Everything dissolved. Except for seeing the man once or twice in a dream, Tyler never thought about the incident again.

Chapter 19:

One-Two Punch!

Number of Conspirators:	*2+*
Danger Level:	*Medium*
Arrest Level:	*High*
Lethality:	*High*
Annoyance Level:	*High*
Economic Damage:	*High*
Equipment Required:	*Car bomb*
	Forklift

Everybody's paranoid about car bombs these days. Oklahoma City showed that they can be a great way to get your message across. So now the Man has put up barricades to stop a similar event. Never noticed them before? Look again! All those pleasant-looking giant concrete planters they've put in front of those government buildings aren't just for aesthetic reasons. They are designed to stop a car dead in its tracks. You can't get close enough to the building to actually really damage it. Or can you....?

The thing about those planters is that people put them there. Who? Workers with a forklift. They aren't nailed down or anything, they're just sitting there. So you need a one-two punch. Get your suicide bomber ready a few blocks away. Then have your team dress up like workers and drive a forklift up and move the barricade out of the way. Security will eventually figure out you aren't real workers, but you only need a few seconds if you time it right. Get the planter moved and then like a running back going through the hole opened by the offensive line, ka-boom! Seven points for your cause!

Tyler sat on the bench in the courtyard in front of the townhouse. He did this occasionally when he'd been out and wasn't quite ready to be home yet. From this vantage point he could see the cars coming up and down the street. When Ann's car pulled in, he would have time to run through the front door, kick off his shoes, and pretend he'd been there all along by the time she parked and got upstairs. Ann didn't really care if Tyler was home when she got home. At least that's what she said. Tyler wanted to be there when she arrived though, just because he knew that he would like it if she was home when he got home and he wanted to do for her what he hoped she would do for him. He figured that secretly she felt the same way he did, even if she wouldn't say it to him. Plus, Tyler didn't want Ann to suspect that he'd been out with Molly again.

They'd had three 'meetings' so far. Not dates; no flirting, no kissing, no touching of hands, no obvious expectation that it would lead to anything. Just meetings between kindred souls. They talked about culture and fashion and how un-hip most of the people in DC were. They talked about how they both wanted to travel around the world to really obscure places. He told her some of the interesting stories from his past, stories he'd rehearsed for years, without having to watch Ann roll her eyes and complain later that he'd told those stories a million times already. They talked about literature and even though Molly wasn't as well read as Tyler was, she seemed eager to learn and experiment with the books he promised to lend her. And bands, bands, bands! Finally someone who caught all the references that Tyler made about the indie scene, and someone who was so into it that she could even recommend bands Tyler wasn't familiar with yet. Molly had even once seen the Stone Roses in concert before they broke up. Tyler was so thankful to finally have someone he could really talk about music with. As soon as the next concert he wanted to see came to town he was going to finally have someone to go with who'd be as passionate and interested as he was. Except. . .

Tyler sat on the bench that was supposed to look like it was made of wood but in reality was made of recycled plastic. When he sat down it was a few minutes before dusk, and now it was a few minutes after. If Ann didn't return soon he'd have to give up and go inside because it would be too dark to identify her car. Lightning bugs blinked on and off around the bushes.

Tyler thought about Molly, or more specifically what he was going to do about Molly. She wanted him, he was pretty sure of that. She wanted him and didn't know that he had a girlfriend because he hadn't been honest with her from the start. Now it was too late to deflect her affections. She was going to be hurt when he eventually had to rebuff her. Tyler didn't want her to be hurt, he never intended it to go this far, never expected it to go this far. He didn't even know how to reject someone. He'd never broken up with a girl before, never, not even once. Every relationship he had ended when she dumped him. He had asked Jason once what it was like to break up with a girl, how he was able to deal with the guilt.

"Guilt?" Jason replied, "Why would you feel guilty?"

"Well you know, because you did things, either purposefully or not, and you got her to like you and then she finally fell for you and now you say 'no.'"

"Dude, that's part of the game. It doesn't always work out. Hell, almost all the time it doesn't work out, it's par for the course."

"Yeah, but I mean, you've got to know what it's like to get dumped, or to want someone who doesn't want you back,

144

right? It sucks, I mean it really sucks a lot. I hate that feeling. So then to know that someone is out there feeling that way about you, and there's nothing you can do about it, don't you feel guilty, I mean, for being the cause of their hurt?"

"I think you're taking this way too seriously. First of all, most people get over it pretty quick, it's not like you are the love of their life after two dates. Second, if some psycho actually falls that deep that fast, it's their problem not yours. They've got to learn to deal."

Jason didn't understand what Tyler felt. He probably never really loved as deeply as Tyler. Or maybe the correct word for what Tyler had felt was 'yearned,' not 'loved.' Tyler knew what it was like to yearn, and he just had to assume that most other people felt what he felt, at least sometimes.

Part of him wanted to ditch his entire relationship with Ann, move out, find Molly and say, "Yes, Yes, a thousand times Yes!" to her. It would be really great. But then what about Ann? He'd be hurting her. He'd be hurting her a lot more than he could possibly hurt Molly. He didn't want that either. He imagined that maybe one of his loves would die in some horrible accident, as gruesome as that sounds. It would at least solve his problem, and he'd be able to spend the rest of his life imagining what could have been with a fallen lover instead of regretting how much he hurt a living one. He daydreamed for a while about ways someone could die that would be completely sudden with no pain or anything like that. Ways that they wouldn't even know that they were dead. He read once about this guy driving down the beltway one rush hour when this truck flew off an overpass and crushed his car from above. Sucker never even knew what happened. If that happened to Ann, Tyler would be free to date Molly. Not immediately of course, he'd have to wait the requisite mourning period, but eventually, and with no remorse.

Tyler stopped himself from being a horrible person. "No, sudden death isn't what I want," he thought. He didn't want anybody to die, not in real life. Everybody fantasizes about horrible things now and then but they don't mean them. Not really. Tyler thought a better solution would be to maybe clone himself. If there were two of him, everybody could be happy. Wouldn't that be a nice solution? I mean, besides polygamy, which would of course be ideal for Tyler, but Ann was seriously unlikely to go for that, Molly neither.

But dammit, what was he going to do? He didn't want to be a horrible person. He didn't want to disappoint anybody. Was that the reason why he was still with Ann after all these years? Was it just pure inertia? Was he still with her because he didn't have the balls to just get up and say, "I'm not happy here. I need more excitement. I need someone more attuned to my desires. I need someone more interested in helping me be the person I want to be, as opposed to the person they want me to be!" and then just leave? Tyler had never broken up with anybody before. For him relationships were all about full-court press to get the target of your affections to like you. He was so focused on getting close that he'd never learned how to pull away. He didn't know how to turn off whatever skills he had (meager as they may be) in seduction. He flirted hard with everybody because he knew that if he didn't, no one would ever love him. But when it became obvious that they were starting to love him, he didn't know how to turn it off. How to pull back, how to say, "do I really want this?" Was he with Ann because he really wanted to be with Ann, or just because Ann still wanted to be with him?

He wished he could talk about his problems with someone, but he had no one to turn to. He didn't have very many friends. Obviously Ann was not eligible to talk to, being as she was one of the sources of his problems. Jason

146

wouldn't understand, seeing as he never felt the same way about things as Tyler did, and nothing Tyler ever said seemed to get interpreted correctly in Jason's brain. And no matter who he talked to he'd have to admit that he was flirting with someone he probably shouldn't have been flirting with and feeling things he probably shouldn't be feeling. Almost everybody he knew, even casually, would probably just think he was a big jerk and that he should just go home and be happy with Ann. Everybody thought she was a pretty great catch after all, and they'd just tell Tyler he was lucky to have her.

Since he couldn't talk to anyone about the turmoil inside of him he just sat on the recycled bench and yearned for a while. Tyler didn't really have a solid set of coping skills. So he sat and stared at fireflies and he felt bad until his chest hurt. Then he decided it was getting too dark to recognize Ann's car. He went back inside and put on a pot of water to make pasta. He didn't want to explain to Ann what he was doing outside. She'd never understand his need for self-reflection.

Ann arrived about 10 minutes later. She didn't want pasta and made Tyler dump out the pot of boiling water. He thought that was a waste of electricity, but didn't feel like arguing the point. Ann wanted to try this Thai place that supposedly people were raving about. Thai wasn't Tyler's favorite, but he didn't argue the point.

-=-=-=-=-

After the waiter took their order, Tyler asked, "Why do you love me?"

"I don't know, cuz you're here?" Tyler looked at her skeptically. "Cuz I'm used to you?" She tried to get back to her Blackberry. He just kept staring. "Because you're not

147

needy and I don't have to pay attention to you all the time?" she joked.

"No. I'm serious, what the hell do I bring to the table? I'm moody and weird and we don't have much in common. You make way more money than me and have your own house and I don't really think you need me for anything in the traditional sense. So why do you keep me around?"

Her email was going to have to wait; Tyler was having another one of his crises. "Companionship I guess. I can't go to restaurants alone. I can't go on vacations alone. Just having money doesn't mean you can do things, you also have to have someone to do things with."

"So that's all? I'm just a. . . somebody? Seems pretty generic. Couldn't you find someone better? One of those lawyers in your office? They're mostly single and rich and good-looking. Wouldn't you have more in common with one of them?"

"They're all 'guy' guy jerks who talk about nothing but sports and drinking beer."

"You could do better than me though, I bet."

The waiter arrived with the spring rolls. Ann, who was a lot less sensitive to very hot food than Tyler, immediately dipped one in the spicy green sauce. She tore it in half, releasing a visible puff of steam. "I don't want to go to all the trouble to find someone better," she said. "To have to beat my way through that jungle of singlehood again? That's really a lot of work. You are here, you'll always be here. I'm comfortable knowing you are always here." She bit into the roll and tried to turn the conversation around. "Why do you like me? What's your reason for staying with me then?"

Tyler ignored her attempt at redirection. "You could at least have an affair with one of them I suppose. An illicit office romance maybe. . . ?"

"Like I've got time for that. I work like 12-hour days, I don't have time for lunch. And once I'm done I want to go home and put on my pjs. How am I going to seduce some guy who's just as busy and stressed out as I am? It's not practical. Plus, I like to live drama-free, you know that. I do not need one of the partners finding out about something like that going on at work. The gossip would be crazy. No way."

Tyler sighed. "Sometimes I just worry that we're just both afraid to be alone."

"You want to know why I love you?" Ann said. "It's because you indulge me and I can be myself around you. I don't have to act all professional and buttoned up all the time when I'm with you. I can do stupid stuff, like wearing footie pajamas around the house without having to feel like I'm being judged. Remember how a few years ago I got really into watching that Pokemon show, and you didn't complain once when I taped every episode and watched them all constantly? You even tried playing the card game with me."

She reached out and took his hand. "You know what means something to me? Remember that time we went to New York for the weekend, and we walked past some street vendor and he had a set of those Russian nesting dolls made up to look like the characters from Seinfeld? And I looked at them for a really long time and even though I loved the show I decided not to buy them because I didn't really need them, but after we got home I started regretting not buying them and got all whiny and complainy for a few days? And now, every time we go back to New York for vacation, every single time, I can see you looking, I can tell you are still trying to find that vendor, still trying to get me those dolls. I'm over them now, I don't even really want them any more, but seeing you asking around for them when you think I'm not in earshot, knowing you want me to be happy, to have everything I want in life, even the stupid stuff. I know that you'll always be there for me, encouraging me to do the things I want to do even when you think they're silly or frivolous. That's what I love you for. Stuff like that." She pushed his hand towards his fork. "Now eat your spring roll because the waiter won't bring the next course until you're done."

That answer seemed to satisfy Tyler enough that he went back to Ann's previous question. "You want to know why I love you? Or I mean the first time I knew I wanted to be with you at least? It was like on our third date or something and you brought me back to your place. You went to the bathroom and I took the opportunity to look at all your cds. There was a His Name is Alive album.[22] At the time I really loved His Name is Alive, and I never met anyone else who had heard of them, and no one I ever played them for liked them even one bit, because, let's face it, they are super-experimental. But you had it. You had it before I even showed it to you. I really respected that."

"You liked me because of one cd? What about all the nice things I've done for you over the years?"

"Not just the one cd, what the one cd *represented*. It showed me that you were experimental, that you sought out things that weren't mainstream, that you didn't just listen to Top 40. That's the sort of person I wanted to be with. Someone who could show me new things and respect me for the things I showed them."

---

[22] Actually Ann owned both "Livonia" and "Mouth By Mouth"

"But now I only listen to dance music."

"Yeah. I suppose that didn't really work out the way I expected. But now I guess it's the same as with you. You are comfortable and familiar and I can be myself with you and say all sorts of crazy things and you just let me say them without arguing back. I really hate getting into arguments."

Tyler stared down at the spring roll. "Remember when these used to be called egg rolls? They were bigger."

"Egg rolls are Chinese, these are Thai. Spring rolls are the new egg rolls."

He pushed the finger-sized roll around on his plate with a fork. "I liked egg rolls better."

That night, as he lay in bed with his eyes wide open listening to Ann breathing beside him, he didn't think about the sirens. He thought about Molly lying in her bed, eyes wide open, pining away for Tyler, not realizing that she could never have him. Did she have a His Name is Alive cd in her collection too? Maybe she'd like a mix tape. Tyler decided to make her a mix tape.

Chapter 20:

Ricin: The terrorist's best friend

Number of Conspirators:	*1+*
Danger Level:	*High*
Arrest Level:	*Low*
Lethality:	*High*
Annoyance Level:	*High*
Economic Damage:	*Medium*
Equipment Required:	*Beans*
	Nail polish remover
	Coffee grinder

The perfect poison for the individual anarchist has got to be Ricin. It's incredibly deadly, odorless, colorless, and has a delay of 24-48 hours, giving you plenty of time to get away from the release point. And best of all, it's so easy to make. We here at CHOAS have plenty of ideas on how to use ricin to achieve your political or anarchistic goals, and we'll be discussing them elsewhere on this website. But first, a primer on how to make ricin:

First, obtain some castor beans. Castor plants grow wild all over the US, so it shouldn't hard to either find some or to grow your own. You can even buy them from gardening stores in some parts of the country. We suggest that you do not grow castor plants on your property since that could give investigators a way to track back to you. Public lands such as highway dividers, national parks, and corporate property are great places to plant your seeds.

Once you've harvested the beans, grind them in an ordinary coffee grinder (note: don't ever use that grinder to make coffee again!) Place the ground ricin in a coffee filter and pour some acetone through the filter. You can just use nail polish remover, which is easy to get and untraceable. Collect the liquid coming out of the filter and you've got a solution that's 11% ricin! You can evaporate some of the acetone off by leaving the container uncapped for a while (but don't heat it on the stove, acetone is flammable!).

Just a drop of ricin is enough to kill a person if ingested. You can increase the potency by adding a chemical called DMSO. This will turn the ricin into a contact poison. Be careful though, as ricin doesn't care what your political goals are and will kill you just as fast as it will kill your enemies. Good luck!

The hallway to Molly's apartment was dark and smelled like a combination of mold and sour milk. The rug was also inexplicably soggy in places, as if there was a leak somewhere. But no water source was evident, and no one who lived there seemed to notice. Molly's keys jangled in her hand as they walked. "You're sure it's ok I come up?" said Tyler, "I mean, it's no problem if your place is all messy or you've got porn lying all over the floor or whatever." He was trying to be funny. Molly just gave him a sideways look.

"You apologize a lot, you know?" she replied. "For stuff that's not even your fault."

"I know, I'm sorry, I don't mean to," replied Tyler without thinking too much.

"You need to act more self-confident. If I didn't want you over I would have told you to go." Every time he saw Molly, which was going on four of these coffee dates now, he always made sure to clean the house top to bottom, hide all of the dirty laundry, wash all the dishes and strategically place conversation starting items in plain view, just in case she wanted to come over to his place. She never asked, and he never offered. Ann wouldn't be too happy to see a strange girl in the house if she got home from work. And with Ann, you never knew when she would show up, sometimes it wasn't until midnight, sometimes, when she was really too frustrated to take it any longer, she'd be home by six.

Molly lived at the very end of a very long hallway on the very top floor of an old apartment building. "They gave me the bait and switch with this apartment. They showed me a place right next to the elevator, but then after I signed the lease they told me it wasn't ready so they gave me this one. The fuckers. Carrying groceries home is a bitch."

She opened the door to her place. Tyler had imagined what it might be like. He was picturing something done up in wacky colors with strange, homemade art all over the place. But it was pretty bare. It was painted that same off-white that all apartments come in. The ceiling was stucco, with more than a few water stains. Molly had a number of framed pictures, but they were all leaning up against the wall near the door. She saw him looking at the pile. "Yeah, I've been meaning to hang stuff up, but I've just never got around to it."

"I could help sometime, I mean, if you want. It's pretty easy to bang in a few nails."

"God, you are so submissive," Molly moaned, bending backward, eyes towards the ceiling. "Grow a dick. If I really cared I'd hang 'em up myself. It's no big deal."

Tyler changed the subject. "How long have you lived here?"

"Like three years I think. I keep meaning to move out every time they raise my rent, but then I'd have to look for a new place, you know?"

"Yeah."

She gestured over to a reddish-brown futon. "Go. Sit." She wandered off into the kitchen. Tyler took off his jacket and sat on the futon. Her tv was small. She had DVDs lying all over the place, none of which was properly placed in its case, and most of which were scratched. It looked like one had been recently used as a coaster. There was also a Playstation. Tyler thought about saying something about it, but something sticky had once been splattered on its top, and that in turn was covered by a layer of grime, so he figured that she didn't ever really play it. That was too bad. Girls who play video games are pretty cool.

"White ok?" she shouted from around the wall. They had originally met for coffee, but after fifteen minutes Molly announced how much she needed a drink and suggested that they go back to her place for some wine. Tyler, restless and curious, got up and wandered around a bit.

On a folding table in the corner sat a dollhouse. Its frame was faded plastic, and there was a pair of pants piled on top of it. He moved the clothes out of the way. It wasn't a regular dollhouse. The place seemed to be all dusty and cobwebby, and not just from the fact that it wasn't played with often. The furniture in the living room was covered with sheets, as if the place had been abandoned. From under the master bed a clawed arm stuck out. The basement appeared to be a dungeon of some sort.

Molly clicked on the cd player and walked over.[23] She put her arm around Tyler's shoulder as he was leaning in towards the dollhouse. "I didn't know you played with dolls," he said without turning towards her.

---

[23] Clutch, "Big News I" Clutch

"It's haunted, get it?"

"A haunted dollhouse?"

"Yeah, I used to have a dollhouse when I was a little kid and I was home like a few years ago and I found it in the attic all abandoned and stuff. I thought, 'hmm, it looks like a haunted house.' So I brought it here and made it into a real haunted house. The monster under the bed is called Marvin. Check this out," she opened the closet door. Inside was pile of Barbie doll parts. "That's where he hides the bodies," she said with an evil grin. "And look in the chimney."

Tyler looked inside. There were some black boots sticking out the top. He pulled out a Santa. "See," she said, "Santa was delivering gifts for the kiddies, and got stuck and now he's dead."

"That's disturbing. It looks like you've really put a lot of thought into this."

"Nah, I gave up on it a while ago. Now it's mostly just in the way." She wandered over to the couch and plopped down. "Sit. Drink," she ordered.

Tyler glanced at his watch. It was almost 8pm. Ann might be home any minute now, probably wondering where he was. He had taken the precaution, like always, of shutting off his cell phone and bringing a book with him. That way, if she called, he'd just say that he was getting some coffee and reading and didn't hear the phone. He hadn't told Ann about Molly yet. It was sort of a Catch-22. He didn't want to get Ann all alarmed that he was spending time with another girl if it was only going to be a one time thing, and Tyler was pretty sure Molly would tire of him soon enough. But then, after meeting with Molly a bunch of times, he

156

couldn't go back to Ann and say, "um, I've been lying to you and spending time with this other girl." Ann would be pissed that he didn't bring it up sooner. She'd probably think he had something to hide.

More importantly, Tyler had neglected to tell Molly about Ann's existence. She caught him looking at his watch. "Got a date or something?" she said.

"No no," Tyler replied defensively. "I got nothing better to do." Chances were pretty good that Ann would be at work til at least nine. As long as Tyler was home by then, he'd never have to explain where he was. "But I do have to go to the bathroom if you don't mind." He stood up. Molly gestured towards a dark hallway with her wineglass.

As he felt around for the bathroom light he heard her say, "And don't snoop through my cabinets." Of course snooping through cabinets was most of the purpose of Tyler's need to use the restroom. He wanted to understand Molly a bit better, wanted to get into her life a bit, see underneath the veneer. There was a pile of clothes on the floor that Tyler nudged around with his toe. Several pairs of her underwear were partially visible. He didn't want to actually pick them up lest he be labeled a pervert, but he had a weird need to at least see them, to know they existed. He also found a bra in the pile. That he couldn't resist. He picked it up, holding on the label, to read it. 34B was the size. "Hmmm" he said. His motive was purely curiousness and not prurient. He put it back down and rearranged the pile back to something approaching its initial configuration.

He looked under the sink. There was a box of maxi-pads and some generic toilet paper. Again, Tyler didn't know what he was looking for, he just wanted to see Molly as a human being, as a functioning biological entity. Seeing what brand of toilet paper a person uses really humanizes them, regardless of what brand they actually choose.

He was into her medicine cabinet when he heard her cry from the other room, "hurry up, I'm lonely!" He quickly glanced around her shelves. They were pretty dirty, and there was a lot of rust under the peeling white paint of the cabinet walls. There was a well-worn toothbrush that was not properly washed out from the last time it was used, some aspirin, a package of birth control pills, and pile of rubber bands to tie hair back. There was also a small, sooty pipe for marijuana. He quickly flushed the rust-stained toilet to make it more convincing, and checked to see how many pills were left in the month. He made a mental note of when Molly was likely to be PMS-ing. Then he hurried back to the living room, already regretting not taking the time to see how clean her shower was.

Spiritual electronic music was playing out of a Target brand stereo.[24] Molly was half sitting, half sprawled on the couch. Her legs were straight out and just the tips of her toes were visible from beneath the ridiculously-long bell-bottomed jeans she was wearing. Her flip-flops were sitting under the coffee table. Tyler figured that if he tried to sit back at the end of the couch he had been sitting at, he'd have to move her feet out of the way. So he sat down across the room in a threadbare armchair that could, under certain definitions of the word, be considered 'funky'.

As soon as he sat down, Molly remarked, "Why are you sitting over there? You can get closer, I don't bite." She half-smiled in a way that some would interpret as seductively.

---

[24] Banco de Gaia, "Big Men Cry"

"I didn't want to get in your way, you're all comfortable." Tyler joked. Molly sighed. She put down her wine glass, and lifted herself up by her elbows into more of a sitting posture. She bent her knees and brought them up close to her chest. Tyler had nothing left to protest.

As soon as he sat on the couch, Molly threw her feet into his lap. Then she leaned back and said, "ahhhh. . . ." Tyler looked down at her toes. They were calloused and misshapen. Most girls' toes looked horrible. It was probably the bad shoes. Tyler had often said he would never wear those horrible strappy things that most girls wore if he were female. Molly's toes weren't any worse than Ann's. They seemed a bit longer, but it was hard to tell without having them both side by side. The nails were painted a turquoise color. Ann never painted her toes. She claimed it was too much trouble, and who was looking at her feet anyway?

Tyler was. He often wished that Ann tried a little harder. Not that he ever really told her outright. He was much too PC and passive-aggressive for that. But Ann never seemed to pick up on his vague, subtle comments that only peripherally related to toe color. Tyler looked up from Molly's toes. She batted her overly-mascaraed eyes at him playfully. All of a sudden Tyler began to feel trapped. He had always felt free reign to flirt with other women because he knew that his success rate was so low. Since there was no way that any girl was ever going to go for him, it didn't matter how hard he tried. It was a theoretical exercise. But on rare occasions where it looked like she might be interested, things tended to spiral out of control because he didn't know how to turn the flirting off. At least not without getting the girl completely pissed off at him. Maybe he was just imagining things. He didn't know Molly all that well, and he was a horrible judge of people in general. He must just be imagining things.

"You know, with these toes right here, you are dangerously close to getting tickled." He didn't know what else to say.

"Go ahead. I'm not ticklish at all." She said matter-of-factly.

"Ok. . . I'm gonna do it. . ." he gave her a chance to pull away, but she just pointed her toes to the ceiling, turned her head as if she couldn't care less, and took a sip of her wine. Tyler touched the sole of her foot with one hand while holding her ankles steady with the other. Molly didn't flinch. He tried tickling for a bit, but nothing.

"Wow, you're pretty freaky." Ann was horribly ticklish and would flinch anytime Tyler got within six inches of her feet.

"Not only that," Molly said, "But I never get ice cream headaches."

"Never?"

She leaned forward to imply seriousness. "Never."

"That's very bizarre. Maybe you've got some nerve damage."

"Boy. You really know how to sweet-talk a girl." She frowned. "Tell me something interesting about you. What do you want in life?" She leaned back and put her arms behind her head. She was wearing a black tank top. Ann never wore tank tops. Ann thought her arms were flabby. They weren't. They weren't as emaciated as Molly's were, but people a lot flabbier than Ann shamelessly walked around in tank-tops every day.

160

"You know what I sorta want?" he said hesitantly. "What I've been thinking would be kinda cool in a way. Something that would solve all my problems?" He waited for Molly to respond. Her eyes opened a little wider and she made it clear that she wanted him to go on.

"I think I'd like to be addicted to heroin," he said.

She looked at him skeptically. "Have you ever even done heroin?"

"No. I don't even know where I could get it. But it would give me something to shoot for, you know? No pun intended. I mean. . . it's like all day I'm worried about my life and my friends and what I'm wearing and what I'm doing and how the President is going to fuck with my retirement savings and how I'm wasting my life in a crappy job I hate and how I need to take my car in to get inspected again and how I'm bored out of my mind all the freaking time. But heroin addicts have it easy. They don't worry about any of that. All they worry about is where they can get more heroin. It's like it brings your life into focus. You know exactly why you're here and exactly what you are supposed to be doing. I never know what I'm supposed to be doing most of the time."

"You are so fucking clueless. Have you ever seen people on drugs? Half the kids in my high school were tweakers and they're all desperate disgusting assholes. You really want to wake up every morning in a pile of your own puke?"

"No, you're not getting it. I'm just looking for something that I can't ignore. Everything in my life seems kinda optional you know? I don't have to do it. Like hanging out with you. I don't have to be here."

"Feel free to leave anytime. I'll deal."

"No no, it's not that. I mean, like, I don't have to be here. If I didn't meet you my life wouldn't be much different. Or take the books I read, I didn't have to read them. I enjoyed them and all, but they were optional. Heroin isn't optional. You can't say, 'I think I'll skip the smack today.' It won't let you."

"Well, go ahead, if that's what you want to do, why don't you?"

Tyler laughed. "I have no idea where I could even get any. Everyone I know is a professional, I bet none of the people in my life have ever even seen a hard drug."

"You don't know anybody who uses. . . *anybody*?" Molly said skeptically. "Hell, I bet a lot of your coworkers are on coke. You just haven't noticed it because you don't know what signs to look for. But if you want some weed let me know. I've got a pretty good dealer."

"That's not really my style." He paused and took a sip of the wine Molly had given him. It tasted tinny. "I did once actively try to become an alcoholic in college," he said hesitantly. "I had been dating this girl for a while and she dumped me for what I'm sure were perfectly legitimate reasons, but I was pretty depressed, and no one seemed to notice. So I thought if maybe I had a drinking problem then people would hold an intervention or something, I don't know. So I tried to put down a fifth of liquor a day. I figured if I just started really drinking every day eventually I'd get hooked."

"What happened?"

"Nothing. Mostly I was just too full or too busy or too sleepy most of the time, and I kept forgetting to drink. And

162

then when I ran out of alcohol it was raining and I didn't feel like going out to the store, and it was kinda expensive, so eventually I just sorta forgot about the whole idea. No one seemed to notice anyway, even though I tried leaving empties all over my dorm room."

"You have to be the most disturbed individual I know." Molly said. "Even more twisted than all those tweakers I grew up with."

"I don't normally talk about how insane I am. I guess even though I've only seen you like what, three times now, you're like my therapist. I hope you don't mind."

"No, I don't mind," Molly leaned in close. "I love being on people's inside."

She rested her head against her arm against the back of the futon and looked at him with tilted eyes. The wine glasses sat on the tie-dyed sheet stained with candlewax that covered the old chest that doubled as her coffee table. The rim of Molly's glass was covered in smeared lipstick. Tyler was starting to get the impression that he wasn't imagining things. He wasn't an expert or anything, but he was pretty sure he'd seen that look in the eyes of a girl before— that expectant look of someone wondering when their partner was going to finally get up the nerve to kiss them.

By any standard Molly was pretty hot, and to be honest, if Tyler had met her years ago, before he had gotten involved with Ann, he would have undoubtedly chosen Molly over Ann, regardless of the fact that it would never work in the long run with Molly. She was too dippy, too much of a free spirit, too hard to pin down. He'd get jealous of all her other friends and she wouldn't give him enough attention, and he'd worry too much about her career and the bills and what she was doing with her life. He wouldn't be able to have a real conversation with her because he was usually speaking over her head, and when he dumbed down his vocabulary to try to get her to understand, he'd be accused of being condescending. She'd try to get back at him by fucking all of his friends and he'd get jealous and freak out and it'd all go downhill in the end. But she was pretty hot.

Tyler decided to handle the situation by not handling it. Just ignoring her obvious attraction to him. Maybe he was wrong. Maybe she'd get the hint he wasn't interested and things could remain at the 'coffee friend' phase. If it all came to a head and he had to reject her overtly, it'd get embarrassing and he wouldn't be able to go back to any of the places he'd seen her in ever again for fear of running into her. "I've got to go to Tucson next week," he said, after an awkward silence.

"Why is that?"

"I've got a business trip. Some kinda class, or seminar, or something."

"You're not sure?"

"Hey, I just do what they tell me to do." Tyler did know of course, or at least he knew more than he let on he knew. It was a class in how to use a new project development software package that Tyler's boss had bought. It was supposed to help people like Tyler manage the time constraints of multiple projects with tight deadlines. Tyler didn't feel like explaining it because he'd have to get into why he thought it was a waste of money and things would get technical and he'd come off sounding like a computer dork. Plus, whenever he tried talking about work to other people, the subject of what he did all day would always come up and it was impossible to effectively explain how little he actually did, and pointless to explain what his job description said he did. Nothing he could say about his office life would make people like Molly like him more.

"I once went to Albuquerque, when I was a kid. I don't remember much about it though," she said.

"That's not the same state. Tucson's in Arizona," he replied without considering the consequences of his dismissal.

"Oh. . . ."

"But, it's pretty close. I bet they're basically the same. I bet that if you didn't have a map you'd be hard pressed to tell which one you were in." She smiled slightly.

"How come you know so much? Everything we talk about, you seem to know a lot about it."

"I just don't see how people could not know. I mean, it's the *world*. Whenever you read newspapers or watch tv or just talk to people, stuff like where Tucson is just comes up." She stared at him blankly. ". . . I suppose most people don't pay much attention." It was a subtle dig, but Tyler felt safe making it because she wouldn't assume he was talking about her. "It's like all those terrorists in the Middle East. All they know are car bombs and suicide bombs. Bomb bomb, bomb. But there are so many more cool things that they could do. Easier things, safer things, more disruptive things. But they never think of them, it's just bombs bombs bombs. If they just did a Google search on terrorists they'd find my web page, which has all sorts of different ideas for them. Stuff that's fun and innovative and cool that'd make people say, 'wow, why didn't I think of that?'"

"I don't think terrorists usually live in places that have internet."

165

"Well they should. I think that if you are going to do something, especially something so extreme as blowing something up, you should at least do some research. It's like they don't care enough to bother, which is weird since they care enough to die for their cause."

"You can't try to figure out terrorists. Those guys are just nuts."

"Maybe. I don't know. I just know I'd make a great terrorist leader."

"Like Che Gueverra. The guy in the Rage video."[25] She put down her now empty glass of wine and moved closer. Tyler was leaning back against the armrest and Molly was sitting with her knees folded under her, head against the back of the couch. Her mouth was less than a foot away from Tyler's. He felt a combination of nervousness and excitement. He thought to himself that he hadn't been imagining things, that she did really want him. He could have her, all he needed to do was lean in and kiss her. Now was the time. Seconds counted.

"Well, he wasn't a terrorist exactly, but yeah I guess. The problem is that no one is really paying any attention. . . ." He trailed off, having completely lost his train of thought. It didn't matter, it seemed like Molly wasn't paying much attention to his words anyway. She was just sort of staring up at him.

"Professor Tyler, Rebel leader." she said softly. "You are simply a fascinating person." This would have been the perfect time to kiss her, to seal the relationship. Tyler

[25] Rage Against the Machine, "Bombtrack"

wanted to, she was hot as hell. But he didn't. He was with Ann, and despite the banality of their life together, despite the lackluster vanilla sex and the lack of conversations about existentialism and never staying out all night at a rave and never reading comic books together on a Saturday morning, he was pretty happy with her. They rarely fought, they had fun together. He knew that he'd never last with Molly for more than a month. She didn't get his jokes, he had to dumb down nearly everything he said, and she was too much of a whirlwind for him to ever be able to keep up. He was too responsible for her, too old and grownup and set in his ways. Although he'd never admit it out loud, he found comfort in going to bed early in his stars-and-moon pajamas.

He was also, despite his vehement denials, a risk-averse person. He hated confrontation and would never give up a bird in hand for even a dozen in the bush. There was no way he could be with Molly without giving up Ann, and that was too great a risk, despite the fact that Molly was all the things he always told himself he wanted in a woman.

He looked into her eyes. She waited for him to say something. Tyler imagined what those things could be. He was in quite an awkward position. He felt ok to flirt because it never led anywhere, now that he was suddenly successful, to break things off would seem totally out of the blue. How could he let Molly down gently? Damn, he was going to have to look like a total asshole. And he'd better think up something quick because the moment was happening right now!

"Agh, I can't do this!" he cried, jumping up from the couch.

Molly looked confused. "Can't do what?"

"We can't hook up. I'm sorry. I've got a girlfriend. I should have probably told you before, but I didn't. It's not you, you're hot and all, I just can't." He paced about the room not looking at her, not wanting to see the disappointment in her eyes.

"Hook up? Who ever said anything about hooking up? Are you on medication!?!"

From the tone in Molly's voice Tyler realized he had been making up the entire thing is his mind. "I mean, you're ok and all but I'm not interested in hooking up with you." She looked a bit disgusted.

Damn. Tyler needed to do some damage control. He was confused. "I guess I misread the signals. I just thought. . . you know, with the inviting me back to your place and wine and all and how you wanted me to sit next to you on the couch and everything, it just seemed like a set-up."

"You need to get out more. And, no offense, but you're like not my type. I'm mean you're fine, there's nothing wrong with you or anything, it's just I sorta like my guys a little scruffier."

"Oh."

"No no, I mean you're a great guy and all, it's just. . ."

"No that's ok. It's not a problem. I mean. . ."

"It's not like you're not cute. You're just a little corporate that's all. You've got a job where you wear a tie and use a computer and all that stuff. I just think that it's like, you know, different worlds and all."

That was about the worst thing she could have said. He knew what she meant, and he hated the same things about himself that she hated. He wanted to break out of the mold, but the mold kept drawing him back in, making him the good son, the good employee, the good citizen. He hated the mold, but the mold had him. He wanted to be a cool, indie, counter-culture person, and if a cool, indie, counter-culture person like Molly wanted him, it'd finally be validation that he was the person he wanted to be, even if it would never work out in the long run.

He couldn't blame her though. "No it's cool. I was just figuring I'd let you know, you know, before you got too into me." He chuckled a chuckle. It was obviously fake, but it wasn't obvious if he was just trying to be funny, or if he was actually trying to convince himself that he was just acting in her best interest.

Molly, being far more used to cockblocking dorky guys than Tyler was used to being this close to scoring was unfazed. Whatever emotional distress Tyler was feeling, it was completely outside her sensory perception. She simply continued with the conversation. "If you haven't told me about her yet, I bet you haven't told her about me too? How come? If you weren't trying to get into my pants and all I mean?"

"I don't know, fear of rejection maybe?"

"You think she's going to reject you if you look at other women?"

"No, I mean fear of rejection from *you*. Or at least, having to admit that I've been rejected by someone. I bump into people all the time, but 99% of them blow me off after a few minutes, worse are those that seem like they like me, but then just sort of disappear after a week or two. I never want to tell Ann that I've met a potential friend because I'm pretty sure that once the person gets to know me, they'll give up on me pretty quick. And I don't want to have to admit that I've failed again. Ann would be all like, 'are you going to talk to that Molly girl again soon? Did you have a fight? What ever happened to that girl you had coffee with that one time?' and I'd have to admit that I'm a huge failure and no one likes me. So it's easier to just not mention it so I don't have to get continually reminded about it."

"Man, you're weird."

"Yeah, but I'm not weird in a cool, disaffected way like Holden Caulfield. I'm not weird in a funny way. Not like the guy in 'Confederacy of Dunces.' If I was weird in a funny way, at least I'd be endearing. I'm just weird in a weird, annoying way that makes people not want to know me."

"I meant weird in an insane way."

"It's like. . . I mean like with my dad and all. I always got the impression he was pretty popular when he was in school, and I wasn't. He never said anything, but I think maybe he was a little disappointed. Take the prom. Junior prom came along and I asked out five girls and got rejected five times, so I gave up and didn't go and I never mentioned it, and no one in my family ever noticed that I didn't go. I wasn't going to go to senior prom, but I told this friend of mine and he told his sister who was a year younger. She came up to me after class and was all like, 'but you have to go, it's a night you'll remember for the rest of your life.' Then she magnanimously offered to go with me."

"So I got all excited and thought that maybe she liked me and I actually had a date. Prom night my dad was all like, 'feel free to stay out as late as you want. . . wink wink.' But as soon as we got to the dance, she took off to be with her friends and left me sitting at the table alone. I must've talked to her for all of five minutes. It sucked completely, a total waste of time. Then, after it ended, I had hoped that maybe I'd get invited to a party or something, but I didn't. She was totally uninterested in spending time with me, I think she was just looking for a way to get to the senior prom as a status symbol. So she feigned a headache and made me take her straight home. I didn't even get a kiss or nothing. It was like 10:30."

"I didn't go to prom at all," she interrupted. "It was all too bourgeois for me." Tyler assumed that Molly didn't really know what 'bourgeois' meant. "Me and my friends drove up to woods and smoked pot and built a bonfire. We were so wasted."

"You're missing the point, I haven't gotten to the point yet. The point is that I didn't want to go home and admit that everything was a failure and I couldn't even get a legitimate date for prom. Not to my dad. So I just drove around for hours and got an ice cream sundae by myself at three in the morning at an all-night diner. When I finally got home, I pretended like I didn't want to talk about it, and I guess dad just assumed I'd gotten lucky. See? It's just easier to not talk about stuff than have to admit you are a loser."

Molly didn't have a response. All she could do was note to herself that Tyler's life and experiences were so far removed from her own that trying to figure him out was pointless. She looked at her empty wineglass and wondered whether or not it would be a good idea to offer to get him high.

Chapter 21:

Timing, Preparation, Patience, Ka–Bang!

Number of Conspirators:	*1–10*
Danger Level:	*Low*
Arrest Level:	*Low*
Lethality:	*High*
Annoyance Level:	*High*
Economic Damage:	*Medium*
Equipment Required:	*Explosives*
	Remote Detonator
	Shovel(s)
	Utility worker uniforms

If you are an astute observer, like we here at CHOAS are, you've certainly noticed that security is only present when there is something happening. Take that big WTO protest in DC last year. Sure, it was impossible to get a bomber or a sniper anywhere near the meetings because the police blocked off all the roads, right?

Wrong! It was impossible to do it AFTER the cops put up the barricades. But if you had inserted an agent into the zone a day or a week in advance, it would have been easy. The trick is just knowing long enough in advance that something is going to happen, and setting up before they have a chance to set up security. For example, you know that the national lawn in DC is always having a rally of one sort or another. Now it's not going to be easy to get in there and cause damage once the rally starts. But here's what you do: You put on some utility worker uniforms and go to the lawn way in advance of the rally (weeks or months even!). No one will notice you digging holes because nothing is happening there that day. Plant bombs in the holes and refill. As many as you got. Then just wait. On the day of the big rally, there'll be security all over the place, but no one will be looking under the grass! Once the place is full of targets, remote detonate the bombs.

This technique would also work with major sporting events, presidential visits, or just anytime you can predict your target's whereabouts far enough in advance to be able to get in and plant bombs before security arrives.

The phone was ringing. The phone was ringing but it was all the way at the other end of the couch. Jason seriously considered not answering it. But the ringing was interrupting the sound of the tv, and if he didn't pick it up they'd probably call back and annoy him again. And he had money on this game. He flopped across the sofa in a way similar to how a walrus would move across a rocky beach and reached the receiver with the tip of his outstretched hand.

"What," he said loudly. He couldn't hear the person on the other end. "Hold on," he grumbled. Under an empty bag of chips was a remote and he lowered the volume on the tv. "What." he said again.

"Jason, it's Ann."

"Ann? Really? Is Tyler dead?" Ann had never called Jason. He didn't know she even had his number. She mumbled something inaudible. "Speak up, I can't hear you." He lowered the volume some more.

"Tyler's in the other room. I don't want him to hear."

"Are you coming on to me, because like, I don't think I could do that to Tyler. He'd go all psycho and shit. Well, I mean, you know him better than I do so I guess if you want to take the risk, I'm in." Jason was just kidding, but he had a

173

very deadpan delivery and often his jokes came off as inappropriate statements. Ann knew enough to ignore him.

"Shush. I don't have a lot of time. You know how you guys are going to Tucson next week?"

"Um. . . yeah. . . ?"

"Well did you know that the day you come back is Tyler's birthday?"

"Hell, I don't even know when my Mom's birthday is."

"Well, I'm going to throw him a surprise party."

"Awww. . . that's nice."

"But you are the only guy I know who works with him. Can you invite anybody at work you think might be interested in coming?"

"I don't think that'd be hard." There weren't that many people in the office who would really even know Tyler's name, but he supposed he could ask around. As long as there was beer at least a few people would show up.

"Cool. I figured I'd pull a bunch of names off his phone when he wasn't looking, but the only people he's got stored are you, his mom, and someone named Molly. Is this Molly a work person too?"

Tyler hadn't told Jason about Molly, mostly because he knew that Jason would just think he was trying to get some on the side, which was exactly what he didn't want people to think. As with a lot of other things, Tyler kept Molly to himself, mostly because he figured that nobody cared or at least that nobody would understand.

174

Jason didn't know who Molly was, and assumed that since Tyler hadn't mentioned her, he was getting some on the side. Jason was interested in gossip, but not interested enough to keep missing the game. "Never heard of her. You'll have to ask Tyler about it yourself."

"I'll just call her. Ok, I gotta go before Tyler comes back. I'll email you the invite. I pdfed along with directions, just print it up and pass it out."

"Done." He hung up the phone and went back to the game, making a mental note to ride Tyler about this Molly person on the plane ride. Within five minutes though he had totally forgotten about Molly. The Caps lost that night.

Ann peered through the doorway into the bedroom. Tyler was lying motionless in front of the television. He was watching The Real World. He had his finger on the remote though, ready to switch back to Crossfire as soon as he heard Ann coming back in. He didn't want anyone to think he actually watched crap like The Real World. Just a minute here or there to reacquaint himself with how awful American culture was these days was how he justified it to himself. Tyler was lying with his head bent against the headboard in an awkward angle. Sometimes he complained to Ann that his back hurt and she would tell him it was probably because he lay in bed at that awkward angle. He agreed, but kept lying in that same position night after night. Ann wanted to nag him about it, so as not to hear him complain tomorrow, but if she disturbed him he might get up and start walking around. She'd never get the rest of her secret phone calls completed that way.

Ann dialed the phone to call Molly. She would rather wait to have asked Tyler who Molly was, but that would require she admit that she was snooping through his phone. Hopefully it wasn't his great-aunt or something.

Molly was sitting on her reddish-brown futon when her cell rang. She could have picked it up on the first ring, but she was still taking the last hit off her bowl. The phone rang three times before she bothered to exhale. The caller ID said it was Tyler.

"Hello?" she said dreamily.

"Hi, uh, you don't know me. My name is Ann, I'm Tyler's girlfriend."

"Aaannnn. . ." Molly replied.

"I'm having a surprise party for Tyler and I'm trying to find people he knows, and he's got your name in his cell phone."

"Um, I don't really know any of his other friends, so I don't think I can help you."

"No no, I'm trying to invite you to come to the party. It's the Saturday after next." Molly crossed her eyes trying to figure out when exactly that was. "Can you come?"

"Uh, I guess. Unless I have to work or something. But do I gotta bring a present or something cuz I'm flat broke right now."

"No no, you don't have to bring anything. And don't worry about bringing food or something. I'm baking some cakes and there's going to be appetizers."

"Well, as long as there's booze, I'm cool."

"Ok, um. . . what's your email address, I'll send you all the details." She had her pen uncapped and the back of a receipt to write on.

"I don't have an email address." She thought about repacking her bowl but the baggie was getting kinda empty and her source wasn't the most reliable guy in the world. She decided to hold off and see if what she already smoked would be enough.

"hmmm. Ok, well I guess I can call you or something later and let you know."

"That's cool. If I don't pick up just leave a message."

"So, like anyway, how exactly do you know Tyler anyway. Do you work in his office?"

Molly might have been out of her head just enough to feel like screwing with the random caller, or she might have been just in her head enough to make sure not to get Tyler in trouble. "Naw man. I'm like in his terrorist group. CHAOS."

"Oh, ok. I thought it was CHOAS?"

"Mmm yeah. That's what we want the squares to think."

"Well if any other CHAOS people want to come, could you coordinate them? I can't be making a lot more phone calls without Tyler getting suspicious."

"No prob. But we don't like to get together more than two or three at a time." Molly suppressed a giggle. "We've gotta be all spread out in case the cops try to bust our asses." She pointed her finger like a gun and made a 'pew pew' noise that was too quiet for Ann to notice over the phone.

Ann could hear that Tyler turned off the tv. "Ok, whatever," Ann said hurriedly, "I gotta go." She quickly hung up the phone and put it back on the coffee table just in time.

"So, are we going to dinner anytime soon?" Tyler said as he entered the room.

Molly put down her phone and let out her giggle. She sat for a few minutes with her eyes closed grinning from ear to ear without thinking about anything particular. Then she looked down at her baggie and decided to refill her bowl after all.

Chapter 22:

Foul Harvest!

Number of Conspirators:	*1+*
Danger Level:	*High*
Arrest Level:	*Medium*
Lethality:	*High*
Annoyance Level:	*High*
Economic Damage:	*High*
Equipment Required:	*Ricin*
	Pesticide sprayer

If you've been doing your homework here at CHOAS, you undoubtedly have a large bottle of ricin by now. But what to do with it? The problem is that it's really only good if people ingest it, and how can you get lots of people to do that? Easy!

Get a job at your local supermarket and work in the produce section. Then head over to the local gardening store and get one of those pesticide spray bottles that hooks into a gardening hose. The rest is trivial. One day when no one is looking, fill the bottle with ricin and attach it to the hose that mists the fruits and veggies so they stay fresh. It'll get all over all the produce in the store. And remember, it takes a few days for ricin to work its magic, so you can keep this scheme going for days and take out a lot of targets. Plus, think of the publicity and economic damage when people all over the country are afraid to buy veggies! And think of the health consequences when no one trusts the best source of vitamins, minerals, and fiber anymore.

"Well, it looks like they've got a Sbarros, a Burger King, a Chik Fil-A, and a Panda Express. What are you up for?"

179

Jason looked over at Tyler. Tyler never had an opinion, although he often had complaints.

"This sucks, I wanted a burrito or something."

"I think we passed a Taco Bell on the way over. I guess that would be ok."

"That's not what I mean, man. I want something with a 'southwest flavor.' I mean, jeez, this is the same crap they've got in Virginia." He moved dejectedly over to the Sbarros. It had the shortest line. Jason followed. "Gimme two slices of the mushroom," he said to the clerk. She was a cute looking Asian girl with way too much eye shadow. Tyler would probably have attempted to make some sort of witty comment to get her to smile if Jason hadn't been around to report him back to Ann. It probably didn't matter anyway, she seemed like she was still in high school and most likely had a boyfriend lurking about nearby.

Jason ordered the Chicken Parmesan platter. They took their green plastic trays and sat down in the middle of the atrium on pink plastic seats at a table still littered with crumpled napkins. Everything in the mall was pastel. Everything in every mall is pastel.

"What are you pissed off at today?" Jason said.

"Isn't it obvious? Look at this place."

"It's not so bad. It's a lot like the malls back home."

"Exactly. It's a lot like the malls back home. Nothing is any different than anywhere else. It's all like homogenous now. The stores they have here are the same exact stores that they have back in Virginia. It's like exactly the same."

". . ." Jason knew better to stop Tyler when he was on a roll. He just let him complain himself out and soon he'd be back to his normal mopey self. He turned his attention towards his parmesan.

"The cool thing about traveling, I mean, the thing that *should* be cool about traveling is that you get to experience other cultures right?" He didn't wait for a response, "you get to eat at different restaurants, you get to shop at different stores, you get to do different things. But this is the same man. I can get Sbarros pizza at home. What's the point of being here?"

"I thought the point was to go to that seminar. Plus we got those nice bags." Tyler didn't take a bag. It had the seminar company's logo on it. Everything had to have a logo on it these days.

"I was pretty excited about coming out here. I've never been to Arizona before. I don't think anybody in my family's ever been to Arizona before. I wanted to be a *traveler*, you know?[26] But it's all the same. If it wasn't for that mountain you can see from the hotel room window, and the disturbing lack of grass in people's front yards, I'd never know the difference between here and back home."

Jason interrupted. "Those people over there are smoking." He motioned towards an old couple with plaid flannel shirts and gritty visages. The man had wide, dark fingers wrapped around a cigarette.

"That's certainly different." Tyler looked closer. "Marlboro of course, the only choice for the grizzled old man look."

---

[26] Tyler intentionally used the word 'traveller' and not tourist in hopes that Jason would catch the Paul Bowles reference. He did not.

"I think the lady's smoking Camel unfiltered." Jason smiled. "I wonder what she hacks up in the morning."

"I was once in this bar in San Francisco, it was in the Beat section of town. I bet that Kerouac used to drink there. But I go in, and it's this real grimy kind of place with almost no light and a pool table and some back booths that you can just sit at all night and talk philosophy. But it was really weird because there was no cigarette smoke. You can't smoke in bars in California anymore."

"I thought you couldn't stand smoking." Every time Tyler wanted to leave a bar early he'd use the excuse that he couldn't deal with all the smoke anymore.

"I know! I hate cigarette smoke. I can't understand how someone can be in a smoky room like that, where they can barely breathe, and say to themselves, 'you know, I think I want to inhale even more smoke,' and light up. But this didn't seem right somehow. Like the place wasn't authentic."

"Well, there you go man. It's pretty freaking authentic here." He glanced over at the old couple. Smoke wafted in their direction, but the ventilation was good, and they could barely smell it. "This is something you don't see back in Arlington." Jason pulled a point-and-click camera out of his bag with the seminar company's logo on it and placed it on the table. He motioned to Tyler to take a photograph.

"That's not what I'm talking about. Could you imagine what it was like to come out here like 60 years ago? It would be like coming to another country. There'd be regional delicacies to eat, and restaurants with flavor and style and built into mud pueblos and everything. But now it's all the same. Everywhere you go it's all Sbarros and Taco Bell and Pizza Huts. I blame Ray Krok. That McDonald's model of his made everything too homogenous. Everybody wanted to be the same, be like everything else. It's like after World War Two nobody wanted to be alone, nobody wanted to be an individual."

"It's capitalism man. Bad business ideas get discarded and good ones get replicated. Its like more efficient or something."

"But there's no reason to drive across the country anymore. It's like a repeating pattern over and over again. It doesn't matter what exit you get off the highway, it's the same thing. Like some kind of weird fractal."

Jason saw Tyler's point, but didn't think it was anything to get worked up about. "What are you going to do? World changes man. Maybe it got too big. I mean, like hundreds of years ago, people never left home, it took weeks to get from place to place. You lived your entire life in the same village. I think that we're programmed to only be able to accept a certain number of choices. Today we can get anywhere in minutes. So imagine what things would be like if there were no chains, no repetition. Imagine what it would be like if every exit was different, and you could get to any of them. How would you know which one was good and which one sucked? How would you deal with not being able to try them all? It's too hard to deal with. So we made the same village over and over again. No matter where you go, you are going to be in the same village, it may be a different building, but it's the same place. It's comforting I guess."

"People need to grow the fuck up." Tyler started to feel he was being tedious and switched the topic of conversation to college football. He didn't ever watch any games, and really didn't ever have a stake in who won or lost, but he checked the scores each week so he'd have something to say when people at work wanted to talk about college football.

Guys are supposed to know about football and he felt weird and awkward if he didn't have anything to add to a conversation. As they finished eating, Tyler looked at his watch. "I don't want to go back to the hotel just yet. Let's see if there is anything here that isn't horrible and corporate."

They walked through the mall mechanically, not really having a specific destination in mind, but just not wanting to get to the car too fast. "They don't have arcades anymore," Tyler said.

"Yeah."

"I used to love arcades. That was the whole point of going to the mall, remember?"

"I was never really into video games." Jason swerved over to a garbage can and dropped in his empty soda cup, without breaking a step.

"Man, I loved all those old games. I guess they're just too complicated now. People want a more, I don't know, 'immersive experience' or something. I guess you can't get that in an arcade."

"Hey, remember those virtual reality games, with the glasses?"

"Yeah. I never played any though, it was always way too expensive."

"You didn't really miss anything, they sorta sucked."

"I used to always go to the bowling alley with my Dad when I was a little kid. He was in a league. I always claimed that I wanted more family time, but really I just wanted to play the games. I'd stand over by the machines looking pathetic and people would give me quarters."

"So that's where you get this martyr complex. You're looking for more quarters."

"Bite me." Tyler stopped dead in front of the Pottery Barn Kids and stared at the display in the front window for a few seconds. "Hold on a second, I gotta ask a question." He marched inside, past the bunk beds and the purple painted chests and the oversized stuffed animals. Past the overpriced pink and blue bathrobes and fancy tableware shrunk down to child-size.

A saleswoman came up to Tyler. He was still wearing his jacket and tie, and could be mistaken for a young professional father looking for something expensive. Jason followed at a distance, unsure of what was going to happen but not wanting to miss it. "May I help you?" she said in her best southwestern accent. She was well dressed and had bright white teeth. They were almost too white, it was obvious that she had had them bleached recently.

"Yes, I wanted to complain about this bunk bed of yours." He pointed to the model near the front window.

"Was the item damaged during delivery? Let me get you our 1-800 number, you'll have to speak to them about. Once it leaves the store it's out of our hands."

"No no, I want to complain about the bed itself. Come here I'll show you." He practically grabbed the woman's hand and brought her over to the window. The bunk bed was unremarkable, except maybe for the price. Designed to be placed in a corner, it had the beds perpendicular to each other. The bottom bunk was covered in a yellow bedsheet and covered with dolls, while the top bunk was covered in a blue sheet and had a stuffed dump truck placed near the headboard. Tied to the ladder to the top bunk was a large, clear, plexiglass sheet with the words, "FOR YOUR SAFETY, DO NOT CLIMB ON THE LADDER" written on it. "I want to ask you about this sign," Tyler said. Where do you get off selling dangerous products like this to children?"

"I don't understand sir?" she said cluelessly.

"This sign. . . you are saying that the bed is too dangerous to climb on, even once, here in the store. But yet you are going to let people put this in their bedrooms where their kids are going to climb on it day after day unsupervised?"

"Sir, let me assure you that all of our products are perfectly safe and kid tested." She tried to smile with her unnaturally white teeth, but her uncomfortableness came through.

"But if it's safe and all that, then why the sign?"

"That's just for liabilities. Our insurance company makes us do that. But don't worry, it's very safe." That answer was good enough for her. But Tyler wouldn't let it go.

"But liability implies risk, and risk implies danger. The insurance company wouldn't make you put this sign up if the bed really was safe, and so you're almost admitting that you're selling. . ." He was cut off by a young man in his mid twenties, also wearing a suit.

"Sir, I'm going to have to ask you to leave." He raised his hand towards the door respectfully, as if he was showing a patron to their booth at the opera.

186

"Don't you get it?" Tyler pleaded with the young manager. The man remained stone-faced. "No I don't suppose you do. Ah forget about it, I don't have any kids anyway." He left the store. Jason, who didn't want to be banned from Pottery Barn, had already left and was waiting patiently on a bench outside the entrance.

"Why do you have to pull crap like that man, It makes me embarrassed to be seen with you."

"Don't you get it? Does it make any sense to you?" Tyler wanted some validation.

"I get it."

"Then why don't they get it?"

"They get it. They just don't care."

"Well, dammit, they should care. That's the problem with this country. It's all fucked up and nobody cares. Not even a little bit. Nobody's bothered by any of this hypocrisy." Jason didn't say anything. "Fuck this, let's go to Mexico."

"I'm not going to Mexico," Jason said coolly.

"No no. It'll be great. I looked at that map we got at the rental car place. It's like only about an hour drive to the border. We can probably make it before it gets dark."

"I don't want to go to Mexico, what the hell's in Mexico around here? It's probably a piss-hole."

"I know, I don't care. I just want to go. I've never been to Mexico. You've never been to Mexico either. This is our chance."

"I don't think there's anything there worth seeing. Maybe, maybe if it was like Cancun or something I'd drive down there, but there ain't nothing in a border town. . ."

"Nogales."

"What?"

"Nogales. That's the city."

Jason mumbled. "There ain't nothing in a. . ."

"It means walnuts. Nogales is Spanish for walnuts."

"There's nothing out here in the middle of the desert worth driving an hour to go see. Hell. There's nothing even here in Tucson worth driving to go see."

"I know. I know it'll probably be a dump. But it's someplace we haven't been to before."

"The only place I'm going tonight is back to the hotel room to watch the UNC game."

"But you didn't even go to UNC."

"I know, but they're kicking ass this year. Here. . ." He tossed Tyler the keys. Drop me off at the hotel, then I don't care what you do. Just don't get kidnapped or nothing, I need a ride to the airport tomorrow morning."

Chapter 23:

Mouthing Off!

Number of Conspirators:	1
Danger Level:	*Low*
Arrest Level:	*Low*
Lethality:	*Low*
Annoyance Level:	*High*
Economic Damage:	*High*
Equipment Required:	*Plane Tickets*
	Rag(s)

Need to wreck a first-world economy on a third-world budget? You can do it. Yes you, all by yourself. Have you ever flown on an international flight? Remember how when you are coming in for a landing they ask you all sorts of weird questions on the customs form, like if you've been on a farm? Why are they asking? Because they are really really worried about you bringing in some animal disease.

You see there's a bunch of animal diseases that really mess up agriculture and spread like wildfire. And that can cost a huge amount of money. But the thing about these diseases is that they are usually already epidemic in a lot of crappy third-world countries. The only thing keeping them out are those dopey customs forms.

So here's what you do: you head over to one of those countries were foot-and-mouth disease is around. Then find a cow in a field somewhere covered in mucous. Rub the mucous off with a rag and put the rag in a bag. Don't worry about getting sick, it doesn't infect humans. Fly back to your target country and head over to one of those big cattle feed-lots or something and toss the rag in. If you are a really industrious anarchist, or you have some co-

189

conspirators you can use a bunch of rags in a bunch of feed lots. Once the disease has taken hold, it'll spread all over the place and ruin the beef industry in that country for years to come. This plan should be exceptionally attractive to revolutionaries and culture-warriors in third-world countries who are tired of seeing the big, rich countries step all over them on international commodities markets.

Except for the plane tickets, this plan is virtually free, presents no danger to the operatives, and it is almost impossible to stop because, who is going to rifle through your luggage looking for filthy rags? As a bonus, you can buy up some cattle-futures first, and when they skyrocket in value, you'll have plenty of cash for your next operation.

Tyler drove through the Sonoran desert at twilight. There were no radio stations out here, at least no radio stations worth listening to. He had considered bringing a tape with him, but usually these rentals didn't have a tape deck. So he was listening to silence. Sometimes when he was driving like this he'd sing songs to himself.[27] But this night he was just enjoying the silence. It was sort of appropriate, considering the terrain was so desolate. It was like *nothing* was here. Who owned this land, why didn't they build houses on it? There were sections of highway where no matter how far you looked in any direction, you couldn't see a single house. Tyler, who had lived his whole life in the megacities of the American East Coast, found these places inexplicable. It was like a waste of natural resources. Not that Tyler wanted to see virgin territory destroyed, he was just confused as to why no one else had bothered to destroy it yet. He mouthed the words, "Gadsen Purchase," half-remembering something from junior-high history class.

---

[27] E.g. Neitzer Ebb, "Join in the Chant," or Stone Roses, "I Want to Be Adored"

The Sonoran desert is a very stereotypical desert. It looks just like you'd expect a desert to look like, with the sand dunes and the cactuses with the bent arms that look just like they came out of a Road Runner cartoon. At the seminar he overheard someone say that it took those cacti something like fifty or a hundred years to grow. Tyler was amazed that they could go that long without some jerk somewhere knocking them down for fun. They looked pretty fragile. He drove past several signs advising him to turn off here to get to one resort or another, but when he slowed the car down and squinted, he couldn't see anything other than empty desert as the side road stretched to the horizon.

The sun got lower and lower, and it was just below some western mountain or mesa or whatever they call those things out there when he reached the border town. The first thing he saw, the first sign of civilization all the way out here after at least fifty miles of open, empty desert was a giant Wal-Mart. It just came up on you suddenly, and it seemed so incongruous when compared to the desolation he'd been driving through. Soon after that though he saw the houses and stores that make up Nogales, Arizona, the US border town.

He read that driving a car into Mexico is a huge pain in the ass, and the best thing to do was just park on the American side of the Rio Grande and walk across the border. He wasn't sure where to go, where the border actually was, but he assumed that if he just kept going south he'd have to run into it. A big sign and a parking lot led the way. He knew that he must be right at the edge because there was a wall. A huge twenty foot high brown wall that stretched as far as the eye could see. The end of America, the end of civilization, the end of safety and police protection and English-speaking people. Tyler started to feel a little giddy, but he contained himself so as not to look like a rube

191

who'd never travelled internationally before. He left the car in the big lot. He didn't even have to pay to park. There was a huge sign that pointed towards a small door in the wall that led to Mexico. Tyler had his passport with him of course. He brought it in the hope that maybe he'd get a chance to go. Ann told him that he didn't need a passport to enter Mexico, but he figured he'd bring it just to be safe. He wasn't so much worried about getting in, he was more worried about getting back out. Tyler's passport hadn't been used very much, certainly not as much as he'd have liked it to have been used, but it was still all wrinkly from this one time he had kept it in his back pocket for like four days straight in France because he'd heard that nefarious elements often stole people's passports out of hotel rooms.

He walked through the door that said, "To Mexico." It led to a hallway that was filled with those waist-high metal barricades you see at banks and Disneyland to keep people in line. But it was all empty. "I guess that this isn't the right time of day for people to be headed to Mexico." He looked around for some Mexican border officials to show his passport to, but he didn't see any so he kept walking. He crumpled his passport a bit in anticipation.

He followed the arrows through another door and another nondescript corridor. That led to an open air corridor with plywood walls and no roof. This then opened up into a street. He was in Mexico.

He turned around and almost started back. Clearly he had missed the Mexican border guards. No one had tried to stop him from entering the country. Hell, no one seemed to have even *noticed* that he entered the country. He stuffed his passport back into his back pocket. "I guess that they don't really have a problem with people smuggling stuff *into* Mexico," he said to himself. It was a little disappointing not getting a stamp though.

The first thing that he noticed about Nogales, Mexico was that it smelled like an open sewer. That's not a value judgment, he thought to himself, just a fact. Maybe it was just the Rio Grande that smelled. There were probably a lot of cattle farms upstream. He had been hoping to maybe get something to eat in Nogales, some 'real' Mexican food, but he quickly lost his appetite when he remembered that they don't have the same health regulations here as he was used to.

The street he was on, the first one from the border station was, he supposed, typical of the first streets that were across from all border stations. It was almost exclusively filled with stores offering souvenirs or alcohol. Tyler imagined that the street would often be filled with eighteen-year old Arizona kids looking for cheap booze. For a few moments he fantasized what it would be like if he were single so he could hit on some drunk eighteen-year olds, but there didn't seem to be very many people in the bars, and those that were there looked older and more sober than he had been imagining. American music spilled out into the streets through the open storefronts.[28] "Maybe it is only hopping on weekends," he thought to himself. There were also a lot of pharmacies. All up and down the street, signs in windows claimed, "Get your Viagra here!" and "Cheapest Propecia in town!"

There was another reason why Tyler had wanted to come to Mexico, a reason he wasn't real sure about, something he hadn't allowed himself to spend a lot of time thinking through. He knew he was depressed and miserable all the time; it was obvious even to him. He also knew that most other people he interacted with weren't miserable and

---

[28] Van Morrison, "Brown-Eyed Girl"

depressed all the time, despite the fact their lives were as boring and pointless as his was. Mostly he attributed this to the fact people weren't paying attention to how dull and lifeless their existence was, but a tiny voice deep inside Tyler's head kept suggesting that maybe there was something wrong with him. He had tried to track his mood and see how it matched the outside world. If you were feeling down when your life sucked, then that made perfect sense, but if you were sad when good things were happening to you then you were obviously clinically depressed and needed medication. Unfortunately for Tyler, nothing good ever happened in his life, so he didn't have a control sample to do a proper study.

But, he had often wondered what would happen if he had some meds. Even if he wasn't really clinically depressed, maybe they'd just make him loopy, and loopy could be good, at least occasionally. If it stopped him from thinking about how bad things were, how bad the environment was, and how bad American politics were getting, and how much more insipid and stupider people and tv shows and pop music and popular culture were becoming year after year, well. . . at least that'd be something wouldn't it?

One time, a few years back, one of his coworkers, someone he didn't know all that well, was loudly announcing to people that his life was so much better since the "shrinks put him on Wellbutrin." He always left his pill bottle in his office. After he'd left for the day once, Tyler slyly went through the guy's drawers and took one pill, just to see. He didn't swallow the pill at first, he decided to wait until something horribly bad happened to him. If the thing worked, he'd be able to get over the hump. A few weeks later some minor crisis or other happened, and Tyler swallowed the pill. It didn't seem to have any effect at all. He was still pissed off and grumpy all day. He didn't feel the slightest bit better. He looked it up on the internet later and found out that you've got to take Wellbutrin regularly for a while before it really makes any difference.

Tyler would never go to a psychiatrist of course. Mostly because he thought that the reason he was grumpy was that the world sucked, not because of anything wrong with him. But also because part of him would always know that the therapist didn't really care about him and his problems, he was just in it for the money. In that way mental health professionals were like prostitutes. They pretend to like you, pretend to care about you, but really all they want is to spend an hour billing time to a client. In both cases, Tyler imagined doing his business and having the person servicing him looking at their watch thinking, "geez, is this guy going to be done anytime soon?" Tyler could never open up to a person like that. And if he couldn't open up, he knew that going was a waste of time.

But Tyler understood that he was an expert on most things, and he felt that he'd be perfectly able to diagnose himself if there were just no regulations on prescribing drugs. He knew that in Mexico you could get anything without a prescription, so this was his chance. He stood outside a pharmacy for a while, looking in the window. It was clean inside, cleaner than he expected. He thought maybe he'd just go in to see, see how much it costs. The girl at the counter smiled at him when he walked in. There was a big sign over her head offering to write a prescription on the spot for Viagra, so you could bring it back to the US legally. Tyler had assumed he'd have to smuggle his drugs back in.

The store was filled top to bottom with darkly-varnished wooden shelves. They looked thick and solid and ancient. His hand brushed across one. It was well worn. This store, like all the stores on this block, had probably been here for a hundred years. All of the shelves had little boxes on them, all in English, all familiar brands from the US. It was mostly vitamins in this section. Tyler walked the aisles, or actually the aisle, the store wasn't more than ten feet in width. He looked up and down but all of the products for sale were non-prescription things; vitamins, cold remedies, panty liners, aspirins. He noticed a large glass-covered cabinet behind the counter, behind the girl. The boxes there looked way more official. That must be where all the drugs were kept, all the serious drugs. It seemed that you had to ask.

Tyler spent about ten minutes walking back and forth trying to work up the nerve to ask for some Prozac. But he didn't know how to ask for it. He couldn't think of any way to say it that wouldn't make him sound weird. If you wanted Viagra, it would be easy enough to ask for that, I mean, you'd look like a pervert, but that was ok, perverts are normal. He knew how to ask for Minoxidil, all you needed was a bald-spot and the clerk would understand. But how do you ask for high-potency mind-altering depression medicine? There'd be so many questions as to why you wanted it. The clerk, who probably would assume Tyler hadn't done as much research as she had done, would probably try to caution him. It wouldn't be anonymous. He'd have to stand up and admit what he wanted and defend why he wanted it, and he wasn't ready to do that. The clerk eyeballed him. He slunk out of the store.

He wandered down the street, figuring he'd see the rest of the town. But even ten blocks into the city, it was still the same things— souvenirs, pharmacies, bars. Over and over again, like a repeating fractal. The city was flat, there were no tall buildings to orient from, and it seemed to go on forever. Tyler thought about getting a drink, but he didn't want to sit alone. All of the Americans sitting in the dive bars were in groups. Tyler had been happy to leave Jason back at the hotel because he wanted to buy things he didn't want to be seen buying. But now that that had fallen through he sort of wanted Jason around to get a drink with, and to remark about how sad this town was.

He headed back to the border. Along the way he passed an old woman in an alley who was selling do-dads from a large blanket. Tyler bought two little wooden armadillos, or turtles or something, garishly painted and with bobbly heads glued on with springs. He'd give one to his mother. She'd never been to Mexico, never really been anywhere actually. He'd jazz up the story of his time here when he told her about it. Make it seem interesting. She'd like that.

Chapter 24:

Icarus!

Number of Conspirators:	*1+*
Danger Level:	*High*
Arrest Level:	*Moderate*
Lethality:	*High*
Annoyance Level:	*High*
Economic Damage:	*Medium*
Equipment Required:	*Plane Tickets*
	Lithium metal

One of the gold-medal schemes any revolutionary organization can pull off is taking down an airplane. That's what will really put you on the map and gather worldwide attention to your cause. But it's pretty damn hard with all the security and stuff the airports have. If it weren't so hard, it wouldn't be such a big feather in your cap would it? Taking down a plane is possible, in fact it can be quite easy, but you have to think outside the box. You have to look at different methods beyond just putting some C4 in your luggage. In the next few months, we'll be focusing on all sorts of new and exciting things you can do with airplanes to communicate your goals to a world too complacent to listen without a shock to the system. Here's our first idea—

One word: Lithium! Have you been to an airport lately? They actually swipe bags with a chemical sniffer looking for explosive residues. They x-ray your stuff looking for suspicious brick-shaped objects with wires hanging out. It's really hard to get a conventional explosive on a plane. So the answer is, don't be conventional.

There's lots of stuff that explodes, but isn't an explosive. Do you remember high-school chemistry? They taught us that certain metals explode on contact with water. So here's what you do. Go get a pound of powdered lithium metal from a chemical supply company. Open the handles of some luggage (which are made of hollow aluminum) and dump it in. During the flight, instruct your operative to take their luggage into the bathroom, fill the sink with water, and dump in the lithium metal powder. Kabam!

It won't be as big of an explosion as C4 or RDX obviously, but you don't need that big of an explosion to take out a plane, they are light and flimsy. And since there are no explosive residues, timers, or fuzes involved, none of those doofuses working the security line at the airport will suspect a thing.

Ann noticed that Molly wasn't interacting with the other people at the party. She just sat there in a corner of the living room on the low, green futon that was a leftover from Tyler's college days. Her legs were crossed and she was bouncing her sandal up and down on the toe of her foot like a marionette on a string. Her bouncing was not in time with the music filling the room.[29] Tyler always played bee-bop jazz during parties— he said that was because he felt it made him appear more sophisticated and classy, but in reality it was because he wanted something so universally acceptable that no matter who showed up, no one could find it offensive and criticizable.

Molly held a disposable, red, plastic cup in both hands. It was half-filled with the cheap wine from the box in the kitchen. It also had three ice cubes. The cup was sweating a little and her hands were wet. She stared off into space, seemingly fascinated by one of the paintings that hung on

---

[29] Miles Davis, "The Birth of the Cool"

the opposite wall. Or maybe she was just lost in her own thoughts.

Ann was a meddler. She saw problems and she fixed them. That was why she was still with Tyler after all this time. He was a problem she hadn't been able to fix just yet. It was obvious to her that Molly was simply feeling detached because she didn't really know anyone. You'd think that the guys would be talking to her at least, but no one seemed to be paying her any mind. Not even Jason, who, if you believed Tyler's stories, was quite the Lothario. Molly maintained an invisible force-field of inaccessibility and aloofness. She was probably feeling discouraged because when she made an effort to interact with others, she came off as being far too counter-culture for the dorks Tyler knew from work and the prep-school attorneys Ann had invited from her own office to fill out the crowd. No one had any idea what to say to her.

Ann decided to interfere. "So, what's your deal?" she said.

Molly looked up at Ann but didn't shift over on the couch to allow her to sit down. "I don't know what you mean?" she replied in a tone of naivety. She might have batted her eyes in a faux Betty Boop expression of knowing innocence, but it was hard to tell if there was any intent in her blink.

"You're being all disconnected. You're supposed to mingle. This is a party you know. . . Woooo," she waved her arms back and forth slightly in a mock approximation of partying.

"No, really, I'm having a great time," Molly said sardonically. She lifted her hands above her head in a similar mock gesture. "Woooo." Droplets of water tumbled off the cup onto the green futon.

Ann half-smiled. "You're one of those moody types like Tyler. No wonder you and him get along. He can't ever have fun, even at his own party." They both threw a glance over to Tyler who was leaning on the wall by the bookcase, unsuccessfully trying to explain to one of Ann's lawyer friends that the metal detectors at airports didn't really make it any safer to fly.

"No. Your boyfriend is just weird. Or maybe he's not. . . Maybe he's got a big dark secret like I do. How much do you know about his history?" She aimed her eyes downward, hoping Ann would feel a little disturbed and end the conversation.

"You've got a big dark secret?" Ann said, trying to hide her interest. She was at heart a big gossip and loved hearing things about other people. It took her mind off all the non-events of her own fairly boring life.

"I can see you are barely able to hide your excitement. But yeah, I've got a big dark secret that makes me be all unapproachable and crap. But you've got to promise not to tell anyone, especially Tyler. Cuz he'll want to talk it out and stuff and I don't want to talk it out. I just want to keep it inside and let it stick with me and slowly eat me away like a malignant cancer of the soul." She moved over on the couch and pulled Ann down next to her.

"You're really a man!" Ann guessed in jest. All of a sudden it seemed to have gotten rather tense, so she wanted to lighten the mood a bit.

Molly pushed her away and half-turned around. "Ah fuck off, I don't need to tell you anything."

"Ok, ok, seriously, what happened?" Ann put on her lawyer face. The one she used when she was taking depositions. It said, "I care about what you have to say and I'm listening closely."

Molly's eyes shifted back and forth a few times, and then looked down at the floor. "Ok, but I don't want this getting around?" Ann nodded.

"I was five years old, we were living in New Jersey at the time. It was summer. I was playing outside with my best friend Jenna. We were out front of her house playing in the sprinkler. I remember everything, every detail, which is weird because it happened so long ago, you know?" She stopped to take a sip of her watered-down wine. "Jenna had long blonde hair. She was wearing a bathing suit covered in neon-colored flowers; pink, yellow, orange, purple. We were jumping back and forth through the sprinkler. I don't know where her Mom was. I guess inside cleaning or watching tv or something I suppose. The important part was that she wasn't outside with us. But then, who the hell would've thought anything could go wrong? I mean it was the middle of the day and all. You figure the worst that could happen is a bug bite or a skinned knee. But we're out there and all and this guy drives up. He had this old, beater, brown Chevy El Dorado. You know, that thing that looks like a car in the front and a pickup truck in the back? One of those. Anyway this guy gets out and walks over to us. He says, 'Could you girls help me? I've lost my puppy.' My mom had told me never to talk to strangers, and I'm sure that Jenna's mom had told her the same thing, so I started to back away. But I don't know, maybe it was the puppy thing, Jenna loved animals, but she didn't back away. She just kinda stood there and asked the guy what the dog looked like. And then, I mean it was like a snake striking or something, I don't know, he just grabbed her. Grabbed both of her shoulders like she was a freaking rag doll. She couldn't have weighed more than 50 pounds. He just grabbed her. . . grabbed her. . . " Molly trailed off. Her bottom lip was trembling a little bit. Her eyes had gotten big and round, bigger and rounder than usual. She started to tear up a little. Not enough to actually cry, but enough to blur her vision.

This was a bigger can of worms than Ann was expecting to open. "It's ok. It's ok," she said, patting her on the shoulder. Molly buried her face in her arm.

"No, it's not ok. It'll never be ok."

A guest Ann didn't know passed by in a hurry, with Tyler closely following, "Don't you see? Even if you somehow made it 100% impossible to get a bomb on a plane, you aren't solving the problem, you are only moving it to somewhere else, like a train or a bus, or Oklahoma. . . " They walked into the kitchen and out of earshot.

"Did he touch you or something?" Molly didn't answer, she just shook her head back and forth. "What happened?"

"What happened? What happened! I ran that's what happened!" She had raised her voice to the point where a few people turned their heads. But she didn't notice the stares. She just looked Ann square in the face. "I ran. I screamed and I ran and I got the hell out of there. I ran all the way home and I ran upstairs and I hid under the bathroom sink. That's what happened."

"Oh my god." Ann said.

"They found her body three days later dumped in a drainage ditch off 287."

"God, that's horrible. I'm so sorry you had to go through that." She pulled her hand off Molly's shoulder, remembering that people who've been abused tend to not like to be touched. "No wonder you don't want to talk to strange people. I'd be scared too. But I mean at least you're ok. You lived through it. That's the important part." She tried an awkward half-smile.

"You don't understand," Molly fired back defiantly. "I'm not afraid. I don't think I'm going to get abused or grabbed or anything like that. I know fucking kung fu man. I've got a switchblade in my purse. No fucker's ever going to grab me. I'll cut his nuts off." A guy standing nearby had turned and was listening in. "That goes for you too asshole!" she said to him, sneering. He quickly moved on.

"Then what's the problem?"

"The problem is that I failed. I failed, she was my best friend and I was there and. . . and. . . I don't know, I could've done *something*, I should've done something. I don't know, I could have grabbed her back, or kicked the guy or hit him in the head with the damn sprinkler or called her mom or something I don't know."

"You were only five years old. You can't blame yourself."

"That's what all those shrinks kept telling me. And yeah, it's easy to say that. But the thing is that I never get close to people. I never let people get near me because I know, I mean, some part of me knows, that I'm going to let them down, that they're going to get grabbed and I'm not going to be able to do anything about it and then they'll be gone and I'll be alone again and there'll be this big hole in my heart and I don't want that. So I keep everyone at an arms length. That's my 'deal' since you must know ok? I just don't like getting close to people and that's the way it's going to be. I'm just going to stay this cool, disaffected loner chick. That's who I am. That's who I'm going to be. So don't try to get me all engaged and social because that ain't the way I work."

Ann had a million questions. Did they ever catch the guy? Did the dead girl's family blame her for what happened? Did her mother become super-overprotective? How many psychiatrists had been burned through in a quest for answers? But she didn't want to press the issue. Molly was clearly upset talking about it. Ann had never had someone open up to her like that. None of her friends ever had any real problems. A few had mild eating disorders, they were all overworked, and none of them liked their parents or jobs very much, but she didn't know anyone who had undergone any kind of real trauma. This was the sort of stuff that you hear about on the news, but it never really happens, at least not to anyone you know. All those kids on the milk cartons. They don't really exist. They occupy a ghostly half-life. They aren't real, they only take on physical form as fuzzy mug shots and creepy-looking age progressions. They only exist because they've become famous. They didn't have physical form beforehand. Ann never knew anyone who had died.

"Wow. I'm sorry," she said apologetically. She sat there for almost a full minute, unable to think of anything relevant to say. Eventually she settled on, "Let me know if there's anything I can do to help. I'm always there if you need someone to talk to. Just get my number from Tyler."

Molly wiped the tears from her eyes. "Thanks." She cracked a small smile. "You could maybe refill my drink?" She held up her plastic cup.

"Sure, sure, no problem." Ann took the cup and stood up. She took a step towards the kitchen, but then turned around and leaned over. "And don't worry about me telling

Tyler. I can see why you don't want him to know. He wouldn't get it at all and say something way inappropriate." Molly just nodded in appreciation. Ann headed for the kitchen, patting Tyler on the back as she passed. He had a couple trapped in a corner and was going off on some tirade about the UN.

Molly sat and smiled as she watched Ann walk down the hall. She crossed her hands in her lap. Her story had garnered the undying respect of Ann. It was a pretty good story. It was also total bullshit. Molly was never involved in an abduction, and she sure as hell would never have associated with anyone named 'Jenna.' But it was a good story and it got Ann out of her hair. The real reason she wasn't mingling was because all of Ann and Tyler's friends were total tools. But she was too nice to actually say that to Ann's face. . . or to Tyler's.

Chapter 25:

The End of TV!

Number of Conspirators:	*1-3*
Danger Level:	*High*
Arrest Level:	*Medium*
Lethality:	*Medium*
Annoyance Level:	*High*
Economic Damage:	*Medium*
Equipment Required:	*Chemical Weapons or Explosives*

Obviously, the objective of a terror attack is to instill fear, anxiety, and a sense of loss in the target population. But a lone terror cell can't possibly hope to kill more than about a hundred people, even with a pretty successful attack. Chances are pretty good that most of the target population won't have any personal connection to any of the victims and will forget about the attack pretty quickly. So, how do you amplify the effect of your attack and really freak people out?

Simple: kill tv celebrities. The average human watches a lot of tv and probably feels closer to their 'tv friends' than their actual family. Simply wait until the Emmys or Golden Globes or other award shows that concentrate tv stars. Destroy it. Sure it'll be harder than a regular attack since they'll be some security. But it won't be impossible (see my previous article- Timing Preparation and Patience: Ka-Bang!) And killing off the cast of Seinfeld will cause hundreds of times more fear and anxiety in a target population than just killing a bunch of random yokels will. Imagine what it'll be like for people on Thursday night-watching repeats, knowing there will never be an episode resolving that wacky comedic romance because the bubbly, lovable actors are all dead. Now that's a sense of loss!

The concert was the other part of Ann's present to Tyler. There were so many times when he would be sitting there reading the City Paper and he'd exclaim something like, "oh my god, I can't believe, that this band or that band is finally coming to town! Those guys changed my life," or "I've heard their live show is incredible," or something like that. But Ann would count down the days and Tyler would never mention it again. That confused her to no end. Especially when afterwards he would complain about how he never got to go to concerts. She had already told him, multiple times, that she would go, all he had to do was buy the tickets. But he never got off his ass and ordered them. The one time she confronted him about it he blathered something or other about how he couldn't figure out to work Ticketmaster. But that made no sense to her because it wasn't that hard, and even if it was, he knew that she used it all the time, and she'd help if he just asked. Ann figured that it wasn't all that important to him, and that maybe he just liked complaining, so she didn't spent too much time worrying about it.

But this year he had had the fortune to complain about never getting to go to concerts that he liked just at the same time that she was looking for something to give him for his birthday. He never gave much information about what he wanted, falling back on, "I've already got too much stuff, I just want some love," whenever she asked. This time she was proactive, listened closely to what he was complaining about, and got some tickets to the Yo La Tengo show at the Black Cat the day after Tyler's birthday. She also made reservations at this restaurant that she figured Tyler would like.

"Of course," Tyler thought, "There's got to be a dinner first." They sat in the trendy middle-eastern restaurant that was sort of downtown. Ann was supposed to come home so

208

they could go together, but of course, things at work got busy, like they did every night, and Ann had to just go straight from work, which left Tyler having to drive into the city, during rush hour, and park downtown. Tyler knew that Ann knew how much he hated driving in traffic, and he couldn't understand why she kept making him drive in, knowing that it would upset him. For her part, Ann knew that Tyler hated driving into the city, but what could she do? She couldn't leave work early if the partners needed her to stay late. She just couldn't. And having him drive in was better than skipping the entire evening, that was something she felt that they both agreed on.

Of course, Tyler was completely inappropriately dressed. He was going to a concert, so he wanted to look cool for the concert. In a way, he felt that the concert goers, the people who listened to the same cool and hip and exciting music he listened to, were therefore cool and hip and exciting by default, and they would certainly be judging him, deciding if he were cool and hip and exciting. These were the people he wanted to be with, or at least the people he thought that he wanted to be with, and he couldn't go dressed like a complete tool. He felt awkward enough going to concerts, considering that he had always identified himself as a geek growing up, and now he was probably older than most of the people there, and with his professional job and large paycheck and such, he was already a bit removed from them. He didn't want to be that guy, the old guy sitting in the back, in a sportsjacket, balding, still trying to fit in but failing. He wanted to be the coolest person there.

So Ann's choice of a trendy after-work restaurant really screwed him over, because everyone here, including Ann, was dressed straight from work as high-powered attorneys, financial accountants, bankers, whatever. Tyler ate his hummus feeling very underdressed and self-conscious. He had come to the decision that he would have to be inappropriate for at least one part of the evening, and he decided he'd rather look cool later than fit in now. Of course Ann didn't notice. She rarely thought about what people who saw her thought, and to be honest, no one in the restaurant was looking at them anyway, so maybe she was right. "And besides," she thought, "I'm taking his lazy ass to a concert I don't want to go to, at least I'm going to get a tasty dinner out of it."

For a while, Tyler had tried to make his annoyance at this contradictory dressing problem palpable by brooding and not being too talkative. But Ann had brought a coworker with her and didn't really notice his non-participation in the conversation. She hadn't intended on bringing Ravi along, but she got to talking at work about the restaurant she was going to and he said he had been wanting to try that place for a while and Ann figured that Tyler always likes more people to talk to (so he'd have someone new to tell the same boring stories she'd already heard a thousand times over and over again), so why not bring him? After dinner was over, Ravi invited himself along with them to the Yo La Tengo show. He hadn't ever heard of them, but he was interested in going because he thought that he was a hipster, even though in his button-down shirt and argyle sweater, he clearly wasn't. Tyler had tried to dissuade Ravi from tagging along, mostly because he knew that he'd feel even more awkward if he had a doofus in an argyle sweater hanging on him, but Ann insisted. "It'll be great. If Ravi is there, you won't have to pay attention to me, you can enjoy the music more."

So, they were there at the show, up in the balcony section, elbows to elbows with all people who had arrived earlier. Tyler usually headed to the balcony section, mostly because Ann was short and there was no way that she could see anything at all from the main floor. It didn't make much of a difference though, she couldn't see anything from the balcony either, and she was more interested in talking to Ravi than listening to the music. She wasn't a fan and hadn't heard their cds. Tyler partially hoped that maybe she'd listen, and somehow become a cooler person, but that wasn't going to happen. It would've been so awesome if once, just once, Tyler could introduce someone to something and they really fell in love with it. It was so hard to be passionate about something that everyone else was indifferent to.

People are like molecules, they move around and around in random patterns, occasionally interacting for a brief second. If you look around you at the people nearby, assuming you aren't at work or home or somewhere familiar like that, then they are probably random people walking the streets that you've never seen before and are unlikely to ever see again. But for one brief minute you have come into contact walking down the sidewalk together. As the band took the stage, Tyler tried to imagine the life of the lead singer. The man had lived a whole life. He was born somewhere, grew up and went to school somewhere, started a band, traveled the world. Tyler imagined his life as a line starting from his place of birth and zig-zagging around for 30 years or so. Tyler superimposed his own life's line on top. The two lines never crossed, until tonight, the one brief moment of connection. This was as physically close as he'd ever come to the band, or they'd come to him. Soon, like molecules, their interaction would be over and the lead singer would travel to another city and Tyler would drive back to Virginia and that would be it. Their lives were completely separate, completely different, but for a few hours, they'd be in the same place at the same time. This was the sort of stuff Tyler thought about while listening to concerts. He'd bob his head back and forth, but he wouldn't dance. He'd listen, but he wouldn't let the sound consume his thoughts, no matter how loud it was. He was always thinking about some obscure topic, or planning out how he'd react if someone tried to mug them on the way home from the show, or maybe just mapping out routes for how he'd climb down from the rafters if he found himself stuck there for some reason.

Like all bands, they finished up and left the stage without playing one of their most obvious hit songs. The crowd started screaming and cheering and begging for more. It was so perfunctory. Everyone knew that they'd be back. Encores weren't optional in the same way that tipping your waitress isn't optional. It's simply going to happen. They didn't even try to hide the fact. The lights didn't go up, and Tyler could see one of the roadies sitting on the side of the stage re-tuning a guitar. Tyler always said that if he were in a band, he'd never play an encore, just because the concept was stupid. He'd simply alert the audience when there were two songs to go in the set. More than anything else, Tyler hated pointless things, things that had little meaning or purpose. Which was of course one of the things he hated most about himself.

After the ninety seconds of cheering, the band came back on stage and pretended like they were fulfilling the crowd's request and not just their own egos. They immediately ripped into the song that Tyler knew they would play, which was cool because it was Tyler's favorite song anyway.[30] The lead guitarist played so hard that he must've broken three guitar strings. It was a stunning performance. Quite inspiring. Tyler felt that there was no way anyone could listen to 'Sugarcube' without becoming a huge Yo La Tengo fan. He looked around for Ann to see if she had the same reaction, but she was leaning against the back wall chatting with Ravi, apparently oblivious to what was happening on stage. As the lights came up, Tyler sighed and watched the crowd begin filing out of the club.

---

[30] Yo La Tengo, "Sugarcube"

Chapter 26:

Death From Above!

Number of Conspirators:	*3+*
Danger Level:	*Suicidal*
Arrest Level:	*n/a*
Lethality:	*High*
Annoyance Level:	*High*
Economic Damage:	*High*
Equipment Required:	*Airplane tickets*
	Weapons
	Flying lessons

Ideally, all CHOASian groups out there would love to have a weapon of mass destruction. But I'm sure you've found it almost impossible to acquire one. So how do you cause WMD-level damage without an actual WMD? Take a look at the skies brother, there's your answer.

With a small cadre of devout followers it should be pretty easy to smuggle some weapons aboard a commercial aircraft laden with fuel for a cross-country journey. Simply have your minions take control of that plane by staging a hijacking. Then instead of negotiating your demands to release the hostages, just fly that giant firebomb into a large building. The explosions should be enough to knock down even something as large as the Empire State Building or the Eiffel Tower, and possibly rain debris over several city blocks. You'll never get more value for your terrorist dollar. Ka-BOOM!

"Get up, let's go!" Molly said. "Come pick me up." Tyler had just gotten home from work. An offhand comment made by a coworker that morning had percolated around in his brain until by the time he drove home it had formulated into a great idea to poison a food supply by adding genes that make cancer-causing chemicals into corn plants, then spreading that poisoned mutant pollen around farms all around the country until it was too widespread to eradicate. No one would be able to ever trust an ear of corn again. On the other hand, maybe it would be better if instead of corn, something else like tomatoes. . .

"Hey, pay attention," Molly said into her phone. "I said come pick me up. Let's have funnnnn." Tyler looked over at his computer. He'd just turned it on. The cursor blinked on and off, waiting for him to post his update.

"Yeah, ok, I'll be there in a few minutes." He hung up the phone and sighed. He drove into DC, already dreading trying to find a parking space near her house. Tyler often complained about how parking was way harder than it should be, and someone should come up with some kind of technology or something to fix it. "I don't know," he'd say, "something like that Jetson's car that turned into a briefcase or something." But no one ever invented anything. No one ever invented anything that really solved any of the problems Tyler saw with the world.

He circled around for a bit until he found a parking space on this shady street that most people never bothered to drive down because it was one-way the wrong way from where most people wanted to be, and it was dark and narrow. It was also a number of blocks from Molly's place, but Tyler usually checked there first because he knew there was usually a spot available. He walked at a fast pace, almost jogging, knowing that Molly was waiting for him. And there she was, sitting on the stoop of her apartment building.

"Where are we going?" he said to her. They usually would go get coffee somewhere nearby, or just walk around the Circle if Molly didn't feel like spending money. Tyler often just bought them both coffee because he'd rather spend the $2 than sit there empty-handed.

This time though, Molly said, "I heard this cool idea. I want to try it out. Where's your car?" When Tyler told her it was on the shady street she seemed annoyed. "I'm not walking all the way over there. You should just park closer next time. Go get your car and drive back to pick me up."

As Tyler returned to his car, he thought about what a chore these meetings with Molly had become. He'd long since gotten over the excitement of having someone 'cool' who wanted to hang out with him. Like pretty much everyone Tyler ever met, she seemed less and less interesting the more time he spent with her. She didn't even seem to do cool, quirky things anymore like wear prom dresses or make up stories about fucking prisoners. Today she was dressed in sloppy-looking jeans. She didn't even have on any make-up.

Tyler drove around and picked up Molly, again dreading hearing where she wanted to go. Usually she picked someplace clear across the city, where traffic would be a nightmare. He wasn't worried anymore about Ann finding out he was out of the house. If anything, she wanted him to spend time with his friends so he'd stop complaining about not having any friends anymore. But Tyler never stopped complaining. "Where to ma'am?" Tyler said in his best cab-driver accent.

"We're going up to Silver Spring. I gotta show you something. This girl at work was telling me this thing and I want to try it out." Silver Spring is just about as far from Tyler's house as you could get and still be considered part of the DC metro area. It was going to take him an hour to get home. An hour that he could be spending working on his website. What if there was a great email just sitting in his inbox waiting to be read?

Molly took the tape out of the player and retuned the radio to an oldies channel. She didn't even ask. Worse, she didn't even put the tape back in the case Tyler had meticulously written all the songs on. She just tossed it in the compartment beneath the armrest. "I'm into oldies now," she declared. Tyler appreciated being into uncool things ironically, but this wasn't even uncool enough to be cool by irony. It was just sort of boring. She bounced back and forth to the music.[31] "For a while I was getting to rockabilly, but then I thought that was pretty lame and unauthentic and I might as well just go all the way and listen to the originals as opposed to what people are trying to recreate today. Right?" Molly figured that Tyler would be impressed because he was always talking about being authentic and stuff. He just drove on silently.

"Where are we headed?" he asked mechanically once it became apparent that Molly wasn't going to give him any directions unless he asked.

"It's a surprise."

The surprise turned out to be this bakery on a side street that was pretty hard to find. They drove around for a while looking for it. The entire time, Tyler kept glancing at the digital clock in his car, watching his evening tick by minute after frustrating minute.

-=-=-=-=-

---

[31] The Boards, "Motion by the Ocean"

216

A bell jingled as they opened the door. Molly grabbed Tyler's forearm and gripped it tight as they entered. Her hand felt somehow alien to him. It wasn't the same texture, wasn't the same temperature as Ann's hand was. He'd been with Ann long enough to mostly forget what other girls' skin felt like. It wasn't unpleasant though, nor was it overtly sexual enough to make him feel uncomfortable, so he didn't pull away.

"We're getting married next month." Molly said to the cashier.

The cashier smiled. She seemed like the sort of person who would be excited to hear about someone's marriage, even if it was someone she didn't know. Tyler never really understood why people got so excited. It wasn't that he didn't understand the value of long-term, deeply committed relationships, he just didn't understand the excitement over the ritual. If he and Ann ever decided to marry, the exciting thing would be their deep commitment to one another on a daily basis year after year, not some expensive party and an affirmation in front of a bunch of people Tyler didn't even really like all that much. "Ohh, congratulations!" the cashier said.

"We're shopping for wedding cakes." Molly hinted.

"Of course, let me get you some samples." The cashier turned around and took down several cakes from the rack behind her. She started cutting some pieces. Tyler shot Molly a look that said, "what are you doing?" Molly answered back with a look that said, "shut up and just play along." The cashier handed the lucky couple about five slices of cake. She even poured them some coffee to wash it down with. It was all free of charge.

The pair sat down at a table. "Isn't this awesome?" Molly said, "You just go to a bakery and tell them you are getting married, and they totally give you free cake!" She smiled at Tyler, but could tell that he wasn't as excited about this adventure as she was.

Tyler was actually quite annoyed. First, he was absolutely mortified to be part of a fraud like this. What if the cashier overheard them? Or realized they weren't getting married? Heck, Molly didn't even have an engagement ring. She should definitely have told him about this scam before she pulled it. Also, why did we have to drive all the way to Maryland? Aren't there bakeries in DC that sell wedding cakes? It was ridiculous to make him drive all the way through all that traffic. Plus, when you think about it, with the price of gas and wear-and-tear it would have been cheaper for them to just have stayed near Molly's place and paid for cake. That would have been a lot faster and more efficient in the end. And then he wouldn't be sitting here feeling awkward as all hell, in a strange place with the cashier staring down on him like the eyes of Dr. T. J. Eckelburg judging him and trying to work out if there was a chance they'd be getting a cake order or if they were just getting scammed out of cake.

He didn't say any of this to Molly of course. She wouldn't get it and she'd just feel bad that he wasn't into her idea. So he just half-smiled and stayed quiet. No one ever got Tyler. The weird thing was that Tyler didn't even get himself. And he knew he didn't get himself either. He understood that if someone had told him about Molly's idea, he would have thought it was the most fun, most romantic thing. It was an idea that sounded pretty cool actually, and Tyler always said he wanted to be with people who did cool things. But when it actually happened, when he was actually with a pretty girl who wanted to be with him and wanted to do cool, exciting things with him, the idea seemed dumb and dangerous.

Wanting to lighten the mood a bit, Molly said, "Tell me the bravest thing you've ever done," between mouthfuls of cake.

Tyler paused for a moment and quickly made a mental accounting of his life. "I almost stopped a rape once, or something that might have been a rape or an assault or whatever."

"That's not really what I. . . " He kept talking, cutting her off.

"It was back in my old apartment, I was walking down the hall and I heard this noise coming from one of the other apartments. I'm like, you know, nosy and all so whenever I hear something that I figure might be audible, I always stop and listen in just in case something juicy is going on. My old roommate swears that once he could see this couple having sex across the street from the balcony of our apartment, but I've never caught anybody like that. So anyway, I'm listening in to hear if there's like something interesting going on and I hear this girl screaming, 'Stop it, stop it, get off me, get off me,' over and over again. I mean it really sounded like she was in trouble, and it wasn't the tv or some rough sex game or nothing like that."

"So I figure what am I supposed to do? I listen in for another minute and the girl is still crying and screaming, 'get off me get off me,' so I bang on the door really hard, but there isn't an answer. There isn't even any kind of reaction at all, which I think it kinda weird because if I was raping someone and I heard this big knock on the door it'd at least get my attention, but nothing. The screams keep going on uninterrupted. So I knock again, even harder this time, but it's like they don't even hear me."

Tyler paused to take a sip of what he judged to be marginal coffee, and Molly finally got a word in, "Did you break down the door?"

"So I walked up and down the hallway a few times wondering what I should do. I can't really just leave right? But I'm not used to dealing with the police, or at least I've never really dealt with the police before and I don't know if maybe I should call them or not and maybe they're busy with real crimes and don't want to be bothered with something that I might just be making up in my head, or maybe they want people to call in no matter what the level of suspicion. I mean I just don't really know if this is the sort of thing they get a lot of calls about."

"So then you broke down the door?"

"No no, what if it was just the tv or something? I'd get arrested for breaking their door. So, ok, I call 911 and they tell me to stay on the line because they are sending some cops over. They tell me to watch the door and make sure no one leaves the apartment. They keep asking me, 'what do you hear now? What do you hear now?' It was probably only about five minutes, but it was pretty uncomfortable because if like someone else was walking down the hallway what am I gonna say to them? I'm going to look like some kind of weirdo listening through a door. But no one else came down the hallway, which means maybe it was good that I called the police because no one else would have. And I'm listening in and the screams abate and it's just some sobbing that I can hear from behind the door."

"Three police show up and they ask me to point out the apartment, which I did, and then they told me to wait

220

around the corner. They bang on the door really hard, but probably no harder than I banged on it, but this time it opened up and they all went inside. So I waited there in the hallway with my cell phone just kinda standing around, not really knowing if I should be doing anything."

"After a few minutes one of the cops comes out and asked me for my name and phone number which he wrote down on this little pad. He told me that if they needed a statement from me they'd call, but I could go. He never said what was happening behind the door or anything, I mean, it might have been just a tv show. So I wandered off. I checked the papers for the next few days and there wasn't a report in the crime blotter, but maybe I just missed it, or they didn't put it in to protect the anonymity of the victim or something. No one ever called me for a statement, so I figured there was never a trial, because they would have probably called me if there was a trial. So I really don't know what happened."

Molly furrowed her eyebrows. "I don't know if I'd say calling the police was all that *brave* really. I mean it's probably good you called, but I was thinking something like, you know *brave* brave, like jumping out of an airplane or something."

"Don't get me started on people jumping out of airplanes," he said. "That's so not brave at all, not anymore."

"I did it once and it was really scary!" she protested.

"Nowadays people don't really jump out of airplanes. It used to be that if you wanted to go parachuting you had to take some training classes and stuff and when you jumped it was just you. I mean, it's probably pretty easy to remember to pull the cord, but you were there falling and falling and you had to say to yourself, 'man if I don't pull the cord I'll get dead real fast. The only person who is going to be able to save my life at this point is me. I'd better keep in control. But now when you go parachuting they just strap you to some dude who's like a pro or something. You don't have to do anything but lie there limply. Hell you could probably be unconscious and it wouldn't make a difference."

"Yeah, but it's still really scary. And it's you actually doing it. It's still you jumping out of the plane. In your story you didn't even do anything but dial a phone."

He ignored her accusation. "I never even told anybody before today," Tyler said, continuing his story. "I didn't know what to say. I guess I didn't want to alarm people about it because they wouldn't want to come over if there was a rapist loose in my building. Or maybe because I was never sure that I wasn't just being a moron and broke up someone practicing for a play or watching tv or whatever." When he was being honest with himself Tyler understood that he never told anyone because he didn't really want to toot his own horn and tell people how great he was and how conscientious he was because all he really did was make a phone call and stand in a hallway for a few minutes, it's not like he was in a gun battle or anything. "Plus, I mean, wouldn't pretty much anybody who wandered by feel obligated to put in that much effort. So I guess I kind of felt good about myself afterwards, but not enough to actually say anything about it to anybody."

Tyler was a little upset. Well, not upset exactly, but perhaps more disappointed. He'd never told anyone what had happened that day, but inside he'd always been proud of what he did, and figured that if he did tell people they'd be all like 'ooh Tyler you were such a hero and you stood up for women's rights and then how cool and humble you are that you never even told anybody about it.' And he'd be a hero. But finally, years later, he told someone his story and she

222

didn't seem to be even the slightest bit impressed. It was like finding an old coin and keeping it safe for years figuring it was worth a lot of money and then having a coin collector see it and telling you it was only worth a dime.

Tyler poked at the last bits of cake with his plastic fork. It was way too sweet and he didn't even want to finish what was left. If he had really been getting married, he would tell his fiancé to veto this baker. "I never even found out who lived there," he said. "For a few weeks afterwards, I used to daydream that the girl I heard crying would stop by my apartment to personally thank me for saving her and putting that guy in prison and we'd get to talking and have a lot in common and she'd be really pretty and the kind of person who'd never have given me the time of day but I'd saved her life and all. We'd end up dating and she'd always be grateful and think I was like her hero and everything. But no one ever came by to say thanks. Maybe the cops wouldn't have even told her who I was to protect me. Or maybe she was just pissed at me for listening in at her door when I should have been minding my own business. I don't know. I don't suppose it really matters. I doubt it would have worked out between us anyway."

Tyler flicked a crumb off the table onto the floor. Molly didn't understand him any better than anybody else did. "How come the more I get to know people the more disappointing they become?" he thought to himself. He glanced down at the ragged, half-worn nail polish on her fingers. "C'mon," he said, "it's getting late, I better get you home so I can be back by the time Ann leaves work."

Jason's Story

I live about two blocks from the Pentagon. I really do. It's not a bad place to live. There's a lot of big, high-rise buildings, and there's not a lot of stuff you can walk to, but there is also a mall and it's easy to get into DC by 395 or the Memorial Bridge past the Lincoln Memorial and the gold statues of horses' asses that Tyler likes to mention every time we drive past.

I was even working from home that day, I really was. I heard later that the plane flew right over my building, but from the trajectory of the impact, I can't see how that was true. I was working from home that day for no particular reason. I usually get more work done when I'm at home actually. If I go to work, I find that I feel satisfied just showing up. Even if I waste the whole day chatting with co-workers or surfing the internet for my fantasy football league, I still think, "Hey, at least I showed up." But if I'm home, then I feel that I really have to come in the next day with product: completed reports, cogent comments on other's reports, nice pie charts, whatever. I'm very worried that if I don't have something to show, something that says, "I may have been home, but I can prove I was working," then people will think that I just took the day off. And even though I actually get more done than most people there I worry that they think I'm a slacker because I have a pretty relaxed attitude around the office. If I was as tense and unfriendly as Tyler I'm sure people would be singing my praises too, even though no one can really recall what Tyler's working on. He just exudes this attitude that he's super busy, even when I know he's in his office not doing anything except goofing around on that website of his. But I digress. . . .

Anyway, as I said, I was working from home that day. I had already had two cups of coffee and was lounging on the futon more than one girl has told me 'eats' people. I was listening to some cd to provide some 'white noise.' I usually use Dave Matthews for that, but I can't remember exactly what I was listening to.[32] I suppose it doesn't really matter.

I was probably one of the last people to know what was going on. I got up to get a bowl of cereal at maybe like 10:00 am and I turned on the tv just for background. Sometimes when I am working from home I like to take a break and watch Springer, but I can never remember what time it starts. Of course, it was all over the news. It was on every channel, every damn channel. I've never seen that before. I know that when something happens, a lot of networks preempt stuff to go 'live to the scene,' but this doesn't usually affect the cable networks. I mean, MTV, Animal Planet, hell even the channel that does nothing but scroll the tv listings; they were all off the air.

Both towers were still standing when I first turned on the news. There was a lot of smoke. They didn't have any real good footage yet showing the impact. That would come later, every few hours a new angle would filter in to the stations and we'd have to watch it all over again, like a recurring nightmare played from a slightly different perspective each time. I was amazed that somehow, each new camera angle seemed to be better than the last, as if by fate the people with the best angles took longer to get their tape to the network. I suppose that the people who had bad angles and were slow didn't get their tape on tv at all. I wonder how those people feel? Disappointed that they missed their brush with fame? Did the people that shot the good angles brag to their friends later, "That's my video

---

[32] Ed. Note— Jason was actually listening to Hootie and the Blowfish, "I Only Want To Be With You," but is not willing to admit that publicly.

you're seeing on CNN right now." Did they get paid? I wonder how much those videos were worth. I suppose it depends on how good of a camera angle you had.

They also said that the Pentagon was on fire. I didn't hear a thing. That was really weird. I mean I was listening to my music and concentrating on work and all, but I didn't hear a thing. How could I be less than half a mile from a major plane crash and not have heard a thing? I just don't get it. I would've expected that I would've had heard something.

I'd never been to an actual disaster. I mean you always hear about disasters and how the people are affected by them and I don't know I guess I wanted to be there. Not in a ghoulish way, but just to be there, just to be able to say that I was there. Somehow, being there makes you a different person. A guy I know at work once told me his father was at Pearl Harbor when it was attacked, and somehow just knowing that fact makes my friend seem more famous. Ok, I suppose maybe it is a bit ghoulish.

I just knew that I had to get there, I had to be there, see for myself what it was like, experience a disaster first hand. I didn't want to be alone. Not because I was frightened or scared or anything, but because I wanted to share, I wanted to talk about it, I wanted to stand there and say, "Oh my god, what do you think about that? Here's what I think about that. . . ." I had tried calling some people, but the phones were down. Even the landlines were clogged up. I was able to receive a desperate call from some girl I know in DC who wanted me to call her Dad and let him know that she was all right. The lines in DC were down too apparently.

In the elevator I ran into a cleaning guy. "Did you hear what happened?" I said. I really expected him not to know, being as he was busy vacuuming the hallways and all, but he did. I guess word was spreading quicker than I thought. In the street in front of my building there was a huge traffic jam. People were driving everywhere. I almost ran down the road to the Pentagon. I was giddy. I'm sort of ashamed to admit that, but I was giddy— with excitement I guess, I don't know. I mean, here I was about to experience something that I would be able to talk about when I was an old man. Here was a life experience in progress. I know I know, at that time in Manhattan, a much bigger event was going on and a lot more people were getting to experience it, but I wasn't in Manhattan. This was as close as I was going to get.

I don't know what I was thinking really, I mean, I thought that I was being innovative. I had brought my camera and I was taking pictures of the crowd and of the streets and of the plume of smoke that I could see from blocks away. I was actually thinking that I would take some pictures, get them developed in an hour, write up some personal story, and then sell it to a magazine. Really, that's what I was thinking. I had a friend who had a story published on salon.com a few years ago, so I was figuring that I could use him as an 'in.' I was figuring that the Salon people didn't have a man on the scene at the Pentagon and they would appreciate a timely, well-written article. Of course, as the days and weeks wore on, thousands of similar articles clogged the airwaves and magazines and I'm glad that I didn't try to write anything that day. I would've either been disappointed that Salon wasn't interested, or else I would've felt like a trendy, self-serving jerk for selling my story in the middle of a crisis. But hey, I'm just trying to be honest about what was going through my mind that day.

As I got closer to the scene, there were more and more people in the street, and on the sidewalks, and sitting in the plots of grass that surround the tall buildings like some sort of communal front yard. If you don't know the geography of the region (and you probably don't), let me explain. There is

227

a highway that separates the Pentagon from the rest of the world, and it is raised up a bit on a berm. There is a mall on the opposite side of the highway from the Pentagon. A huge pile of Pentagon workers were loitering around on the grass on the highway's edge on the far side. They had obviously been driven out of their offices, across the vast Pentagon parking lot, and under the overpass. They were waiting on the grass on the mall side. I meandered among them for a while, making my way steadily up the hill to the highway. You couldn't get under the overpass because there were police there and they weren't letting anyone in. So I tried to climb up the hill and look and see what I could see.

As it turns out, you couldn't see anything from the highway. The Pentagon is big, but it is low to the ground, and even standing on tiptoes I couldn't see anything but the plume of black smoke dispersing into the sky. I took some pictures of people as I walked around, but felt guilty and ghoulish doing that, so I kept it to a minimum. I was worried that the people would hate me for it and I might get punched. Although, looking back I guess no one really noticed me.

Everybody was on their cell phones, or at least complaining about the fact that their cell phones weren't working. There were a lot of rumors floating around. People were talking about 23 other planes that were still in the air that weren't answering ground control, or about how we had already started bombing Afghanistan, or about how we would definitely go nuclear now, if we hadn't already. Looking back, I guess the really weird thing that struck me was that none of the rumors seemed ridiculous. It was like the world had changed into some Michael Bay sci-fi movie or something, and something so unbelievable and improbable had happened that it gave your mind license to believe that *anything*, no matter how unbelievable or improbable *could* happen. No one seemed to know, or at least no one was mentioning that the towers had already fallen down. I didn't find that out until hours later when I returned home.

Up in the air, a lone fighter jet flew by, really fast. I've seen fighter jets in the air before, but usually near army bases where they are training. But this guy was ready to fight. It was really eerie. Everyone stopped and looked up at it. I can't explain the effect it had on me. In a way it was comforting, because it meant that people were ready to defend us, but in another way it was very disconcerting. Fighter jets do NOT patrol over the Capital of the United States! This was different, this was something that had never happened before. I guess that was my sign that the world had changed.

We were all standing at the edge of the highway, up the embankment from the mall when all of a sudden everyone started running. I couldn't hear what people were saying, but I got the impression that something spooked someone. Perhaps there was word that another attack was imminent, perhaps the police decided that they didn't want a bunch of gawkers like me getting in the way, but whatever the reason, everybody moved away from the grassy embankment and across the street to the mall. I decided that I couldn't really see anything, and I had taken a dozen pictures or so, so I just went home. It was getting hot out and my feet hurt because I went outside without socks on. I thought about going into the mall just so I wouldn't be alone, but of course it wasn't open.

I went home and watched the story unfold on tv. I had meant to get back to work, really I did. But as events started to sink in, I started to not feel like working. About noon the girl I was sort of dating called and said that everyone in her office in DC had been told to go home. Everybody was going home. I guess there was no point in working anymore. She took the subway to my place. The strange thing about this is the Metro has a stop right under the Pentagon. I would've figured that they would have closed the system down, but it didn't take her long to get here. We sat on my old beanbag chair that leaks BB-sized balls of styrofoam and watched tv and hugged in silence for many hours. I remember that I kept waiting for George Bush to come on and say something. Why did he wait so long? Why wasn't he reassuring us? I'm not a fan of Bush. Hell, I even once protested at the IMF and everything. But every fiber of my being wanted him to come on, wanted him to tell us that it would be all right, that everything would be all right.

The thing that struck me the most about that day was that the majority of the people loitering around outside the Pentagon were in uniform. Obviously. But I don't know, I've seen tv and people in the military are supposed to be more. . . I don't know, 'on guard' or something. But they were just as confused and dazed and bored and chatty as the rest of us. They stood around in their polyester uniforms not knowing what to do or where to go or what to say. I saw one female sergeant crying. Soldiers aren't supposed to cry. They are supposed to be marching in rhythm, guns at the ready, prepared to defend me and my way of life. But they were just as human, just as traumatized as everybody else. Where were the people in charge? Where was Rambo? Where was Superman? I kept looking up at the sky, but Superman never appeared.

My apartment smelled like smoke and jet fuel for almost a week.

Ann's Story

To tell you the truth, I didn't even notice anything until the internet went out. Tyler says that he has a lot of time at work to read news or watch tv or whatever it is he does there, but I don't. I'm usually working from the minute I get in until the minute I leave. I mean, every now and then I'll stop and check my email or something, but I don't have time to sit around and read every news story and chat with co-workers about what's going on in their lives or anything. Most of the time I don't even have time for lunch. Everything is always so "do it now" around here. The deadlines are so quick. We've got to respond to things in like an hour or two most of the time, so we can't afford to slack. Mostly I blame the clients for that. You tell them that there is a filing deadline in 30 days and they need to give you the information and they do nothing until the day of the deadline and then expect you to work til midnight getting the forms filled out properly.

But anyway. . . I was just sitting at my desk doing some research for this merger we were working on. There might have been people in the hallway talking or whatever. I've learned to tune out what's happening outside my office. I needed an address, so I tried to google it, and I just got one of those white pages, you know, with like some error message or something on it. I figured it was just a mistake, so I closed the browser and reopened it, but it still didn't work. But I really needed that address. So I went out into the hallway to ask my secretary if her computer was working, but she wasn't at her desk, which was like, weird because she usually tells me when she has to step away. I'm sure I thought she was probably at the bathroom or something.

I went back and did some more work on our response document, but after fifteen minutes or so I tried again and kept getting the error screen. My secretary still wasn't at her desk. By then I noticed that there seemed to be some noise coming from over in the conference room. Most of the other lawyers were standing around watching the tv. It looked like a fire or something, just billowing smoke and pictures of people all covered in ash, and I wondered what the big deal was that was causing everybody to just be standing around. Then the news anchor came on and said what was basically happening.

I don't talk to people a lot at work, I mean, I talk to people, but it's almost always related to some work topic. I just don't have time to discuss politics or sports or whatever. Plus, I'm embarrassed about a lot of the things that I'm interested in, like Pokemon or some new flavor of potato chips, and it's just best to keep things professional. I didn't talk to anyone in the conference room, but I did listen for a while. No one seemed too worried or anything. I suppose that's because they didn't live in New York. They just casually wondered about whether it was an accident or on purpose, and if it was on purpose, then what sort of person would do that kind of thing, and how'd they pull it off, and where'd they even get the idea for a stunt like that anyway. You know, Tyler and his website never even crossed my mind.

I had a filing due that day, so I didn't really have time to sit around and watch tv. I figured whatever was happening the police or whatever had things in hand and there wasn't anything I could do about it anyway so why waste time when I had this deadline hanging over my head.

So I went back to my office and worked for the next few hours. I heard some sirens outside every now and then, but I work in the center of a big city, and there's always sirens going off, so I didn't worry about it too much. I didn't even have time for lunch. I had brought a lunch with me, but I didn't really want it. I was always trying to eat healthy and all, but whenever I opened my lunch bag and saw some cottage cheese and a carrot staring back at me, I'd always lose my appetite and my resolve and wind up going across the street to this buffet-by-the-pound place that's great because you can get a little bit of everything all on one platter. But I needed to get this filing done, so I just snacked on candy out of my candy bowl and a bag of Doritos that I got from the machine.

It must have been like 1:00 pm or so when I was finally ready to submit the filing to the FDA website, but the internet was still down. I started to panic. The FDA was pretty strict about their filing deadlines, and excuses like, "the internet was down" just don't fly. I called the help desk, but they said there wasn't anything they could do. I went out to talk to the partner about it and she looked pretty shaken up. She was packing her things. She was distracted, but she told me that, "the FDA is closed, the whole government is closed down. Don't worry about the filing, you can submit it tomorrow." I wandered past the conference room on my way back to my desk. There were less people there than before, but still a decent number. Nothing was new on the tv, it was the same footage again and again. "We're not supposed to leave the building," one of the legal assistants said. "They don't want the streets clogged in case emergency vehicles have to get through." At the time I thought that was weird because last time I checked the World Trade Center was in New York, but I hadn't been watching the news and didn't know that people were thinking that planes might crash into DC as well.

I didn't have anything better to do, so I went back to my office and called Tyler to see what he was doing, but his cell phone didn't pick up. I spent the next hour cleaning my

233

office. I'm one of those people that prints everything out, and there are always huge stacks of paper all over my desk. I never have time to get really organized. I also ate a few more pieces of candy, which I felt guilty about. I was hoping that maybe the internet would clear up before the end of the day so I could submit my filing. I supposed that since they were shut down the FDA would probably accept it late, but if I could get it in on time, I'd just feel better about it that night when I was trying to sleep. I mean, there was no *official* word from FDA that they'd be taking things late, so why take the risk if I didn't have to?

About 3:30 a senior partner came around to announce that the office was closing and we should all go home. By then most people had left anyway. I checked the FDA website one more time and then I headed out. The streets were totally clogged with cars going every which way. There were even a few army guys sitting on a big army truck in Washington Circle. It looked like we were in a war zone.

I don't think that I was really worried at the time. I suppose I hadn't spent enough time thinking about what was happening to really get all that worried about it. I do remember being really annoyed by the traffic though. It took me almost four hours to drive home, and I only live like two miles away. By the time I got home the FDA website was back online so at least I was able to submit my filing from my home account.

Tyler and I were scheduled to go to New York for a short vacation that weekend. I had tickets on the Delta Shuttle and everything. But when it looked like most of Manhattan was going to be shut down, and the planes weren't going to be flying, we decided not to go. I had gotten tickets to Rent that we couldn't return, and Tyler, because he's cheap, was upset that they had been wasted, but I couldn't get a refund. We wound up seeing Rent anyway a

234

while later, when we eventually did go to New York, and neither of us liked it, which made Tyler even more annoyed that he had paid twice to see a bad show.

Molly's Story

If you're looking for some sort of self-reflection you're not going to find it here. I'm not all deep and stuff and you aren't going to get into my psyche or figure out what makes me tick or nothing just because I'm telling you all this. I didn't even know about it or anything when it happened. I was sleeping most of that morning. Plus I don't even like, have a tv. Ok, that's a lie, I do have one, but its old and the screen is shit and I don't watch it much.

The Spitfires had one of their ska-punk shows the night before and afterwards I wandered around U Street and got stoned and could barely find my way home before I passed out. I was probably asleep until like, noon maybe. I would've slept more but I had to be at work by three. I'm pretty sure the first thing I did after I got up was to smoke another bowl, if it was like most days I mean. I didn't smoke enough to get fucked up or anything, but just something to take the edge off. Then I microwaved a frozen waffle and took a shower and probably had to hunt around the floor for my work smock, which is usually lying crumpled up in one corner of my place or another.

I'm real slow getting ready in the morning, so that took up most of my time before I had to go to work. I might have put on a cd and chilled out a bit.[33] I don't really remember that part of the day real well, because it was just like other mornings I suppose.

But I got my smock on and I headed over to work and I still had a headache even after I took like five Tylenols and

---

[33] Spacemen 3, Recurring

smoked that bowl, plus a few cigarettes. I walked over to work and there was like traffic everywhere. That was probably the first thing that I noticed. I didn't care really cuz I was walking, but I definitely remember noticing. There was some asshole a few years back that tried to jump off the 495 bridge and shut down the beltway during rush hour. Holy shit there was traffic all over the freaking place that day, and I don't live anywhere near 495! I was thinking that maybe there was some other asshole pulling the same kinda crap or something.

But then, when I got to work the door was locked. And there was this handwritten sign saying they were closed. I figured that Jesse was just pulling a joke on me and all. I mean, c'mon, it's CVS, it never closes. But I banged on the door for a while and nobody opened it up. Plus, all the lights were off inside. I went around the side to go to the back door because I really didn't need to be fucked with on account I was all hungover, but all the stores on the block were closed. And I was thinking, "Is my watch out of batteries or something and it's like three in the morning?" So I asked some dude in a suit who was walking by what the hell was up and he looked at me like I was an idiot or something. I mean, not everyone is fucking glued to the tv set you know. And he said something like, "terrorists blew up New York, everybody went home." And you know, that made no freaking sense to me at all, but I was like, "fuck it." So I went over to get some coffee but Java Shack was closed, and even the Starbucks wasn't open. So again I was like, "fuck it," and I just went home. I wasn't feeling good anyway so I figured I'd just go and lay down and maybe find out what the fuck people were talking about.

I went home and took a nap and woke up at like seven and I was thinking that man I needed some coffee, but then I remembered that everything was fucking closed. So I turned on my piece of shit tv and wiggled the antenna. Every channel was the same. Everybody was showing the same things again and again and again. I figured out what was going on in like the first five minutes but they kept showing the same video over and over and over again. It was like weirdly compelling though.

It was like, here it comes! Bam! Rewind the tape. Here it comes! Bam! Rewind the tape. Here it comes! Bam! Rewind the tape. There was one angle over and over and over again, the same three seconds of grainy footage again and again on every channel. It was shown in super slow-mo, frame by frame by frame. You could see the plane just before it hit, inches away from the building, flying perfectly level, perfectly fine, perfectly intact, as if nothing was wrong at all. If you could just have moved the building out of the way, the plane would've just kept going about its business. Then in the next frame there was just this fireball. There was no plane, it was gone, in space of one frame of video it went from perfectly fine to . . . just gone. Then three frames of nothing, then boom, all this debris flew out of the other side of the building. Just flew out into space. You couldn't see what it was, just tiny black dots flying out into the air. They showed that over and over again and I started to think that wow, maybe that debris, those tiny dots, were people. One minute you were sitting by your desk doing office stuff and then bam, there you are in 50 stories up in the air, falling. That's when I started to like pay attention.

They kept talking about all these people who were jumping out of the buildings or falling out of the buildings or getting sucked out of the buildings or whatever; they didn't know, I suppose we'll never really know. And then they showed these videos of these bodies falling through space. They don't show them anymore. Not on any of the reunion specials or the 'one year later' retrospectives or any of that. They decided it was kinda not cool and maybe pretty gruesome. But they were showing it that day, I swear. And they were showing this guy falling and you couldn't see all that much on account of the smoke and the fact that the camera was like blocks and blocks away, but you could tell the guy was wearing a tie and I thought, "man, you're jumping to your death, you can take off the tie." If I was jumping to my death I'd fucking take off that crappy CVS smock first thing, that's for damn sure. But they kept showing this guy, tumbling over and over and you could see the windows flying by as the camera stayed on him, and it kept going out of focus and all, but it was sorta beautiful you know? I mean, it was like that scene in American Beauty where the gay guy is like filming that bag flying around. That's what I thought of. Just this guy falling and floating around like a bag or a leaf or something caught in the wind and I wondered what it was like for him and all, there at the end. Was it scary? Was it all peaceful, like he had made his decision? Was he all nervous wondering if maybe he'd make it like those guys whose parachutes don't open and they somehow survive the fall? The video looked so freaking calm, but I don't know maybe that's just cuz there was no sound and he was screaming and crying and whatever and we just couldn't hear him. But I was just so sad watching the same guy over and over and over again falling and falling and the camera didn't take it all the way to the ground so you never really knew what happened to the guy even though you were pretty sure, and you just wanted to reach out, reach out your hand into the tv and I don't know, like catch him or something. It was like that plane and all. The guy was fine in the video, he wasn't on fire or missing a leg or nothing like that, he was perfectly fine, all his organs working great, and you knew that if you could just maybe catch him, everything would be ok. But that's what death is like I guess. It's too late to reach out your hand. It's too late to stop the tape just before impact and fix it. It's just over and that's it.

I heard later that lots of the guys who jumped out of the building like landed on firemen and other people and killed them too, which made me change my mind and think that the people who jumped were kinda dicks for doing it. But what the fuck do I know.

Chapter 30:

Not Found

The requested URL was not found on this server.

Additionally, a 404 Not Found error was encountered while trying to use an ErrorDocument to handle the request.

"Fuck fuck fuck holy motherfucking mother of god fuck," thought Tyler as he watched the tv, still half-dressed for work. Every tv channel was showing the same thing; click, click, click. All the same image. The information coming in was sketchy. They didn't have any video footage queued up just yet. But they had the basic facts. Terrorists. Airplanes. Weapons. More in the sky as we speak.

Tyler turned off the tv and looked over at his computer. It still had a sticker on the side for some band called 'Seed' that he'd never heard of but picked up for free in a record store in college. He turned the box on. It was old and slow and took a long time to load. It had another sticker on the top for Moby, which Tyler had placed there back before Moby was a total sellout. Luckily the sticker was pretty vague about who it was advertising, so Tyler hadn't felt the need to take it off, lest someone think he was some pop-eating lemming drone type.

Tyler didn't really need to log on to the internet, he knew that what he was looking for was there. He knew his websites like the back of his hand. He spent a lot of time agonizing over them, making sure that each detail was right, that everything was justified correctly, that every word was spelled correctly.

He looked at the html document on his computer, PLANE.HTML. He read his description of how to take out a building by hitting it with an airplane. All the information wasn't in yet from the news. They didn't really know what happened, how it happened, why it happened, how they did it. But Tyler knew. It was all spelled out right there on his website. All they had to do was follow the instructions. Everything was right there for anyone anywhere in the world to see.

It was obvious what was going to happen next of course. It was pretty clear that the FBI was going to have to investigate this incident. They were going to have to find out who did this, and where they got the idea from. It wouldn't take an FBI intern more than five minutes searching with Google to find the CHOAS website and once that happened they'd come looking for Tyler. Aiding, abetting, encouraging, whatever they wanted to call it, his ass was completely on the line. They had finally taken his advice, someone had finally taken his advice and stuck it to the man and now the man was going to stick it right back, and Tyler was caught in the middle.

The first thing that needed to be done of course was to get rid of the web page. At least try to slow down the pursuit a bit. Make them have to go through the logs and the backup files and whatever. Tyler tried to log onto the internet to get into the server, but it wasn't working. He just got a busy signal. He made a mental note to take care of that later, as soon as he could get to a computer somewhere with an internet connection. Maybe in some internet cafe in eastern Europe? Maybe in some backwater village in South America with dirt roads and live chickens in the streets and people carrying sacks of flour around? Pretty much everywhere had internet access these days.

Tyler had to get rid of the local files next. For years he had kept a large, clunky magnet on the desk in case of an emergency such as this. He knew that if the Feds ever broke down his door he'd only have seconds to get rid of the evidence, and what better way than several gauss of a magical magnetic scrambler? At least that's what he told people the magnet was for. He would never admit it, but he had no real evidence that sticking a magnet to the side of the case would permanently scramble the hard-drive, he just assumed it would.[34]

He scrolled through his directories looking to see if there was anything that he wanted to save. Tyler figured it'd be at least several hours before the cops would be able to match the attack with the website and be able to connect the site to his address so he had a few minutes to scroll through the files of his life and decide if there was anything he should keep.

Old homework assignments, text files with drafts of emails he'd sent (or intended to send) to ex-girlfriends, funny jpg files of the President's head on a monkey. An address book filled with addresses that probably weren't correct anymore. Illegally downloaded music files. It was all too valuable to discard. Although no one single item had much intrinsic value by itself, the collection of electronic detritus was really a roadmap of Tyler's life. By looking back at individual items, he was able to remember parts of himself, certain events that were too painful or shameful or embarrassing or poignant to deal with in his head. He had blocked out most of his memories, but looking back at

---

[34] Ed. note— it would not.

various scraps he could, when he had the time and inclination to let himself feel the emotions he normally kept pretty effectively bottled up, instantly transport back to them. For example, this text file that contained nothing but a single phone number reminded him of that girl whom he met at a party who talked to him for an hour about some band that he'd heard of but didn't like even though he pretended to because he liked her and she never returned his phone calls and he never saw her again.

He decided that owing to the circumstances, he wasn't in the right frame of mind to permanently delete his scattershot scrapbook memories of the last several years. But he did want to at least delete the CHOAS files that would directly connect him to what was happening over New York.

He dragged all the html files that made up the terrorist training website into the trashcan. He was about to hit the delete key, but hesitated. It would be a shame, for historical purposes, to delete the files permanently. He imagined being on the lam for many years but the story would eventually come out. People would read about it, it would become some sort of historically important record. People would want to know, want to see the original files. He imagined historians one day pouring over the contents of his bedroom, looking for something, wondering what exactly was said, what exactly was meant. Who was this Tyler person? He got the thought in his head that perhaps the best thing to do would be to save the files on cd. That way, some day, when the historical record was being finalized, some ambitious grad student would find a mislabeled cd, overlooked by everyone else, and that would contain the motherlode of information on CHOAS and the radical doctrine they espoused. He removed the files from the trashcan and burned them to cd before erasing them again.

He thought about marking the cd, 'PORN,' to discourage people from searching it, but he figured that would just make the detectives want to look at it more. He thought about marking the cd 'GAY PORN', which would solve the detective problem, but would probably reflect poorly on him if his Mom ever came by to pick up all this stuff. He eventually settled on HOMEWORK: CE218, figuring no one would be particularly interested in homework assignments Tyler did for some boring class in college.

Then Tyler looked around his room at the enormous pile of stuff he'd accumulated over the years and started thinking about what few items were so essential that he'd need to take them with him.

Tyler's Story

I don't like to do things fast you know. I'm a planner, I'm a schemer, I'm the kind of person who likes to mull things around for a while and chew on them and get them conceptually into my 'mind-space.' And then, once I've fully formulated an idea, fully considered all the options available to me, something inside clicks and I move, I move with lightning speed. Sometimes Ann accuses me of being lazy, she has to nag me and nag me over and over again to do things like order plane tickets or make dentist appointments or things like that but she doesn't understand is that I *am* doing those things. I just can't wake up one morning and jump out of bed and take my car to get inspected. I have to spend a few weeks imagining what it'd be like to get my car inspected. I have to firm up my schedule days in advance to make sure that I had the time, that the weather would be right, that I'd have been to the bank recently so I had cash in my pocket. All these things needed to align. I'm not the sort of person who just does it.

I want you to understand this because I want you to know how hard it was for me to get up out of bed that day, see the tv, and make the decision that I had to leave. I can't even handle going to a concert without several weeks of time to get comfortable with the idea. To move so quickly on something this big, to change my life, to give up my job, my home, my friends, all with only a moment's notice was almost impossible for me. It was like moving through molasses. Everything seemed to take longer than it should have, everything was inertial. It was like I was trying to move with a sumo wrestler sitting on my head. But move I did. I forced through it. I was able to get my brain to work and my limbs to move because I knew that my life was going to change anyway. The die had been cast, the bomb had

246

exploded, the world had ended just as surely as if an earthquake had struck. The FBI were going to come and get me. They were going to take me away anyway. No matter how much I wanted to stay here, the option was closed. Change was going to happen and it was going to happen fast. The only choice was whether I was going to let it happen to me, or whether I was going to take control of my own destiny and steer my future, for the first time in my life, in the direction I wanted it to go in.

I thanked God for all the fantasy planning I had already done. I'd imagined leaving my life, imagined that something exciting, interesting, dangerous was happening and I needed to get out and get out quickly. I'd spent so many nights lying in bed, Ann asleep by my side, mulling over options for the best way to get out of the country, and the best places to go to hide. The Seychelles was always a popular daydream. They speak English there, it's really far away, and they don't have an extradition treaty with the US. Sleeping on a beach, maybe working at a local hotel carrying bags for European tourists. That was the final destination. It was all just fantasy, it wasn't something real to plan, like figuring out what Christmas presents I have to buy people this year, it was just play for my mind. But it turned out to have value after all. The contingency plans are in effect. I am already in my car before my conscious mind has formulated where I'm going. But my unconscious mind knows. Drive, get away from northern Virginia. That's the first place they'll look. It'll take time for the authorities to issue an APB. The car is safe for a few days, the credit cards should work for a while before they get blocked. As long as I can get out of the continental United States before that happens I should be fine. I used to think that the Canadian border was the place to go, but Canada is just like America, it's all connected and wired, and the system works. Plus, once you are there, where do you go? There are no easy outs from Canada. Mexico is the way; it's further of course, but it's less developed. The cops don't have wireless internet connections in their cars, they are more corruptible. Plus, the border is wide open. Nogales, Arizona. No one could stop me. All I needed to do was get to Nogales, Arizona. After that; Guatemala, El Salvador, Paraguay, all the dark places where a wanted man could disappear are open. The way is clear.

As I'm throwing a bag together the phone rings. Caller ID says it's Jason. I'm sure he's watching this on tv and thinks I think it's pretty funny. I'm sure he's got nothing interesting or profound or useful to say about it. I don't answer. He's part of my past life now, already fading into distant memory like that red-haired kid you vaguely remember hanging out with in first grade but can't recall any details about. Jason was an ok guy and all but he never really got me. Ann used to refer to him as my best friend and I suppose that's technically true. But shouldn't a best friend be someone you are really in tune with? There were a lot of things I'd never say to him because I know he'd take them the wrong way, or he wouldn't get it, or he'd make some kind of joking comment that I'd interpret to mean he didn't care.

That's the problem with most folks, they just don't get what I'm saying to them. Or, I don't know, maybe they just weren't interested. But where were the people that were interested in what I was interested in? I mean, how come I never found any of them? People always seem super-exciting when you first meet them, but that wears off really soon as you realize they are nowhere near as cool and interesting and smart and entertaining as you'd imagined them to be. Take Molly for instance. Like pretty much everyone else I've ever met, the more time I spent with Molly, the less I liked her.

Maybe it's just that I idealize people too much. When you first meet someone you don't know anything about them except for a few visual clues here and there. A band t-shirt, a funky hairstyle, an oblique reference to some artist or politician you admire. And your mind fills in the gaps. You think that well, if they are interested in A, then it's obvious that they are also interested in B, C, and D, because that would make logical sense. I love B, C, and D too so oh my god they are perfect for me! But as you learn more about them you eventually come to the conclusion that not only are they not interested in B, C, and D, but they've never even freaking heard of those things and don't have the intellectual curiosity to even bother to seek them out. Then they stop being interesting. Nobody real is ever interesting.

I once tried to explain to Molly that I never could find anyone who I found intellectually stimulating. She responded that intellectually stimulating people aren't just going to come up and talk to me, I'd have to go out and find them and introduce myself. I couldn't make her understand though that in any meeting someone comes up and talks to someone so shouldn't there be a 50% chance *they* would introduce themselves to me? I mean, why is it that I'm the one who always has to do all the work? I spend the majority of my time making myself interesting and waving giant, brightly-colored flags that attest to my interestingness. How come no one is ever out there trying to find *me?*

But I digress, this isn't supposed to be about interpersonal relationships, it's supposed to be about what happened to me that day.

Chapter 32:

I am driving. I don't want to drive straight there, straight down I-95 or whatever, straight through Texas, straight to the border and escape. That would be too obvious, too predictable. That's where the roadblocks will be. Or at least that's where the APB will go out to local redneck police assholes— that the mastermind behind the plan to crash planes into the World Trade Center is headed your way. I don't have much faith in the police, at least from an intellectual standpoint, but this seemed big enough that they'll actually pay attention and do their job. I mean, it would only take 30 seconds on Google to realize that my website was the clear blueprint for the attack. I couldn't imagine that they wouldn't at least do that much searching to find out who was behind this.

I figure the best thing to do is just follow the plan I'd been fantasizing about for a long time now— drive northward, fake them out, use the credit card a few times to make them think I was moving towards Canada, then veer off around Philadelphia, past my parents old house. Since I grew up around there I know all the back roads and it'd be pretty easy to lose anyone following me. Then, and only then, head west til I get out to Ohio or Indiana or somewhere, then make the mad dash southward, through the fields and flatness of middle America, to the border.

Ideally I'd want some escape music playing on the tape player. But I don't really have anything useful. If I'd only thought to plan a little better to make an escape music tape. Too late now. I'm stuck with what's in the car. For years now I've made a new mix tape every month or two. There are dozens in the car, the playlists meticulously written with an old sharpie marker of the exact type that Dad used to use to meticulously write down his mix tapes with. All of my tapes have got the cleverest names. I don't understand why anyone names a tape something stupid and generic like, 'Party Mix,' when there is so much you can do to make your mixes stand out. I finger through the most recent ones, the ones in the center storage space between the driver's seat and the passenger's. 'Music to Drown To,' 'Acid-Washed Genius,' 'Tangled Up in Bright Red Ribbons,' 'Beaches in Winter,' 'The Unburied Dead Still Litter the Streets,' all the classics from the past year. I look through the playlist of the first tape, then the second, then the third. There is nothing good here. I never make mixes for me, I never put my favorite songs on the tapes. I mean, some of the songs are pretty good, but the tapes are usually designed to sound good to the people who sit in my car. Something catchy, something that won't alienate them, nothing to make them think I'm weird or strange or have bad taste. I always put the commercially palatable songs from each album on my mixes. I've even designed some of them around specific people just in case that person is ever in the car with me for a long trip. A great mix is something a person will listen to that is filled with songs they've never heard of before but somehow is in line with their particular tastes. I want people to grow, I want to teach them, I want to push their envelopes just a little bit, just enough to spark that passion to seek things out and not just take what's fed to them. I want people to want to revolt, want them to question the status quo, want them to say, "I'm not going to take what you give me, I'm going to do it myself!" That was the point of CHOAS I suppose. Not to actually rebel, not to actually start the revolution, or really crash planes into buildings killing thousands, but to just make people want to start the revolution, make them see that there is a different way of looking at the world, at American Hegemony. No one ever got it.

I don't need these fucking tapes anymore. After all this time trying to make people listen, no one ever listened. No

251

one ever came into my car and said, "wow, what is that?" Usually I don't even play a tape when people are in my car. I figure that they aren't interested anyway and a song not listened to is a song wasted. Ann certainly never listened to any of my tapes, not even the ones I gave her, not even the ones I put in her car. No one else I know ever did either. It was all a fucking waste of time. No one ever even sat in my car. I never really drove anyone around that often, never drove a bunch of people to lunch at work. Hell, I don't even think that anyone was ever in my backseat. I take a tape and roll down a window. Throw it out. Break the mold, break out of my stupid little mind. I don't need these anymore, I don't need these where I'm going. I hesitate. I take the little paper playlist out of the case. I know I don't want this thing, I know that it's just a symbol of an old life that I don't live anymore, but I also know that I'm fickle, I also know that I change my mind a lot. I know that I'm filled with regrets and nostalgia for the past. I want to save the playlist in case I need to recreate the tape in the future. I get ready to throw the tape out the window onto the highway. I hesitate again. I'm not going back. I'm not going to get to see my cd collection again, not going to ever get the chance to recreate this tape. Whatever I've got, whatever mixes I've recorded, this is it. This is all I've got left. Even if they aren't the best songs, dumping these tapes leaves me with nothing. And it's a long drive to Mexico. I put the playlist back in the case and put the case back in the little cabinet underneath the armrest. Damn I'm such a fucking coward.

-=-=-=-=-

I am driving. Trees that are starting to turn brown and lose their leaves pass by in a blur. After driving for two hours the panic has subsided and I'm not even listening to the radio because the news is so damned repetitive and there isn't much point. By this time I've pretty much forgotten about what is happening and why I'm driving. I'm just driving. I am in a contemplative mood. I start to see familiar landmarks from my youth. I am home, I am going home. I haven't been here in so long. So much time has passed. Do I even know the way? Remember the route? Of course I do, it is ingrained with me. I grew up here, I am part of this place, or at least I was. I am not anymore. Things are different, subtle things. I am driving. On my left is a strip mall, filled with the latest and brightest chain stores. It wasn't there before. That was an empty field. It still is an empty field, at least to me. The strip mall isn't really there. This one short glimpse as I speed past can in no way crush the years of memories I have of the place. The strip mall is no more than a mirage. It doesn't exist.

I continue down the rural roadway of this sleepy Pennsylvania suburb. My house is just off the highway, or at least it was. Can I remember the turnoff? Do I know what the side street is called anymore? Of course I do, or at least I will when I see it. As I said, I am part of this place. I turn onto Riverbend Road, right after the weatherworn sign for the organic farm. The farm is still there, or at least the sign still is.

I pass the house of a girl who used to drive me to school back when having a car was a symbol of status. She isn't there anymore. No one is here anymore. I turn up the familiar street at the intersection where I had my first car accident. It was only a small dent yet it was devastating to a young child who had to return to his parents with his head held in shame. I drive up the hill. My house was at the top of the hill, is at the top of the hill. It sits where it always sits, slate grey and black trim. I don't live there anymore. No one lives there anymore. I mean, someone does I'm sure, but I don't know them. My parents have long since retired and moved away. I park the car at the side of the road across from the house and stare into the windows. Not too closely of course. I don't want to know what is inside. I don't want to have to imagine the house any differently than I know it to be. There, downstairs in the living room window, I can almost imagine the lighted Christmas tree that my mother used to turn on every night during the holidays. I stare at the landscaped bushes and trees that my father planted by hand years ago. Are they taller than they were in the old days? It doesn't seem so. I haven't been here for six years, you'd think that the trees would be taller, but they aren't. Maybe it is just a trick of my memory.

I don't stay at the house long. I don't want to remember, it is hard to remember. All of the times I spent here. It is my youth, it is the symbol of my youth and my history. And now it is foreign. It is somehow different. The old way doesn't exist anymore. It is different, I am different. I look different, I act different. My car is different. Being in the presence of the house is painful, my history is gone. Seeing the home in someone else's hands is like watching a precious artifact being destroyed. But this is worse, because it is *my* history, it is *my* world that has been changed forever.

I drive around the side of the house (we had a corner lot), and continue on my journey. I notice that the newspaper box was still bent from the time I bumped into it with the lawnmower. It had never been replaced. The bend, however slight, reminds me that I do exist, that I do make a difference, that everything about my past has not been erased. I feel more solid knowing that.

The radio doesn't have music today, not on any of the channels. It's just white noise about what it going on in New York. I put in another mix tape because I don't want to hear about New York right now.

Chapter 33:

I don't know why I had to see my parents' old house again. It was on the way I suppose. I'd blocked out much of my youth in my mind. I mean, I know it's there, I know that things happened, I just can't really recall what they were. I wasn't abused or anything or molested or bullied. I was normal I suppose, just like every other teenager— depressed and isolated and bored and restless and dying to get away from this place and all the bullshit and rules and annoying people and everything else. Still naïve enough to believe that anyplace else I might wind up would be different. They lie to you in school about how you'll be a great success and people will kiss your ass if you've got a college degree and how you can buy beer once you turn 21 and stay out as late as you want and even get a motorcycle and a ninja sword and no one could say shit about it. But then once you do all that and you get a job and you buy beer and stay out all night it just doesn't seem like it's all that special anymore. It's like a fence and you dream about how the other side is going to be so much better and when you finally climb over the damn thing it's exactly the same, and now you don't even have that fence anymore to dream about.

So I guess that's it then. The last bit of familiarity I was going to experience for a long time. I don't know, I suppose I made the detour because maybe I needed something to convince me to get the hell out of Dodge before it was too late. Looking back, I don't know if I was leaving to stay ahead of the law, or just because I finally had the chance to escape who I'd been and never have to sit in that god damn muted blue office one single day more, twiddling my thumbs and watching my life drain away minute by boring minute. I needed to remember how pathetic everything about me was, how nothing's ever been interesting or easy. The high school is only a few blocks from my house and I drive past it on my way back to the interstate. School has let out by now. The guy on the radio had said that nobody knows what's coming next and so everybody is going home to sit and wait. There were a few stoners lounging on the curb next to the parking lot, just sitting and sitting and smoking. Still wearing those plaid flannel shirts they wore when I was a student here. They don't seem all that upset at what's going on in New York. I suppose it doesn't affect them much here in Pennsylvania. They don't know anyone in New York and they are too disinterested in general to bother keeping up with the news or finding out what's really going on and what it means to the geo-political balance of the world. To them it's just a free day off. I bet they're glad it happened.

Across from the school there's another one of those damn strip malls. This one's been there as long as I can remember. But it was always real crappy inside and the stores were old and smelled like the 1950s and I could never figure out who ever shopped there and how the stores stayed in business. But now on the corner was that shining beacon of corporate culture, a Starbucks. I fucking hate Starbucks. They totally ruined everything. It used to be that you could go and get some coffee in a nice local place and people were friendly and there were couches to sit on and every one of them was unique and different and had its own culture and its own crowd and all, and Starbucks was like the god damn McDonalds of coffee. All standardized and cookie cutter and here's your coffee: drink it and get out mentality. And every asshole person I knew, from Ann to Jason to all those annoying people at work I have to deal with every day, they all drank Starbucks like it was going out of style. Without ever so much even setting foot in local place to see how much better it was. Nobody fucking understands. I should have targeted Starbucks on CHOAS while the site was still up. Get some kind of ELF action going where people would firebomb random stores until they went out of business.

Who am I kidding? No one ever read CHOAS, no one would have taken up my call to arms. Everybody is too fucking lazy and contented. Cancel Star Trek or raise the price of gasoline three cents a gallon and you'll get millions of people in the streets protesting, but ask for help getting rid of a soul-sucking corporate leech and no one will give you the time of day.

I didn't want to do it, but it was going to be a long, boring drive. There were no other local places around, or if there were I wouldn't know where they are because the coffee craze didn't start until after I moved out of here. But some coffee did sound good. I pulled into the strip mall parking lot and went in to get a cup to go. I figured I'd pay with my credit card that I'd never pay off since I was leaving for good, so in a way it would be a 'fuck you' to both Starbucks and the corporate assholes that owned the credit card company. Let them sort out who was going to get stuck with the $3 bill.

Chapter 34:

I couldn't remember what that place used to be, for the life of me I couldn't remember what it used to be. It's a strange thing about memory, you remember glimpses of things, highlights of them. I could remember walking around the back of this strip mall years ago when I went to school across the street. I could remember how the dumpster smelled of spoiled milk and how the curb wasn't angled and perpendicular like a regular curb but instead was curved as if meant to be ridden over by a skateboard or a bicycle. I remember one time there was this geeky kid that some of the other kids tried to goad into fighting me and how he wanted to meet behind the strip mall and how I didn't go; partially because I didn't want to perform for the amusement of others and partially because I thought I might lose. I remember that kid's name was Scott. But everything else about this place is blurry. I suppose it's like your vision, you only can see what you are focused on, and what's at the periphery is sort of fuzzy and indistinct. Maybe I went into this store that is now a Starbucks but wasn't back when I was in school across the street, but for the life of me I couldn't remember what it could possibly have been.

I suppose it doesn't matter anyway. It's clearly a Starbucks now. Whatever vestiges of the old store were ripped out, repainted, and replaced by the standard corporate-approved color scheme and plastic, cloned furniture. Even the specials on the chalkboard were written in the same hand as they are in a thousand other Starbucks, as if the managers must all pass a penmanship course before being allow to open a new location.

The store was empty. As the gravity of the day's events began to hit people, more and more of them just went home.

Or maybe a Tuesday afternoon wasn't the busiest time for coffee. Or maybe the place was never very busy, the concept of paying $3 for a coffee being pretty new in this part of the country. I don't know. It didn't matter. The radio was on. It wasn't the cds that they usually played, cds that had been focus-grouped for maximum coffee drinking enhancement. It was just the radio. I ordered a regular coffee, black. I always drank my coffee black. I remember when I was kid, my mom was always such a pain in the ass about her coffee. It had to have milk, 2%, not whole not skim not 1% not cream, and she had to have the pink fake sugar not real sugar not the blue fake sugar or the yellow. And if they couldn't exactly meet her demands she didn't get coffee at all and sulked. I resolved then that if I ever started drinking coffee I'd learn to drink it black, because they always have black. You never have to be a pain in the ass and annoy people if you just ordered it black. On rare occasions I would put some milk and/or sugar in my coffee, but when I did Ann would always make some sort of comment about how that was unusual for me, so I don't do it anymore, just so I don't attract her attention and have to defend myself.

I ordered the coffee to go, but then sat down anyway. I closed my eyes. The announcer was speculating on who could be responsible for what was happening. They had a few people purporting to be experts talking but they didn't announce their names or what their backgrounds were. One of them was going off about how this was such a sophisticated attack that there were only a few groups that could possibly be responsible. Someone else was talking about how this was totally outside the scope of what anyone had ever done before and how amazing (only I'm certain that I'm misremembering because I know no one would have used the word 'amazing') how amazing it was that they were able to pull this plan off because it was so sophisticated and caused so much damage in relationship to the amount of money and effort and personnel it would have taken. "Damn right," I thought to myself, because I was the one who came up with the idea. Everything on CHOAS was a great idea. Not that I wanted credit or anything, but it was, you'll have to admit, conceptually a brilliant idea, and I thought of it first. That was always my problem in life. I had these great ideas, I could have been so much more, but I never had the means or help to actually make anything happen. All I could do was putz around and futilely attempt to encourage others to act. I figured that no one would have made the connection between the attack and the CHOAS site yet. That was going to take some forensics work from the FBI; tracing IP addresses and such to find out where they originally got the information. But at least once they had made the connections they'd know where the plan came from originally. Finally somebody would know who I was.

I didn't really feel like smiling, because you know, even if people finally notice that you can occasionally have great ideas, there were still several thousand people dead. But I'd always wanted to be something, and after a long time of really being nothing, it was nice to know that at least I'd be something. Even if that something wasn't something that a lot of people liked. At least the guy on the radio admitted it was a totally novel idea and how it was the most impressive (although again I'm sure he didn't use the word 'impressive') act of terrorism in history. In a way it was a bit of validation, you know? All these loser assholes get famous for really stupid, pointless stuff and just sort of seem to fall into fame, and here I was trying really hard, shouting, "Look at me! Look at me!" all this time and no one ever noticed. But they were going to notice me now at least. Was that worth living a life on the run and giving up my stuff and my job and Ann and all the other people I knew in life? Maybe, maybe it was.

But then this other terrorism expert was talking and he was saying about how this wasn't all that novel after all. He was reading passages from a report that was given to

Congress a year ago and how it had completely predicted this scenario exactly. He read a passage from the report that talked specifically about what had happened, and it talked about how we knew that terrorist groups had been discussing using passenger aircraft to take out buildings for years now.

And it was fucking written by Gary Hart. Gary fucking Hart! Gary Hart was some asshole senator or something that could have been President only he couldn't keep it in his pants until after the election like at least Clinton did. I didn't even know the guy was still alive. I couldn't believe that my one fucking good idea, the one thing that I had ever done in life that I thought mattered, really mattered, got scooped by Gary Hart. Fuck. What's the point of anything?

A few people came in and out of the store. A few more walked by the window. They all looked pretty shaken up. More shaken up than I would have expected them to be, considering that nothing had taken place anywhere near this sleepy suburb. It was probably the fact that it was being replayed over and over again on tv. Seeing it happen made it much more real, much more visceral for people, I suppose. I started to make a mental note to post something about that on CHOAS, but stopped myself. There was no CHOAS anymore.

But what now? I had all these plans for what to do if I got into trouble, into real trouble. But after that guy on the news made it sound like everybody and their freaking mother knew about this plan for attack there'd probably be no FBI manhunt for me. So what now? Do I just go home and pretend nothing ever happened? You just know that if I did go back Jason and all those pretentious twits Ann worked with were going be asking me all sorts of questions about what I thought about what happened and there'd probably be even more hate mail in my inbox, and did I want to go back to being just a nobody and was I just a big loser for even

261

thinking that I might, thinking for just for one second that I might not be a nobody and how much more pathetic that seemed than if I'd just accepted my lot in life in the first place. . . .

"Hey Tyler, I thought that was you." A large shape passed in front of me and fell into the chair opposite mine. I was shaken out of my reverie. It was one of the workers, still in his green and black apron. "It's me, Kyle."

I had blocked out most of high school, I never kept in touch with any of the people that I knew there, and it was like what. . . almost ten years on? Everybody gets older and changes and the people you remember as pimple-faced teens with braces and dorky glasses and funky haircuts all look old and a bit wrinkled and have less hair and more middle and generally look like a horrible caricature of the person you knew. Even after he said his name it took me a while to connect him up with my memories. "Haven't seen you in like forever man," he said. Looking up at the radio speaker, "That's some pretty fucked up shit today huh?"

I'm nothing if not cool and even-tempered. No matter how bad things get or how confused I am, I always come off looking totally at peace with everything, as if of course it was supposed to be that way. I don't work at it, maybe it's just because I really don't care about a lot of stuff. Maybe most people who had bumped into someone they hadn't seen in ten years would have jumped up and given a hug and been all like, "Oh my god, I haven't seen you in like forever man!" but all I did was look up at the speaker too and say, "yeah, pretty messed up." It was as if I had been coming to that coffeehouse and chatting with Kyle every day for years.

We sat in silence for a few seconds. I volunteered, "I don't live here anymore. I'm just passing through today."

"That's cool man."

My high school was weird I guess. There weren't any people you'd call geeks or nerds, or whatever— smart kids who liked science but failed at social skills and enjoyed Star Trek. At my high school, all the honors students were just as cool, if not even cooler, than the average kid. It wasn't even like I went to some fancy private school or anything and I never really could explain it. Maybe all high schools were like that and the image of the short pimpily kid in broken glasses was really just an archetypal myth that only exists in the movies. At my school the honors class fit more or less into two groups. On one side were the preppy kids who wore Izod shirts and owned their own cars and were going to become businessmen and leaders of industry. Some even wore suits and ties to class and carried their schoolbooks in briefcases. I'm not shitting you on that one, that's 100% true. On the other side were the goth-skater-punk kids who had dyed hair and claimed to be very counter-culture and unpopular but who were secretly just as concerned with looks and status as everyone else. They were all going to be great artists or writers or whatever and scribbled disturbing poetry in the margins of their math textbooks and ditched class to go see U2 when they came to town that year. I suppose I was marginally part of the skater clique, on account of being involved in the school plays, but I didn't really have that many friends in high school and I rarely saw anyone outside of class.[35] Kyle on the other hand was one of the leaders of the skater group. He was about as popular as you could get in high school. He used to sit next to me in math class and used to proclaim strange words to be the 'word of the day.' Words like 'lederhosen' and 'armadillo' and he'd try to work them into everything he said in class, no matter how inappropriate they were to the subject. And we'd all chuckle

---

[35] Ed. Note— Tyler's involvement in the school plays was limited to running a spotlight and developing a huge crush on the lead actress.

every time. He had a mop of the coolest, most unsymmetrical blonde hair and was dating a girl who had an exact mirror-image of his hairstyle. Everybody was envious of them. I heard second or third-hand they broke up after high school.

"What are you doing working here?" I said to him, in as nice a tone as I could manage. "Last I heard you were going to Swarthmore."

"Swarthmore was great man. I mean, I was so drunk I couldn't even see straight most of the time I was there. Of course, after I stopped going to class, they sorta told me to not bother coming back and all. I figured, you know, 'screw them' because I was going to write the great American novel and all and life experience was more important than college anyway."

"Did you get it published?"

"I was going to write a book that was all about the American diner and I was going to like, you know, write the whole book while actually sitting in various diners across the US. I used to go every night, all night and hang out and drink coffee and smoke cigarettes until my hands were shaking so much I couldn't hold a pen, and I kept thinking, 'yeah man, yeah, this is the shit.' But I don't know, I sorta gave up on it after a while. You've got to pay the bills and all. I was working at this one-hour photo store and they moved me to night shift and I pretty much didn't have the time or energy left to really write. I kept meaning to pick it back up, but you know. . . life man."

"Yeah, it's hard to find the time." Actually I didn't know what he meant really. I had all this time and energy and everything, my problem was that I never had a real goal, you know? If I ever decided to write a book about something, and I really knew what I wanted to write about and I had the passion for it, I'd be able to do it, I'd be able to work all day and write all night and I wouldn't let anything get in my way. If you don't believe me, just look at all the effort I put into CHOAS and that was stupid shit. If it were something I really cared about I wouldn't be working at Starbucks while my life passed me by.

"I'm so glad high school is over though. God I hated that place," he said. I was surprised to hear that coming from someone like him. The things I hated about high school were things that happened to guys like *me*, not to guys like Kyle. I always imagined that if I was like him, I would have loved high school.

"What do you mean man? You totally ruled in high school. I figure you'd keep looking back on that time as like your glory days."

"Are you kidding? I was such an outcast dork."

I looked at him in amazement. "Are you nuts, you were one of the coolest guys in high school. You and that guy with the blue hair and the rest of the skaters and that all that crowd, you were the people I looked up to in school. I used to secretly take notes of the bands you talked about and the stuff you wore and tried to emulate you."

"But we were the geek crowd. We were always getting picked on by the popular kids and the football team and all those preppy assholes in suits, like that guy Jack. I heard that he became some big neo-Nazi, as if you couldn't tell where he was headed back then."

"You guys were totally not geeks. The geeks were people like me who were outsiders, even to the 'outsiders' crowd." Then I finally realized something. "Maybe, you know, like everybody thinks that. Like no matter who you are you always think you are at the bottom of the social pecking order. Here you were thinking that you were a loser and secretly I was looking up to you as a role model for coolness. Maybe there were other kids back then who looked up to me?"

"No, I don't think so. You were a pretty big loser." He smiled half-heartedly, trying to make a joke of it, but also knowing that he was speaking an unpleasant truth.

I just sighed. You know, in school you always have these fantasies about how you are going to grow up rich and successful and come back to the reunion and show everyone how great you are and all and how you'll see them working at McDonalds and laugh in their face? That's a great fantasy, but it's not what happens in real life. In real life you see someone who was your 'better' that's turned into a miserable failure at life (as I judged Kyle to be), and you just, I don't know, feel sorry for them, or just don't want to make them feel worse about themselves I guess.

We talked for a while longer. He told me about some of the other people I knew in high school. Names of people I barely remembered really. None of them sounded particularly all that successful to me. Just ordinary lives doing ordinary things in ordinary places. It was pretty amazing really. I think I could make a case for having the best life of the lot. I had a steady girlfriend who wasn't hideously ugly or fat or dumb or unintentionally pregnant. I had a professional job that paid me well. I wasn't still living with my parents. I suppose that maybe Kyle didn't know what happened to everyone and mostly just knew about the people that were still living in town who were undoubtedly not the cream of the crop, but still he talked about a lot of people that I thought would be great successes in life, who really just wound up married and in dead-end jobs like everyone else.

266

In all those honors classes we kept being told over and over again how we were the future leaders of America. How we were going to win Nobel Prizes and become Presidents and cure cancer and star on Broadway and do all those things that the very best of us are supposed to do. They sent us off to the best colleges in America. They filled us with the idea that greatness was just around the corner. If you had asked me on graduation day where people were headed I wouldn't have guessed a dead-end job with a plain wife and three kids and receding hairline and crappy days hunched over a computer in a dimly lit cubicle trying to beat their way into middle management. Every now and then I guess someone makes it, but those people are few and far between and it's never the ones you think. High school turns out to be mostly a lie. It would be better that they don't even bother to give you all that hope. That way you won't be so disappointed when life doesn't turn out like they told you it would.

I think that the perfect time to die would be sometime before one graduates high school. For me I think that it should have happened after sixth grade. If you die young you aren't obligated to fulfill your potential. When I was in grade school, I was once told by a teacher that someday I would win a Nobel Prize. I'm 100% serious about that. Now that my life has gone onward I know that that is not going to happen. When you are young there is a world of possibilities, and you can do anything. Once you are old and broken down you can only look back at your life and wonder what went wrong. If I had died as a youth, my name would forever be venerated as someone who died too soon, someone who never had a chance to achieve greatness. Now that I have had that chance and only achieved mediocrity, I will never be regarded in the same way again. No one is ever going to suggest I'm going to win a Nobel Prize now. Admittedly if one really achieves a level of greatness and wins Nobel Prizes, then I guess it was worth it for that person, but the percentage of people that actually reach their potentials has gotta be very slim.

As a corollary, someone who dies young is less likely to have regrets, to have done the wrong thing. I look back on my life and I see so many instances where I have not done the right thing, where I have hurt people who didn't deserve to be hurt, and been hurt when I should have known better. If someone dies as a young child, one never has the time to have any regrets or to hurt people and so they die in a state of grace. While life is short and fleeting, they maintain a constant state of perfection. They can honestly say that they lived their lives without ever having caused pain. That sounds like a pretty cool thing to me. To be able to say you made it all the way through life and you were never a jerk to anybody. People value life and make every effort to force it to go on, but why bother? Why go for a life that is filled with regret, and pain, both inflicted and received. A short, perfect life would be ideal. Death with unfulfilled potential is better that Life with constant failure. "Life goes on, long after the thrill of living is gone."[36] John Cougar Mellencamp? Holy fuck, I'm quoting John Cougar Mellencamp now? God, I'm more pathetic than I thought. There's really no hope left for me.

I didn't really have anything to say to Kyle. He wasn't like a great friend of mine back in the day or anything like that, and our lives had diverged a lot since then. I could barely remember the people and places we had in common and talking about them was just dredging up a past that was better off being forgotten. We chatted about nothing in particular for a few more minutes and then he had to go back to working the cash register.

---

[36] John Cougar Mellencamp, "Jack and Dianne"

I finished my coffee and then called Ann. She was still at the office because the roads seemed all backed up and she had work to do because the deadlines weren't going to change even with everything going on that day. I lied to her. I told her that I was still at the office too and was going to be stuck there all day. That way if she did get home before me she wouldn't have any idea that I had driven way out of town. I waved to Kyle on the way out and he smiled at me.

Chapter 35:
Epilogue

I was reading that afternoon, reading and waiting. Waiting and half-thinking about some new girl who emailed me the other day saying she liked my new website and if she would ever write again and if I really even cared. I knew I did though, because I always care about stuff like that, whether people like me and want to talk to me. That's just the sort of person I am.

So, I'm sitting there reading the City Paper which was this free weekly sort of thing that I assumed urban bohemians like Molly read in order to find out who was playing where and what was going on around town. I had no real evidence that the urban bohemians actually read it, but if they didn't, then I had no idea what they did read to stay as on top of everything as they seemed to do. One of the nice things about the City Paper was that it never mentioned the war or the human right violations, or any of that crappy stuff the government was doing these days. As horrible as it sounds, I was pretty tired of hearing about politics by then. Mostly because it was just so fucking depressing and hopeless.

I was reading the part of the paper that I always read first. The part that actually makes me pick the paper up when I see it lying around in Metro stations and on street corners around town. It was sort of like a personal ads sort of thing, but it was for people who had seen someone they thought was cute walking down the street somewhere but didn't have the opportunity or guts to actually talk to. I eagerly awaited the paper every Thursday to see if maybe someone, somewhere had spotted me and thought I was groovy enough to take a chance on. Of course no one matching my description was ever there. Partly because, well let's be honest, I was a loser that no one was interested in talking to, but also partly because I never went anywhere interesting. I mean in order for people to see you, you had to go places where you could be seen right? I mostly hung around at home or went out to the few local places where there was never anybody cute or young or interesting anyway.

I'm sitting in this coffee shop, which I didn't think I specifically mentioned before. It was a few blocks down from the Georgetown campus. It was sort of an unusual place for me to be and all, since it wasn't really near my house. But I was waiting for Ann to get done with some of her shopping and then we were going to go to dinner or something afterwards. The place was pretty crowded, it being around finals week and all. I was sitting at this long table that was covered with copper sheeting like a bar. There weren't too many places to sit, and I had to even move some dishes that someone else had left just to find a place. But that was ok. I kept looking around at all the people. It was mostly cute young college girls reading textbooks. It was almost summer, and so a few of them were wearing sandals which they had kicked off and put their tiny bare feet up on chairs and such. Nobody was paying attention to me though, but that was to be expected. I really wished that I had brought my book with me. I was reading "The Dharma Bums" by Kerouac. Back in those days I was always reading books that were considered hip rather than ones that I wanted to read. Now don't get me wrong, Kerouac is fantastic, but even if he really sucked I probably would've been reading it because I would be hoping that someone would see it and say, "Wow you are pretty cool, let's get to know each other." The only time that anyone ever did mention anything, it was some random security guard while I was waiting in line at the bank, and it was really unexpected and awkward and I had no idea what to say to the guy so I'm sure I just mumbled something incoherent and ran away. I never read at home though, because what was the point? I mean. . . no one would see you.

I look up and there's this girl walking towards me, a real cutie. She had a round face and really short pixie hair clipped back with a pair of metal barrettes. She walks right over to me and asks, "Is anyone sitting here?" and of course there wasn't. But it was crowded and there weren't many chairs left, so she had to sit somewhere right? So I tell her that she can sit there and she puts her chocolate brownie down on the table. But just then a whole group of kids get up from this other table and leave. So, wordlessly she picks her brownie back up and goes and sits at the newly empty table. I didn't take offense to that, I mean, it made sense and all, since there was more room there, but it was a little disappointing. I was lonely.

With no other real options, I go back to reading my paper and looking at all the concerts that I wasn't going to go to because I was too apathetic to get off my ass and Ann wouldn't want to go anyway and because they were on a weeknight or in the bad part of DC or too loud or whatever. But I keep glancing up at the girl since she was directly in my line of sight. She was sitting in a big, comfy chair and reading a book titled, "Economic Theory: A Historical Perspective," so I pegged her as a Georgetown student. I keep looking up at her, and she throws me a harmless glance too. I quickly turned away. I didn't want to seem like a stalker and I wasn't going to do anything about it anyway, so I was mostly focused on my newspaper. She was wearing black pants and a white button-down shirt and she had those strappy, high-heel sandals on and she kept twirling her foot around and around as she read, which was a little distracting even though I really don't like strappy sandals. Prefer big clunky boots or platform shoes on girls. Ann typically just wore mules.

After like five minutes, this black, hip-hop guy comes in to the coffee shop. He's got the MJ sneakers and a big floppy hat like LL Cool J and a blue jumpsuit. So he looks around and there are some seats available at this point, but he makes a beeline to the pixie girl and asks her if he can sit at her table. She agrees absentmindedly. The guy spends a minute or two eating his pastry quietly, and then starts chatting the girl up. What are you reading, are you a student, that kind of stuff. But I can tell that the girl is a bit uncomfortable, because even from the other side of the room I can see that this guy is basically cruising for a college chick. I keep peeking over and listening as she is being polite but not friendly. I don't want to sound racist, I guess maybe she would have acted the same way even if it were some preppy white guy, since she was studying and all. But it seemed like an awkward situation. You'd think that the guy would have gotten the hint pretty quick, but he hung around for a while. Guys like that always get the girl. Well, maybe not 'the' girl, but 'a' girl. You've got to be aggressive to get a date, you can't sit in the corner giving out furtive glances like I do, you've got to be friendly and talkative and not embarrassed. Unfortunately for women, these guys also tend to be the biggest jerks and everyone ends up disappointed in the end.

She glances over at me once or twice. I can imagine that she was thinking, "I made a mistake, I should have sat next to you." I start up this little fantasy in my head that she would get up and leave that hip-hopper and come over and sit next to me and let me protect her from random pick up attempts. We'd get to talking and she'd be really interesting and I'd be happy that someone was interested in me. But obviously it didn't happen that way. The guy eventually got the hint, finished his coffee, and took off. She sat silently in her big comfy chair with her knees drawn up underneath her. I kept flipping through my newspaper, wishing that I wasn't so bored and was more aggressive and had more friends and people to talk to and hang out at coffee shops discussing the good and bad aspects of Kerouac's novels. No matter what I'm doing, I always feel like I should be doing something else. No matter who I'm talking to, I always look at other people longingly and wonder why they aren't talking to me. I probably should go to a therapist.

A few minutes after the guy left, she gets up out of her chair and walks straight over to my table. I was quite surprised, and felt like I had been caught doing something I shouldn't. It's really a crazy Catch-22 world I live in. I mean, I've got a girlfriend and I don't really want to date other people, but I always want the attention, I want to be flirted with, I want girls to hit on me. Not because I really want them in particular, but because I want to feel wanted. So I sit and I covet them from a distance, and in the few cases where my flirtation actually produces a positive result, I all of a sudden have to backpedal and get out of there and apologize and run away like a frightened bunny. That must really make those few girls who take the leap of faith to talk to me feel really crummy, but to be honest I don't know what else to do.

Anyway, she comes walking over to me and I'm thinking "Yikes! What am I going to say?" but then she just asks me to watch her things while she gets a fresh cup of coffee. She doesn't even really stop to get an answer from me, like as if there is no way her request would be rejected. And to be honest it won't, I'm a nice guy. I'd probably be watching her stuff for her even if she didn't ask me to. It was a little strange that she would ask me though. I mean, she didn't know me and I was probably just as likely to swipe her bag as anybody else in there. But as I said, I'm a pretty honest guy, so she made a good choice whether she knew it or not.

After she leaves, I'm sitting there looking at her book and her bookbag and I'm thinking that maybe this was a sign, like she was flirting with me on some really subtle level. Maybe she'd start talking to me when she got back from the bar. I'm thinking that if I were really a cool guy, I would sneak over to her book and write a note with my phone number and slip it between the pages and that would be really cute and she would call me. But I don't do it. I mean mainly because I have a girlfriend and I don't really want the complications. I'm also worried that Ann is going to come in any minute looking for me and it would be very difficult to explain what I was doing if she caught me. Plus it probably wouldn't work anyway. I mean, in a way my plan sounded pretty cute and romantic and all, but in another way it was kind of scary and stalker-like. I didn't want to scare the pixie girl. She had to study for finals. So I didn't do anything at all but sit there and wait for her to come back and think about all of the possible futures that weren't going to happen because I was shy and weak and awkward and all. But that's ok, I mean, Ann is great and I wouldn't want to ruin my relationship with her just for a chance at some random girl who wasn't even super-attractive or anything. It was probable that the pixie-girl had a boyfriend anyway. But it's fun to dream about stuff, you know?

So I'm daydreaming about what the pixie girl is going to say to me when she gets back and I'm trying to think of some clever line that will make her laugh a bit but won't seem too forward. Everything I come up doesn't seem right. Then she walks past me, says thanks without even breaking step and goes back and sits down. I didn't get a chance for a witty rejoinder, but that was ok, since I hadn't figured out anything good to say anyway.

A few minutes after that Ann comes in. She is carrying a whole pineapple plant in a pot and everything that she bought at this frou-frou gardening store. It even had a baby pineapple sprouting from the top. She was always buying wacky crap like that, which is one of the reasons I liked her so much. She asked how I was doing and if I was bored. I packed up my things and threw out my empty paper cup and started talking about some of the bands that were coming to town. I didn't mention anything about the pixie girl, but I thought that later I'd bring up the fact that she picked me in specific to watch her bag so I must look pretty trustworthy. I glanced over at the girl as we walked out. She hadn't looked up, it was like she wasn't paying any attention to me at all and she really didn't care if I left. Oh well, maybe she was just absorbed in her book, it was finals week and all. As I made my way out, I made sure not to touch Ann or say anything too loudly that would really give away the fact that we were dating. Who knows, maybe next week I'll pick up the City Paper and they'll be an ad from the pixie girl looking for me and saying about how she wished that she got my number before I left. I know that it probably wouldn't happen, I mean I was sure that it wouldn't happen. But it would give me a little more excitement when I looked through the paper next week. Sometimes all you need is just a little thing like that to keep you going.

End